"I have to tell you something, something that Alex doesn't know and shouldn't know," Gigi started. "Remember the party where Kim got really angry with Ollie and threw her out, well earlier that night something happened between Ollie and I, something . . . sexual, something more than a kiss. We were getting high in the van and next thing I know we were *doing* it. I was so nervous but I still did it and now I'm really scared that Alex is going to find out. It only happened that once and I regret it but I can't undo the fact that I fucked another woman and that was what it was: fucking, pure and simple lust incarnate and now . . . now I don't know what to do. What do you think I should do?"

Silence.

"It's not like we were having an affair. It's more like an isolated incident and believe me I'm not proud of it. Mallory?"

Mallory rolled over and made murmuring noises. She'd been asleep the whole time.

Visit

Bella Books

at

BellaBooks.com

or call our toll-free number

1-800-729-4992

Talk of the Town

by
Saxon Bennett

Bella
BOOKS

2003

Bella Books, Inc.
P.O. Box 10543
Tallahassee, FL 32302

Printed in the United States of America on acid-free paper
First Edition

Cover designer: Bonnie Liss (Phoenix Graphics)

ISBN 1-931513-18-X

About the Author

Saxon has gone rural and really likes it. Having lived in the city most of my life this hanging out where the deer and the antelope play rocks. Sometimes the birds get noisy but they were here first. Lin and I live in the east mountains of New Mexico with our two furry children Gunter and Sarah. Gunter should be canonized as a lion cub with the patience of Job for putting up with his sister who is the lost princess of the wild tribe of calicos. We haven't told her that they aren't really looking for her because she is such a handful. Animals are the best and we hope to have more. I recommend learning to drive a tractor and avoiding chiggers at all costs. Life in the land of enchanted mañana bull crap is never dull and I hope you all come to visit sometime.

One

Dr. Kohlrabi still found it disconcerting looking a patient in the eye when she was sitting in an upside down lotus position, cross-legged and balanced neatly on her head. The doctor had been treating Mallory Simpson for almost a year and she often wondered if the therapy was working or if Mallory was wasting both their time and her overly protective mother's money. But there was something about Mallory that interested Dr. Kohlrabi more than her usual professional interest. She found herself contemplating the lives of Mallory and her friends, all of which Dr. Kohlrabi was highly acquainted with because they were intricately connected with Mallory.

Dr. Kohlrabi had to suppress the urge as a straight woman not to make comparisons between her world and Mallory's although she had begun to take some notes thinking that her insights might make a good paper for her next conference. God knows there was so little

1

written on the lesbian that she was truly Freud's dark continent. Dr. Kohlrabi thought about her own daughter who was Mallory's age and how her life differed from Mallory's life. The comparison was intriguing and definitely warranted further study.

"So anyway I don't think being attracted to Gigi is a good idea. She's my friend and she has a partner who I think is absolutely incredible, I mean how could I hope to compare with Alex, who is stunning, good-looking, smart, has a career and is totally in love with her wife, I might add. So you're a therapist and you cure things like this . . . right?" Mallory said, looking straight at Dr. Kohlrabi.

"Your mother hired me to get you to wear clothes again which I have not been successful in doing," Dr. Kohlrabi replied, once again noting Mallory's unique sense of fashion, striped flannel pajamas with a shiny silk tie.

"Do you like the tie?" Mallory said, holding it up for inspection.

"Yes, it's very nice," Dr.Kohlrabi replied.

"It's a Picasso," Mallory replied.

"Why do you wear a tie with pajamas?" Dr. Kohlrabi asked, suddenly wondering why this had never crossed her mind before. Perhaps Mallory's constant array of pajamas had distracted her.

"It's a power thing. I mean look at it. You see this woman, she's in charge, she's sitting behind a desk, she runs the show, she is a Sagittarius, the archer, arrow poised on the wire ready for action, half animal, half human waiting to rule the world, conquer any thing at any moment. She simply must wear a tie and it needs to be a power tie, a tie that says I know what I'm doing, I am the One. But just to give reality a slip she's wearing flannel pajamas in the middle of the day with no bed in sight. Now that's a picture," Mallory replied with evident satisfaction.

"Okay, would indulging your attraction to Gigi make you wear clothes?"

"No, Gigi understands why I wear pajamas," Mallory said, totally disgusted with Dr. Kohlrabi's assumption that lusting after her best friend would have anything, whatsoever, to do with her sense of fashion.

"But I thought you started your pajama episode when your one and only girlfriend left you, in the morning while you were wearing your pajamas?"

"True and your *point*?" Mallory asked, sitting herself upright and brushing her shoulder length hair off her shoulder's. This was known as a moot gesture.

Dr. Kohlrabi fully understood its implications. In Mallory's opinion she, the doctor, was behaving like an imbecile. Behaving stupidly was grounds for complete dismissal in the Republic of Mallory.

When she first started treating Mallory Dr. Kohlrabi had seriously entertained the idea that perhaps Mallory was a schizophrenic, especially when Mallory described her Republic in complete detail with a governing set of laws, property rights and creative freedoms. Mallory made the Declaration of Independence seem tame as if mere schoolboys had written it.

Later Dr. Kohlrabi withdrew from her initial notion of schizophrenia and came to her present state of mind; that being, that Mallory was overly bright and highly individualistic which made her a suspect in a world that carefully groomed homogeneity.

"How long have you know Gigi?" Dr. Kohlrabi asked.

"Since we were in the fifth grade. We met at Brownies. My mother was the group leader. Gigi's mother marched her into our meeting kicking and screaming. She dumped Gigi in our midst and bid my mother make a lady of her. If you ever meet Gigi you will see what a terrible job my mother has done. Gigi is anything but ladylike."

"Tell me about her."

"Why?" Mallory asked, instantly suspicious.

The good doctor refrained from saying because I'm your therapist dummy. She knew that would send Mallory right out the door.

"So I can better understand why you're attracted to her."

"Oh, well in that case. She's . . . alive, I mean she's vibrant and real, not like the rest of you saps. She feels things. She thinks the

3

world is just as big a crock of shit as I do. She makes fun of the whole thing whereas I am known only for my ability to absorb misery acutely."

Dr. Kohlrabi nodded.

"So you feel there are a lot of similarities between you?" Dr. Kohlrabi queried.

"Not at all!" Mallory replied indignantly.

"I thought with the world view perhaps."

Mallory rolled her eyes.

"You couldn't be farther from the truth. Here's a poignant example of our differences. Gigi's mother is a staunch Roman Catholic complete with bathtub shrines of the Virgin Mary. You can imagine what having a lesbian daughter must do for her maternal self-esteem. Do you think that Gigi suffers guilt? No, she rages. She desecrates the shrine, every shrine she comes upon. She is in a constant state of rebellion. What do I do? I go to therapy because my mother pleads with me. That is the difference between our *world views*."

"I see."

"I doubt that."

"Until next time," Dr. Kohlrabi.

"If there is one," Mallory replied.

Gigi and Mallory sat on the old couch alongside the canal by a dirt road that stretched across Phoenix following the intricate canal system. They oftentimes imagined the canals of Amsterdam that they had once walked along on a summer trip to Europe. If you blurred your eyes and gazed at the reflections bouncing off the water's surface you could almost pull it off. Gigi had tried to explain the method to her girlfriend Alex but to no avail.

But Alex did not understand why they sat on a dirty couch they'd rescued from a dumpster and pretended to fish with children's play rods complete with plastic fish attached to the end. It was perfectly understandable that playing imaginary travel games wasn't Alex's

4

scene either. Not that it mattered because in Mallory, Gigi had found her kindred spirit.

"A mentor?" Gigi said, sneering.

Mallory nodded. She threw a pebble into the canal. She couldn't see the rings it made in the water, she could only hear the plunk as earth met liquid.

"How long have I known you?" Gigi asked.

"Since we were ten," Mallory replied, hearing Dr. Kohlrabi's words shuffling around in her head. Don't you think it kind of odd that you've known Gigi most of your life and all of a sudden you find yourself in love with her?

"We've known each other for too long for such a thing to happen. You need to get a new therapist," Gigi said, reeling in her fish and casting it out again.

"I think you're right," Mallory said, stepping into the Republic and feeling the garden corner of her emotional landscape shrivel and die. She was standing once again in the black forest of her oblivion, a lone character on the edge of burnt out forest. If Gigi thought mentoring was disgusting, a torrid love affair was out of the question.

Gigi looked at her askance. "You know you're my best friend."

"I know," Mallory said, leaning on Gigi's shoulder. It was the gentle rebuke Mallory had suffered a thousand times whenever things threatened to get mushy between them. Gigi turned into a frat boy and Mallory diligently buried her true feelings.

Alex came out the back gate from their yard to find her girlfriend engaged in one of her usual pursuits.

"It's a good thing you two have known each other for so long or I might be inclined to think you were having an affair," Alex teased.

"You doubt my fidelity, oh my sweet damsel I would never tarnish the beauty of our union with anything so turgid as mere lust," Gigi said, dropping to one knee and kissing Alex's hand.

"You would have made a perfect Cavalier Poet," Alex said.

"The Cavaliers were full of shit," Gigi replied.

"Exactly," Alex said. "Ollie called. She wants to know if we're doing anything this weekend. They're planning a barbecue."

5

"I'm going to see Aunt Lil this weekend," Gigi replied, trying to keep her voice even and her pulse from racing. Every time she thought of Ollie strange things happened to her body.

"I forgot. It's that time again. The pilgrimage to Yarnell," Alex said, attempting to disguise the animosity she felt over losing her girlfriend for yet another weekend.

"You could come," Gigi offered.

"You don't want me to come," Alex said. "Besides this way I can take Mallory to the barbecue instead. I'm sure she's got a pair of pajamas with grill utensils on them."

"Mallory wouldn't be caught dead at a potluck," Gigi challenged.

"How do you know? You never invite her," Alex replied, sitting next to Mallory.

"Mallory will you go the party with me?" Alex asked running a finger through the one of her long blond tendrils and batting her eyelashes.

Mallory blushed bright crimson.

"Leave her alone. She doesn't like those guys and I'm the only one who understands her peculiar ways. It would be awkward."

"I'll take care of her and stop talking about her like she isn't here," Alex said.

"Do you want to go?"

Mallory looked acutely uncomfortable but curiosity got the better of her. She did want to see what Gigi found so engaging about these women, and Ollie in particular. For a moment she was back in the Republic standing on the edge of a threatening crevasse imagining that she could jump and spread her carpetlike wings.

"I could try," she said quietly as the wind currents of the Republic gently floated her toward the ground, depositing her safely.

"See there, I'll make her a practicing lesbian yet!" Alex said, jumping up.

"Where are you going?" Gigi asked as Mallory did the same.

"Shopping. I need to find some pajamas that fit the occasion," Mallory said.

"Why don't you go with her? I still have some paperwork to finish before dinner," Alex said.

"I don't want to go. I have to things to do before I go. Besides I refuse to be part of this vileness," Gigi said, stomping off.

"Why is she mad?" Mallory asked.

"I don't think she likes sharing you," Alex replied.

Mallory sat in her new party outfit talking to Dr. Kohlrabi who was extremely surprised that Mallory was attending the party.

"I just don't understand why knowing someone for a long time is a bad thing. Why can't we fall in love? I like Gigi best. I have known her so long now that we have no illusions about each other and we've had all the arguments we could possibly have in one lifetime. Look at this picture," Mallory said, poking the photo at Dr. Kohlrabi.

It was a photograph of four little girls at Mallory's birthday party.

"Tell me the look on Gigi's face is not love," Mallory declared.

"Mallory, you were twelve. I'm certain since then Gigi has been single once or twice. Surely you've had opportunities," Dr. Kohlrabi replied, looking at Mallory over the top of her dark rimmed glasses.

"There was never a *right* time. She's a serial monogamist."

"What's that supposed to mean?" Dr. Kohlrabi asked.

"You're not a lesbian, are you?" Mallory said, narrowing her eyes.

"No, nor have I ever pretended to be one," Dr. Kohlrabi declared.

"Perhaps that's our problem," Mallory said, sitting upright permanently this time.

"Why would me not being a lesbian be a problem? I am a professional. I'm certified to treat anyone . . . even lesbians."

"It's not the same. Maybe Gigi is right. I should get a new therapist."

"Why don't you just explain what serial monogamy is instead," Dr. Kohlrabi suggested, wondering if this would be another one of those times when Mallory disappeared for a while only to return frantic with some new catastrophe.

"I'm not sure I can."

"Try."

"Well, it means that women like Gigi don't stay single for long. They leave one partner or are left and then shortly find another and they stay together for years. The opposite of this would be women that date."

"Are they settling for someone so they don't have to be alone?"

"No. I think they are basically people who are smart enough to know that you'll never find a perfect lover so they make what they have work. Does that make sense?"

"Yes. That was a very good explanation. Thank you. Will I see you on Thursday?" Dr. Kohlrabi asked.

"If not before, depending on how the barbecue goes. You know what I like about our relationship?"

"No."

"I like that it's timed."

"I see," Dr. Kohlrabi replied, pushing her glasses back up her nose.

"It has a beginning, an end and basic agenda to operate under. I wish my life was like that."

"No, you don't. You'd find it boring. Surprises are good things and someday you will cherish them."

"*Cherish*?" Mallory said, grimacing.

"I'll see you on Thursday if not before."

Mallory sat on the bed in Gigi's room and watched her pack. She was seriously trying to overlook the fact that for Gigi packing meant shoving whatever she could find that was clean into a duffel bag. Gigi's lack of neatness had always concerned Mallory. She planned on retraining her when Gigi finally realized she was madly in love with her. Mallory was certain that Gigi's unorganized life had to do with not being Mallory. She thought of her own well-organized closets and inwardly sighed with relief.

"You don't have to go," Gigi said, eyeing Mallory with evident suspicion.

8

"Don't you want me to go?" Mallory countered.

"You're the one who always refers to these parties as the lesbian love fest and the idea of being physically close is repulsive to you."

"It seems you know everything. Have you been spying in the Republic again?" Mallory replied. She got up and repacked Gigi's bag. She folded and rolled so that everything fit neatly together.

"Thank you," Gigi replied.

"You're welcome."

"Tell me more about the Republic," Gigi said, pulling Mallory down on the bed.

"You won't believe this, but Dr. Kohlrabi is convinced that I created the Republic as a way to avoid dealing with my mother. She is certain that I got the idea from the Magic Kingdom on Mr. Rogers and I took it from there. Have you ever heard anything so absurd? I was supposed to outgrow it."

"Absolute nonsense. I was rather hoping you'd write it all down and sell it as a book. Your creepy little world makes Harry Potter look like a day at Disneyland."

"Gigi!"

"Well, it's true. Now tell me more."

Gigi had been fascinated with Mallory's imaginary world ever since Mallory revealed it to her when they were twelve. Gigi had some inkling that Mallory only revealed the part of the Republic that she wanted Gigi to see. She knew there were other deeper, darker parts of the Republic.

That was how Alex found them on the bed, holding hands, the duffel bag between them and Mallory weaving giant yarns that never ceased to delight and amaze Gigi. Alex's heart pounded in her head when she got home and heard voices from the bedroom. She was home earlier than usual, a practice she tried to avoid. Having a schedule was a good thing. People could count on that. It was not that she doubted Gigi's fidelity but Gigi did have the uncanny ability to elicit powerful emotions in other people. It was the other people that worried her.

Alex had found her wrapped in another woman's arms on more than one occasion as they were both experiencing some intense bonding as Gigi referred to it. Intense bonding occurred frequently with Ollie. This concerned Alex but she pushed it to the back of her mind and tried to feel the cleansing water of truth, love and fidelity wash across her nervous heart.

"I thought you were leaving." Alex said, ready to be contradicted.

"You are," Gigi said, getting up and pointing at Mallory.

"I am?" Mallory said, feeling like she was standing on the window ledge of a skyscraper with the wind and rush of traffic below blowing up at her. She closed her eyes and tried to stop the sweep of vertigo passing through her.

"Yes, you are," Gigi said, pushing her to the door. She kissed Alex.

"I'll see you Sunday night."

"Give my best to Aunt Lil," Alex said, smiling to avoid the dose of facetiousness she knew was coming. She didn't get it and Gigi was always mysterious about what went on in the land of Airstream trailers.

Aunt Lil was the black sheep of the family just like Gigi. It was her mother's second greatest disgrace that her own sister was a lesbian as well as her daughter. Mrs. Dupont was convinced the water in Yarnell was tainted and had created these homosexuals in her family and when that didn't work she blamed bad genes. She used genetics as a last resort, however, because that meant her sister and her daughter were victims of God and not degenerates that had willingly chosen sin and strap on devices of mysterious origins.

Alex liked to think that Gigi's pilgrimages to Yarnell were simply a way for her to feel better about her family. With Aunt Lil she could be herself and she had several adopted aunts that acted as family. Alex knew Gigi thrived on the attention and she couldn't really blame her for liking this part of her family when the rest were so blatantly horrid to her. Alex was never allowed in the house and Gigi only went home when summoned.

She and Mallory watched as Gigi pulled out the driveway and waved.

"Are you ready to go?" Alex asked.

"Yes," Mallory said bravely.

"Let's go have a drink first. I've got everything in the cooler so it can sit for a while."

"You seem very good at these potluck things. I didn't bring anything . . ." Mallory said, starting to panic.

"You're my date remember. Each couple brings something. I've got you covered."

"What are we bringing?"

"Some finger food stuff I picked up at the deli," Alex said.

"I thought lesbian potlucks meant everyone cooked some specialty dish that everyone fawned over," Mallory said, helping Alex load the cooler in the back of her car.

"This is the twenty-first century darling, all anyone really cares about is whether you bring beer."

"That's what is really in the cooler," Mallory said, feeling less intimidated now that she knew she was not required to produce a delightful dish at each soiree.

"See this is a lot easier than you thought."

"Where are we going for a drink?" Mallory asked.

"Let's go to Winks. It's on the way. We can talk."

Mallory looked out the car window.

"Not about anything serious. You're Gigi's best friend and I never get to talk to you without Gigi answering everything for you. I'd like to hear you say something . . . anything," Alex said, touching Mallory's arm gently.

"We can't talk about the Republic, not yet at least," Mallory said, looking uncertain.

"No, we don't have to talk about it."

"Maybe we can one day when we know each other better," Mallory said, sensing she was already getting on Alex's nerves.

"That's all I want Mallory, just a chance for us to be friends, okay? No big deal," Alex said, pulling into the parking lot of Winks.

"No big deal. Can I buy the drinks?"

"If you'd like."

"I like to because friends do that, right?"

"Right," Alex replied, stopping herself from asking Mallory if Gigi was the only friend she'd ever had. Alex couldn't help wondering what sort of emotional wasteland Mallory inhabited. Maybe she did want to talk about the Republic. Perhaps it would give her a clue about Mallory and Gigi's relationship.

Mallory had two martinis while Alex sipped a beer. With severe coaching she got Mallory off the barstool and into the car.

"I can do this, right?" Mallory asked tentatively.

"It's going to be easy because everyone is on their third or fourth cocktail which is why we went to the bar. Now we are all even, everyone is at their social best and most of the awkward moments have now passed," Alex said, expertly avoiding traffic.

"You're a good driver," Mallory said, picking up CDs from the console.

Alex looked over, pleasantly surprised.

"Gigi never told you that. She's short on compliments," Mallory replied.

"Find one you want?" Alex asked.

"This one," Mallory said. "Now you'll know another thing about me."

"Yes, music tells."

"Sometimes more than the Oracles at Delphi," Mallory replied.

Mallory made Alex do some deep breathing exercises before they went in.

"Does this really work?" Alex inquired after they had done three sets of twelve.

"Don't you feel better?" Mallory said, looking the picture of relaxation. She almost glowed with inner light.

"No, I feel like I'm hyperventilating," Alex said.

"You're not doing it right then. Come on let's get this over with while I'm feeling centered."

"Do you do this a lot?"

"All the time. At first I was skeptical but with enough practice I've become a believer."

Alex was the perfect partner. She introduced Mallory to everyone she knew at the party. Ollie and Mallory eyed each other like they both knew a lot about the other via Gigi.

Ollie's partner Kim was gracious but already taxed at putting on this social extravaganza. Ollie, of course, was no help.

She is a lot like Gigi, Mallory thought, inconsiderate without being malicious. They don't mean to be laissez-faire but they are and so their partners endlessly pick up the slack. It was one of Gigi's traits Mallory would shortly reform. She endeared herself to Kim by helping her organize the food table and get people set up with plates and cutlery. Alex was mildly surprised at Mallory's forthrightness but then she had never seen Mallory at work where her coordinating skills made her vending company run smoothly and profitably.

Del Farnsworth, a friend of Kim's from work, watched Mallory intently. She liked what she saw. Anyone who wore flannel pajamas with grill items as the pattern was all right in her book. She just wished she could get a better look. Mallory was in disguise with a ball cap and Ray-Bans. Del figured it was intentional. She knew a shy woman when she saw one. She watched as Mallory stood holding her plate and talking to Ollie and Alex. Del had met Ollie before at a party with Gigi. Alex was still at work and the way Ollie and Gigi carried on Del swore something was going on but she knew Kim and Ollie had been together for a while and then Alex showed up. Del found herself quite confused. Neither Kim nor Alex seemed to find anything wrong with having their girlfriends hanging all over each other. Del knew this because she had interrupted one of their embraces on her way to the restroom.

Ollie went to get another beer. Del saw her chance.

"Introduce me to your friend," Del said.

"To Mallory?" Ollie asked, obviously surprised.

"She's single, right?" Del asked, wondering if she'd miscalculated.

13

"She's single but, you know, she's a little *different*," Ollie cautioned.

"That's what I like," Del assured her.

"I think you'll find she's a lot more than you bargained for," Ollie replied.

"I'm a big girl. I'll sign a waiver if you'd like so you won't be responsible."

Ollie smiled. "All right. Come on. You're about to get on the ride of your life."

Mallory felt her pulse quicken as Del approached. Del put on her best cruising look, the mildly interested gaze, the quick lick of the lips, the soft squeeze of the hand. Mallory let Alex do the talking while she stood quietly playing with her potato salad. Del's eyes never left her face. Mallory started to sweat and she felt the onset of an anxiety attack. She tried deep breathing. Now was not the time for such an episode.

The afternoon had grown warm and she was wearing flannel, she told herself. Just take more deep breaths. But the shrinking feeling was starting. She felt herself getting smaller like the ground was slowly sucking her down, first her ankles, then knees and soon she was waist deep in grass and no one seemed to notice that she was being sucked out of the conversation. And then with a final pop she was through. She found herself standing by a river. A woman went running past and Mallory called out after her. The woman kept running. Mallory chased her. They ran round and round until they both stood on the other side of the river without ever having crossed it. Mallory looked over at the other woman. She smiled. The woman was herself.

Mallory opened her eyes. She was flat on her back with her plate of potato salad sitting firmly on her chest. Del was peering down at her.

"We should get you inside," Del said, helping her up.

"What happened?" Mallory asked, feeling groggy and borderline nauseous.

"You fainted," Alex said, taking one of her arms as Del took the other. They put her on the couch in the living room.

"Let me get my bag," Del said.

"I'll get her a drink of water," Alex said.

"Del is a doctor," Ollie explained to Mallory.

Mallory took a deep breath and looked over at Dr. Kohlrabi after she'd recounted what she was referring to as the Barbecue Incident.

"And what happened after that?" Dr. Kohlrabi asked.

"Aside from me being perfectly mortified and ruining a brand new set of flannel pajamas with spicy brown mustard?" Mallory said, turning herself right side up, consternation written across her face in bold letters.

"Yes," Dr. Kohlrabi replied. "Tell me about the woman."

"What woman?" Mallory asked, adjusting her sandal.

"The one you don't want to talk about, the one that gave you the anxiety attack because she likes you."

"I don't think she's an issue," Mallory said.

"Mallory . . ."

"All right. Her name is Del. She's a doctor and she just transferred out here from Chicago. She is a friend of Kim's from the hospital. She doesn't have a girlfriend because between med school and interning her schedule killed most attempts at romance and now women seem to be more interested in her status as a doctor than her being a person with a profession."

"That's a start."

"Do you think it's true about the doctor thing, how people react to you?"

"Yes. How do you feel about the other things she told you?"

"I think they're true. I know I wouldn't be that popular if I was a practicing lesbian because I work a lot. It seems togetherness is a big issue in the relationship department."

"Would you go out with Del?"

"Have you lost your mind? No way!"

"Why not?"

"Because I don't date."

"How do you expect to meet someone if you don't date?" Dr. Kohlrabi asked.

"I don't expect to meet anyone."

"Do you plan to spend the rest of your life alone?"

"No. I have Gigi."

"But Gigi is in a relationship with someone else."

"I know that but one day . . ."

"What if that one day doesn't come?"

Mallory looked at the clock. "Isn't our time up?"

"I have a few extra minutes," Dr. Kohlrabi challenged.

"Well, I don't."

"Don't cross Del off so quickly."

"I borrowed a shirt after mine got soiled. I have to give it back."

"So you'll see her again."

"I was going to have it delivered . . . with one of my bonsai plants as a thank you. She likes bonsai. We talked about their simplicity and meditative value."

"You have something in common."

"So do all the people who go to baseball games. It doesn't make them lovers," Mallory countered.

"Next week?" Dr. Kohlrabi inquired. opening her appointment book.

"If I don't get run over by a truck."

Gigi and Mallory sat on the couch by the canal waiting for people to go by so Gigi could take a photograph. She had her camera set up on a tripod with a long release cord. It was her latest art project. Gigi had a long list of strange projects. She purposely made bad art to see if the art community would accept it and hail the creation as modern. She did this with the intent of poignantly stabbing the art community in its big, fat, conceited ass. Sometimes her projects backfired like her series on fridge doors that made it into one of the downtown galleries and the local papers.

16

Mallory could never tell if Gigi liked this or if she viewed notoriety as a failure. Gigi was testing her notion that the universe was perverse in that it toyed with human desire and that desiring brought about bad consequences and that only the lack of desire brought about desired consequences.

"At least you didn't puke, that would have been really embarrassing," Gigi said, getting ready to snap a photo of an unsuspecting passerby, a woman in giant pink rollers and a checkered dress, walking a white poodle.

"I think fainting was right up there," Mallory replied, not wanting to discuss the Incident any further.

"Ollie said Dr. Del was real interested in you. What's the deal there?" Gigi asked.

"Nothing."

"Kim says she gave Del your number. Did she call?"

"Yes," Mallory said, looking away. She despised the intrinsic matchmaking desires of married couples.

"Well?"

"Well what?"

"What did you talk about?"

"Nothing. She thanked me for the plant."

"What plant?" Gigi asked.

"I gave her a bonsai," Mallory said, trying to be nonchalant.

"You never gave me a bonsai," Gigi said.

"You don't like them. You said they were creepy."

"How did you know she'd want one?" Gigi asked suspiciously.

"We talked about them. She liked the one Kim has."

"And you bragged that you made it."

"I didn't brag. I simply told her the story about Kim's father teaching me how to do it. Del said she always admired the art but never knew anyone who could actually do it. That's all," Mallory said, her face wrinkling in perturbation.

"Are you going out on a date?" Gigi said.

"No."

"Did she ask?" Gigi said.

"Is this any of your business?"

"Only if you have something to hide," Gigi countered.

"All right she asked. I told her I don't date but that I might consider showing up at another one of the soirees."

"Are you really going to?"

"I don't know."

Del went to Alex's dinner party only to discover that Mallory wasn't coming. Alex tried to explain to Del that when Gigi went to pick Mallory up to ensure she would arrive Mallory had made up some not very good excuses for not coming. Gigi hadn't done her best to be persuasive.

"Mallory is a little different," Alex said.

"But that's what I like about her," Del said, using bravado to cover her disappointment. Kim had already warned her that even thinking about courting Mallory was going to be one endless disappointment. Kim told her to let it go but Del couldn't. All she thought about was taking Mallory's cap and glasses off to discover a pretty girl who was smart and odd. She did things that moved Del. She liked being moved.

Del spent the evening helping Alex with the dinner party while Gigi played bad girl with Ollie. Del liked Alex but couldn't help thinking that Gigi was an incorrigible flirt who would do better to pay attention to her wife more and other women less. All Del wanted was a nice girl to fall in love with, someone she could romance and charm who wouldn't think it was old-fashioned and corny, someone who would stay true and not wander like Alex's and Kim's partners. She thought she might have found her in Mallory, but why did it have to be so hard? But Del was no quitter. She had set her sights on Mallory and neurotic or not she wasn't going to give up yet.

In the warehouse of Kokopeli Was An Alien Vending Company, Mallory was dealing with the daily stress of running a business. She was doing a good job, she thought, of avoiding her mixed emotions.

On the one hand, Gigi had been much more attentive since Del had come into her life but on the other hand, Mallory actually suffered a guilt pang about standing Del up. This did not move her enough to call Del and apologize. Mallory thought about calling every day, had even picked the phone up once or twice but the days had slipped into weeks and she knew she was letting time sweep away her options.

Jose was supposed to be delivering a set of machines to a new account but Mallory could hear him on the phone with his pregnant girlfriend. Mallory was sympathetic to their plight—they were just youngsters with a devout Catholic family and an unwed child on the way. There was bound to be a little tension in their family relations but she had promised delivery today and being consistent in an inconsistent industry was what kept Mallory's business on top of the rest.

Running her own business and not using her family's wealth, was a source of great pride to Mallory. In their eyes she might be a psychotic lesbian, however she was good at running a profitable business. This kernel of knowledge had kept her grounded more times than she cared to count. She wasn't about to let Jose's lazy work habits fuck it up. She should have fired him months ago but he had become one of her pet projects. She tried to convince herself that he was worth saving. Today she wasn't so sure.

"Jose, get off the phone and get those machines on the truck and delivered, right this minute."

He nodded and started to move the pallet jack toward the end of the dock while still attempting to get off the phone with his girlfriend. The phone jerked off the table as the pallet jack hit a crack in the cement. The badly placed vending machine toppled and started to come toward Mallory who was busy watching the semi driver pulling into the dock with supplies.

Jose screamed. Startled, Mallory stepped backward, her movements not quite fast enough to avoid the machine that landed squarely on her foot. Jose stood frozen.

Guadalupe had her wits about her enough to pull the pallet jack back and lift the machine off Mallory's foot with Jose's help. They both stared at Mallory who was grimacing while they both peered at the bleeding foot.

She took a deep breath. "Guadalupe will you please get me a bag full of ice. Jose load the machine and get it delivered."

"Boss, I'm so sorry, so sorry," Jose pleaded.

"It's fine. Get moving."

Guadalupe got her ice and a rolling stool and together they put her into the car.

"I'll drive you," Guadalupe said.

"No, you need to check in the supplies and answer the phone," Mallory said, wincing as she got into the car and tried to stop the waves of nausea that were creeping over her.

She puked twice on the way to the hospital. She pulled up into the Emergency driveway and hopped up to the admittance desk. Then she called Gigi.

"I'm at the hospital. I need you to come."

"What?" Gigi screeched.

"Phoenix Baptist," Mallory said, hanging up as the nurse put her in a wheelchair.

They helped her onto the gurney. Mallory positioned herself to look out the window while she waited for the doctor. If she concentrated hard enough on the clouds and trees she could keep herself from crying.

Del came in the room and saw Mallory sitting with her back to her. Her heart skipped a beat.

"You didn't have to go to all the trouble to hurt yourself. You could have just called and apologized for standing me up," Del teased as she came around the side of the bed. She saw Mallory's hand, knuckles turning white clutching the bedrail.

Del looked down at her foot still wrapped in plastic, the ice melting and the bag slowly filling with blood.

"Do you have a bucket? I think I'm going to puke."

"Sweet Jesus," Del said, getting her a bucket, a nurse and a shot of Demerol.

Gigi came flying in the room with an admitting clerk right on her heels.

"It's all right. She's family," Del instructed the clerk who was put off at being so flagrantly ignored.

"What happened?" Gigi asked.

"Jose dropped Big Bertha on my foot. My truck is probably being towed as we speak. Will you go park it if that is still an option," Mallory said, handing Gigi her car keys.

"You drove here?" both Del and Gigi said.

"It was either drive myself here or commit murder. I didn't want to go to prison for strangling a short, fat, lazy bastard. It's bad enough I'll have to fire him."

Del set her foot while Gigi tried not to watch. She held Mallory's hand.

When she was done Del said, "Do you want the good news or the bad news first?"

"The bad news," Mallory said.

"Is the glass half empty or half full?" Del teased.

"Half empty," Mallory replied.

"The good news is it was clean break in the middle of your foot meaning you were extremely lucky you didn't crush your foot. The bad news is you're going to lose all your toenails."

"Toenails I can handle," Mallory said, feeling sillier and sillier from the drugs.

Del wheeled Mallory out to her truck. Gigi had pulled up front.

"Are you taking her home?" Del asked.

"No, I'm taking her to my place. I don't think she should be alone," Gigi said.

"Good. She's going to need some help for a little while and she needs crutches."

"I'll get her some," Gigi said.

Mallory's truck was too high for her to slide into the seat from the wheelchair. Gigi studied the situation. Her Jeep was no lower.

"If I get her in the truck can you lift her out when you get home?" Del asked, taking a good look at Gigi who appeared to be strong.

"Of course I can. She weighs all of a hundred and ten pounds."

"Okay, Mallory I'm going to pick you up," Del said, gently drawing her attention back to the present moment.

She picked her up while Gigi moved the wheelchair back.

"Del?" Mallory said.

"Yes?" Del said, still holding her.

"I'm sorry I stood you up," Mallory said, looking deep into Del's eyes.

"That's okay. Another time," Del replied, setting her in the truck, feeling her heart quicken a beat and her face turn red.

"You know her?" Gigi asked, as she pulled out of the parking lot.

"That's Del. The one I met at the party."

"I see," Gigi said, feeling jealous suddenly that Mallory's affections were being drawn somewhere else.

Gigi managed to get Mallory in the house and into bed, with both of them laughing.

"You don't make a very good knight-in-shining armor," Mallory said, feeling giddy and sleepy from the drugs.

"What? Del does it better?" Gigi asked.

"Of course she does. Del is a much better butch than you," Mallory said, curling up in bed.

"Says you," Gigi said, hopping into bed next to Mallory.

Mallory rolled over and looked at Gigi. "Thanks for rescuing me."

"That's what best friends are for. So tell me more about Del," Gigi said, pulling Mallory close.

"There's really nothing to tell," Mallory said, getting sleepier by the second.

"Do you like her?"

"Not as much as I like you," Mallory said, touching Gigi's face and feeling something that she knew her drug induced stupor allowed but that the sharp edges of reality would have quickly buried but everything was getting fuzzier by the second.

Gigi pulled her closer. They stared into each other's eyes, each trying to read the other's thoughts. For Mallory it was drug-induced confusion; for Gigi it was an act of cowardice. She kissed Mallory knowing she wouldn't remember it and as their tongues danced together they lived a moment that would go no further.

Mallory murmured that she loved Gigi and fell asleep in her arms. Gigi kissed her face. She wished she had the courage to do and say the things she'd been thinking most of their lives. She knew it was the fear of not being the woman Mallory envisioned her to be. It wasn't Gigi's other lovers that kept them apart—it was Gigi's lack of faith in herself. A faith destroyed so long ago that the vacuous hole it created became a gaping abyss that no amount of art, drugs, or lust could fill.

When Alex came home she found her girlfriend in the arms of another woman. At least it was Mallory but there were times when Alex wished her wife were faithful. Gigi called them harmless infatuations but nonetheless Alex wished they weren't there. She couldn't stop herself from thinking that if Gigi really loved her she wouldn't have these minor infatuations and just because she swore she didn't sleep with anyone else it didn't mean she didn't want to, and that scared Alex.

Two

Kim stood in Del's office having been summoned while she was doing rounds. Del was rubbing her forehead, obviously deliberating over something.

Finally Kim said, "What is it?"

"It's Mallory," Del said, looking up apologetically. "I need some advice."

"Mallory . . ."

"Help me here," Del said.

"All right," Kim replied, trying to conjure up her best thoughts about Mallory. She was having a hard time. She kept envisioning a helpless, paranoid, strangely dressed woman who professed to be a non-practicing lesbian.

"She broke her foot the other day," Del began. She bit her lip and studied Kim's face which was the picture of Eastern placidness.

"Okay," Kim said.

"And I helped her into her truck later. She looked at me." Del replied.

"Okay," Kim said, thinking she needed more to work with than a look. "What kind of a look?"

"That's just it, I don't know," Del said.

"Perhaps you could call her and find out," Kim suggested.

"You really think so?" Del gushed, the perfect teenager.

"Is that what you wanted to ask me?"

"Yes," Del replied.

"Maybe you two are right for each other," Kim replied.

"What do you mean?" Del asked, picking up the phone.

"You'll see," Kim said.

"Do you think she's home?"

"No, she's at Gigi's," Kim said, taking the phone. "I'll set you up."

Gigi acted odd but agreed that Del could come over. Kim shrugged her shoulders, thinking the whole tribe was weird. Sometimes Gigi behaved as if Mallory was her girlfriend, sometimes Alex and other times . . . Kim hung up the phone and found she was breathing easier. Maybe what she saw happening between Ollie and Gigi was her imagination. Maybe Gigi's idea of friendship was deep but not sexual.

"What are you doing?" Mallory asked as Gigi hung up the phone and began to madly straighten the house. She was bored stiff and had finished the one and only book in Gigi's house, Tolstoy's *War and Peace*, a leftover from some previous guest. If she was home she'd have had stacks of books to read. She didn't understand how people lived without reading. Gigi was holding her hostage. Every morning for three days she'd begged to go home but Gigi thought it was too soon.

"Del is coming over to look at your foot," Gigi said, puffing up the pillows on the couch and straightening Mallory's collar as she went. Mallory felt like a piece of furniture.

"I didn't think doctors made house calls anymore," Mallory said, immediately experiencing heart palpitations.

"This one does," Gigi said, grimacing.

"If you don't like her why did you agree to let her come over?" Mallory asked.

"Who said I didn't like her?" Gigi said, slamming dishes into the dishwasher.

"I got that vibe," Mallory said, trying to appear cool and collected.

"She's a doctor. You don't have to subject yourself to an office visit. I thought it was good," Gigi said, lying without one moment of hesitation. She let Del come over because she wanted a chance to size her up. The house call was a perfect opportunity.

"Why are you cleaning the house?" Mallory asked.

"Because it's dirty," Gigi countered.

"You never clean."

"I clean sometimes," Gigi said, getting the vacuum cleaner out.

"You actually know how to run a vacuum cleaner?" Mallory teased.

Gigi turned on the vacuum cleaner and purposely screamed, "I can't hear you."

Mallory was forced to concentrate on her own nervousness. Part of her was excited to see Del while another part was standing on the white sandy Beach of Mortification in a faraway region of the Republic. All her interior landscapes were in black and white with the exception of the Garden of Good Things. There everything bloomed in color. These were usually moments when she thought about Gigi and their future life together. It always shriveled when reality came crashing in.

The Beach of Mortification was her place of shame, the place of inadequacy, where all her failures came crashing into the shore captured in the gray waves and echoing across the beach. Mallory couldn't understand what Del saw in her. All Del's efforts to get close to Mallory served to remind her of the times she spent with

Caroline before she walked out of Mallory's life forever, leaving her with only pajamas as a memory. To be chased in Mallory's mind was to be caught, seduced, and deserted. Mallory was walking up the shoreline listening to her failures when Del arrived.

Del examined Mallory's foot, took her blood pressure and her temperature. In the midst of the medical exam Mallory forgot to be frightened.

"How's the pain?" Del asked, shining her penlight in Mallory's eyeball.

"The painkillers make me nauseous so I haven't been taking them," Mallory replied, smelling Del's cologne, CK One. Mallory felt herself quiver at the scent. A nice-smelling woman was hard to turn down.

"So how's she doing?" Gigi asked, peering over Del's shoulder.

"We need to get her some other pain medication," Del said, writing a script and handing it to Gigi, who refrained from making a rude comment about being the errand boy.

"I'll go," Gigi said.

Mallory sat back in the recliner and nodded. "Maybe that's a good idea."

"I'll wait with her," Del said, "if that's all right."

"Sure," Gigi said.

"How long am I going to need supervision?" Mallory asked.

"Until *we* decide you can get about on your own," Gigi replied.

"When will that be, Del?" Mallory asked.

"It depends on how mobile you are, what kind of a setup your house has and how the drugs affect you."

"I feel like a hostage," Mallory whispered to Del as Gigi left.

"We could get you a walker and set your house up to make it more user friendly," Del said.

"Tell me what I need to do so I can get on with my life. Gigi won't let me out of her sight and I never thought I'd say this about my best friend but all this togetherness is wearing thin."

"I bet," Del said, smiling.

"Can I make you some tea?"

"I'd like that," Del said.

"Perhaps I can demonstrate my abilities and you can talk Gigi into letting me go home," Mallory said, grabbing her crutches and hobbling to the kitchen, trying to disguise her wincing face.

"You should have said something about the medication. It will make you feel a lot better. I know you're tough but it puts unnecessary stress on your body when it is trying to heal."

"I know," Mallory said, getting up herself up on the counter and putting the kettle on.

Del watched as she ingeniously scooted about the countertop making tea.

"You're getting about rather well, I see, perhaps I can talk Gigi into letting you go home soon," Del said.

"That would be a great service," Mallory said.

"But I would like something in exchange," Del said, knowing she was pushing the limits but she needed to do something if she was going to see Mallory again.

"And what would that be?" Mallory asked, feeling her face getting flushed.

"That I could have lunch with you. It wouldn't be a date. It would just be lunch. You've got to eat, right?" Del asked, looking as tentative and nervous as Mallory was feeling.

"I think lunch might be okay, as long as it wasn't a date," Mallory said, struggling to get off the counter and back onto her crutches.

"Can I help?" Del asked, coming over. "Put your arms around my neck and I'll lift you down."

Mallory obeyed.

In mid lift, Del asked, "Is lunch not a date because you don't want to go out with me or because you don't like to go out on dates period?"

Mallory could see Del wasn't going to set her down until she answered the question and it was hard between the cologne and Del's blue eyes not to feel a moment of longing despite her basic philosophy that she was a non-practicing lesbian.

"I don't go out on dates but I will have lunch with you," Mallory said, as Gigi walked in the door, stopped in her tracks, mouth gaping.

"That will do," Del said, putting her down. She turned to Gigi. "She's ready to go home."

The Simpsons' house was nestled high against Camelback Mountain with its glass living room positioned like a large pointed nose looking down on the rest of the city. As Mallory drove up the winding road to the house she ran through her list of why she did not agree with the politics of wealth. First she despised her mother's lack of social conscience and sense of reality. People with money have no sense of reality. They have no concept of ugliness, dirt, hunger, or crime. Nothing bad happens around them because they are insulated by wealth so they never go anywhere to see dirt, poverty and violence.

Mallory had learned a lot by sitting on Gigi's dirty couch on the canal. She learned what not having money could do to people. People without money had too much reality in their lives and no delusions because to be deluded you needed money. Her mother and her father were deluded into thinking life was nice. They could not begin to fathom the kind of life Mallory observed and to a certain extent surrounded herself with. Where she lived, the inner city albeit the central corridor, gave her more knowledge of humankind than her entire college education in sociology afforded. Her life and the life she observed were completely outside her parents' ken.

Harrington and Buffy Simpson diligently chose to ignore this fact and did their best to pretend that Mallory was attending country club events and devoting herself to charity in between taking care of her adoring husband and two point five children.

"I told you something like this would happen if you continued to insist on carting those . . . what do you call them?" Buffy Simpson said, suddenly at a loss as she mixed two martinis.

"Commonly referred to as *vending machines*. You put money in them and stuff comes out," Mallory said, plucking two cocktail olives from the fancy silver container and plopping them in her drink.

"Why do you do it?" Buffy asked, her face the picture of perplexity.

"Do what?"

"All these *things*, that are so unlike other girls," Buffy said.

"Because I'm crazy," Mallory replied.

"Don't say that, don't *ever* say that," Buffy said, her eyebrows drawing themselves together until they formed a light blond caterpillar. Her eyes closed and she breathed out slow and even like she was exorcising demons.

"You asked," Mallory said.

"How are your sessions with Dr. Kolhrabi going?" Buffy asked, trying to recover her composure.

"Fine. She's helping me through my latest dating crisis."

"You're dating someone," Buffy said, sidling up to Mallory on the couch with a do-tell-look written blatantly across her face.

"It's a woman," Mallory said, watching her mother's shoulders shrink.

"I know that," Buffy said, quickly regaining her composure, thinking it couldn't possibly hurt to hope otherwise.

"I'm not dating her really but we are having lunch."

"I see. Where did you meet her?" Buffy inquired.

"At a potluck."

"What's that?"

"Never mind. It's entirely beyond your comprehension."

"What does she do?" Buffy asked.

"Does it matter?" Mallory asked, getting up and looking into the dining room. Cook had just finished setting the table. She reminded herself the ordeal would be over soon.

"Yes, it matters. What a person does for a living reveals a lot about them."

"What do you tell people I do?" Mallory countered.

Buffy looked away.

"What do you tell them?" Mallory demanded.

"I tell them you're away."

"I see. Your *invisible* daughter."

"It's not that, Mallory. I don't know what to tell them. It's just easier."

"And certainly less embarrassing than telling them your daughter is a self-employed vending machine person and a lesbian."

Buffy was spared further grief by Cook and Harrington as they simultaneously entered the living room.

Harrington put a clumsy arm around his daughter and said, "So how's business?"

"Booming," Mallory replied, going through the same motions to the same questions that comprised her relationship with her father.

"That's my girl," Harrington said, leading the way to the dining room.

Ollie and Gigi sat on the back steps of Kim's house and shared a cigarette. Neither one of them was supposed to be smoking but so far the sessions with the hypnotist were not taking root yet. They both swore they were trying.

"It's like heroin you know. Not an easy thing to give up," Gigi said, taking a long drag.

"I know. People just don't understand," Ollie said.

"Not to mention I'm getting fat," Gigi said, pulling up her shirt and pinching her stomach.

"Oh my God! You can pinch an inch, how disgusting," Ollie said, grabbing Gigi's inch and then pushing her to the ground for a complete tickle.

"I want you to know that I completely disagree with this treatment," Gigi screamed in between fits of gasping laughter.

"You like it. I know you do," Ollie said, pinning Gigi to the grass. She came dangerously close to kissing her, going in close, rubbing

Gigi's nose and had her wife not miraculously appeared, she would have kissed her.

"What do we have here?" Kim asked diplomatically.

"Gigi thinks she getting fat from not smoking," Ollie replied with equal decorum.

"I see. Are you perhaps measuring her body fat?" Kim asked, trying not to take obvious offense at her lover's current position.

"Now that's a good one," Ollie said, standing up and giving prone Gigi a hand up.

"No, I was teaching her a lesson about vanity, that being concerned about an inch is utter bullshit."

"How is the non-smoking life treating you two?" Kim said, picking up the lit cigarette lying on the step and handing it to Ollie.

"Fine," Ollie said, taking a drag and handing the cigarette to Gigi.

"Are you coming in?" Kim asked pointedly.

"In a minute," Ollie said, taking the cigarette back.

"Fine," Kim said, going inside.

Kim ran into Del in the kitchen. Her normally placid face was not composed. She twisted her long dark hair into a knot.

"You okay?" Del asked.

Kim nodded.

Del looked past her shoulder and saw Ollie reach for Gigi. She shook her head. All Del wanted was a faithful, tender lover. Seeing what Kim was going through only made her want it more. She was done cruising. She wanted a woman to make a life with. She wanted Mallory. She wanted Mallory to be here, but Gigi had told her Mallory was having dinner with her parents. She said she might stop by later, to which Gigi rolled her eyes in a *like never* position. Consequently, Del was enjoying another evening in the bosom of the lesbian love fest hoping Mallory was going to show up.

After the Gigi-Kim-Ollie thing, Del decided to call it an evening. When she walked outside, Mallory was sitting on the tailgate of her truck. Del did a double take.

"Mallory?" Del asked, not trusting herself.

"I wondered when you would show up. Making a hasty retreat are you?" Mallory teased.

"Well, since you're here everything has changed," Del replied.

"But I'm not really here," Mallory said.

"You're not?"

"Not officially."

"What are you doing then?"

"Wondering if you would be here," Mallory said, looking intently at Del.

"In the flesh," Del said, bowing extravagantly.

"Are you staying?" Mallory asked.

"Only if you are," Del said.

"Want to go for walk?" Mallory asked.

"With your foot?" Del said, looking down.

"There's a park half a block from here. I can walk that far," Mallory replied.

"Let's go," Del said.

Mallory threw Del a blanket. "Know anything about the stars?"

"No, but I bet you can teach me," Del said.

"As a matter of fact I can. Come with me little lady," Mallory said, crutching off toward the corner.

"Little?" Del asked, catching up and straightening her five foot eight frame.

Mallory smirked.

They made their way down the dimly lit street. Kim's neighbors' houses had lights emanating from various rooms. Neighborhoods always reminded Del that she didn't live in one and that most of her adult life had been spent in the rented boxes masquerading as apartment living. It made her think of Mallory's queer little house not far from here. A house meant you were staying somewhere, making this space real and permanent. Del wanted permanence.

"Why did you come tonight?" Del asked, when they stopped and spread out the blanket.

33

"I wanted to see if you'd be there because you thought I might," Mallory said, slowly easing onto the blanket and setting her crutches next to her.

"I did," Del said.

"Why?" Mallory asked, getting out her brass spyglass. She laid back and stared at Betelgeuse and Rigel, the two powerhouse stars that made up the shoulder and knee of Orion. Tonight was perfect for stargazing as the moon was no more than a sliver in the sky.

"Because you still won't have lunch with me."

"You never called," Mallory said, handing Del the spyglass.

"I thought you were going to call me," Del said, putting her eye up to the piece.

"Oh, kind of a mix-up then," Mallory said, not knowing if she was supposed to be relieved or all the more terrified.

"What am I supposed to be looking at," Del asked, rolling on her side making her elevated slightly above Mallory's prone body. Her eyes wanted to roam carelessly over Mallory's body but she didn't dare. Instead, Mallory pushed her back and took her right hand, pointed its finger and began to give her lessons in navigating the universe. She drew the constellations by connecting the bright dots of lights that filled the deep blue night. Then they would look through the spyglass.

"I'm not very good at this sort of thing, you know," Mallory said.

"What kind of thing?" Del teased, still holding Mallory's hand in her own. Mallory's hand was small and smooth but with rounded calluses on her fingertips and around the joints. Del had made hands a minor study as she had the opportunity to see so many people in a day. She hoped to keep Mallory occupied so she could keep holding her hand. Del knew it was a stolen moment but at this point she was already beggar, man, thief. She wondered what Mallory thought.

Instead, Mallory rolled over, took Del's finger and stuck it in her mouth. Del turned instantly red and was extremely thankful for the dark night. It created a thickness between them that allowed for such an intimacy without shame or anxiety.

"Now that I've done that I think I can go to lunch with you," Mallory said.

"Tomorrow at high noon?" Del inquired.

"I can manage that," Mallory said.

There was a commotion up the street. They could hear loud women's voices.

"Perhaps we should go," Del said, feeling propriety tug at her when all she wanted to do at this moment was exist next to Mallory beneath an indigo sky.

When they got there, Ollie was screaming at Kim, who stood totally undaunted. She kept repeating, "I'm not the one out of line here."

"Right now I don't give a fuck about lines, points, or circles. I just want to get my car out of your driveway so I can get as far away as I can from you," Ollie screamed.

"It's my truck. I'll move it," Mallory said. "Sorry."

Ollie looked at Del and Mallory, made a brief connection, scowled at her girlfriend and screeched out of the driveway.

"Isn't love grand," Mallory said, still in the truck.

"It can be. Got to go?" Del asked, standing by the side of the truck.

"Think it might be a good idea," Mallory said.

"See you tomorrow?"

"Yes," Mallory said.

As she drove home Mallory tried to understand why she had gone to the party in the first place. Was it her mother's statement that rendered her daughter an invisible part of her life? Was it thinking about how it felt to have a woman truly interested in her?

She went because part of her liked Del, liked the feelings she got from her. But part of her saw too many parallels that comprise the art of courting between Del and the only other woman she had loved in her life. She would talk to Dr. Kohlrabi tomorrow. She would know what to do.

The sky didn't have the same charm as it had when she was stargazing with Mallory. Del and Kim sat on her back porch having a nightcap.

"I don't think it's asking too much to want her to be physically faithful. I know we all have our fantasy moments but does she have to fool around with our friends, not to mention someone else's partner?" Kim said.

"It's not good," Del said, sympathetically.

"If she wants to be with someone else fine, but don't cheat on me. If you don't want me, let me know. Don't pretend, stay for the sake of staying, and then fuck someone else. And to top it off she has the audacity to think me a prude because I take offense at her sitting on top another woman getting ready to kiss her. I'm not wrong am I?"

"No, you're not," Del said. "You have every right to expect to live with someone who is true."

"Thank you, Del. You're such a sweet woman," Kim said, leaning on Del's shoulder.

"I try."

"You like Mallory?" Kim asked, suddenly remembering she had seen them together earlier.

"I do. I just hope she likes me."

"What's not to like," Kim said, pinching one of Del's dimples.

They didn't say much on the way home, but Gigi knew this was the proverbial calm before the storm. Alex would wait until they were safely parked before she began her list of thoughts and desires.

Gigi tried to gather responses. They'd done this before.

"I just don't understand your fervent interest in other women if you're happy with me," Alex said, her voice very even as she locked the car door.

"I'm only playing around," Gigi said, starting slow and easy.

"Playing around enough to get the host's girlfriend escorted from the premises," Alex said, opening the front door and leaning down scratch Vesuvius' ears. She picked the cat up. She looked at Gigi sadly.

"I'm sorry," Gigi said.

"I wish you loved me as much as I love you," Alex said.

"I do."

"No, you don't," Alex said, sitting on the couch.

"Coming to bed?" Gigi asked as Alex petted the cat and slipped her shoes off.

"No, I think I'll watch television. You go," Alex said.

"That's all?" Gigi asked.

"Talking about it doesn't seem to accomplish much. Does it?"

"I suppose not," Gigi said, going off to bed. She was tired and confused by having overindulged in far too hedonistic pursuits. She sensed Ollie was offering more than she was prepared for. Usually these flirtations amounted to nothing more than a slightly indiscreet kiss on New Year's Eve. But when she slips her tongue in your mouth it's more than flirtation. And then the thing in the van was much more . . . She was surprised yet couldn't say she didn't like it. Still, she did love Alex and there were limits to one's partner's patience.

Mallory was sitting upright which did much to disconcert Dr. Kohlrabi. There was something different about Mallory but she had not as yet ascertained what it was. She was wearing her usual pajamas and sandals and her long hair was pulled pack. Her baseball hat sat neatly in her lap and she was attentively looking at the good doctor.

"What's wrong?" Mallory asked.

"Nothing," Dr. Kohlrabi replied.

"Do you think I look different?" Mallory said, getting up, putting her cap back on and looking in the tiled mosaic mirror hanging on the office wall.

"Perhaps a better question would be do you think you look different?"

"Do they teach you that in therapy school?" Mallory asked, peering deeply into her own hazel eyes. They say the eyes are the windows of soul. Mallory wondered what her soul would look like if she could catch a glimpse of it. The Buddhists teach that the soul is a false construction and only when one begins to travel the path does she discover that there is only oneness with the universe and no immutable thing to call your own. This knowledge did much to lighten one's load in the good and evil department but it did little to alleviate the anxiety at the immensity of the universes, planes, infinities that a woman would become a part of.

"Teach what?" Dr. Kohlrabi asked, trying to bring Mallory back from wherever she was traveling.

"Answer a question with a question," Mallory replied, sitting back down. She took her shoes off and assumed her upside down lotus position.

"Yes, I suppose they do," Dr. Kohlrabi said, breathing easier. She knew Mallory was ready to talk.

"Because it's all about me right?"

"Right."

"I went to lunch with Del."

"That's a start," Dr. Kohlrabi said, noting the slight flush in Mallory's face when she mentioned Del's name.

"It was actually fun. She brought Chinese food."

"You liked it?" Dr. Kohlrabi replied.

Mallory thought for a moment. She had liked it. She liked sitting on the floor of her office on an old Mexican blanket bought years before at Rocky Point, bits of sand still nestled in its fibers, the smell of sea lurking somewhere near. The tiny white cartons of the Kyoto Bowl laid out in a circle and Del sitting across from her.

"Yes, but . . ." Mallory said, feeling like she was standing on the Beach of Mortification and her heart was a kite that the wind slammed into the ocean, crushing the wooden bows of the brightly colored kite. She ran to rescue it, only to discover it was beyond repair.

"But what?"

"I'm frightened."

"Of getting intimate?" Dr. Kohlrabi prodded.

"Yes. It's the good feeling that scares me, the kind that makes you crave the other person. And that's dangerous, especially for someone with my past."

"Because they might leave?"

"Yes."

"Not everyone leaves," Dr. Kohlrabi said, thinking of her ex-husband who was off somewhere with a woman half his age.

Times like these made her feel like a hypocrite. Yes, falling in loves means hazarding the risk that you will be disappointed, hurt, skewered and roasted. But not falling in love meant existing in a half-life of safe, antiseptic waters that slowly and inevitably washed you toward emotional oblivion. She would lie and she would cheat to get Mallory out of those waters and into the game of loving chance.

"Name one that stayed," Mallory challenged.

"Eleanor Roosevelt," Dr. Kohlrabi replied. Ellie was handy. She fit into almost any situation. And she was historical enough to avoid any threats of libel.

"Her husband had a mistress and he died in her bed. And Eleanor had a woman for a lover," Mallory replied, undaunted in her belief that being attracted to Del was dangerous.

"But they all stayed together didn't they? Man with wife, man with mistress, woman with man, woman with woman."

"You've got to be kidding. I'm supposed to be the crazy one here," Mallory said.

"You're not crazy. You just need some minor adjustments," Dr. Kohlrabi replied.

"Am I supposed to take that as an indication of my progress?" Mallory inquired, suddenly alarmed with the thought of outgrowing therapy.

"No."

"Good. I can't come next week. Gigi is taking me to Yarnell," Mallory said, getting up.

"That should be interesting. Why don't you take Del with you?"

"You are crazy," Mallory said.

Friday night was ticking past with the setting sun and the clock rings as the girls waited for the pizza man. Del, Alex and Kim sat with their feet in the pool, talking about bad women in their lives. Del wasn't sure being privy to this conversation was a good thing. Young loves should not be subjected to the notion of failure. However, Del had her own failures to relive. She did think it odd or at best spiritually enlightened to be drinking beer with two women who each had partners that were fooling around with each other or at least contemplating it. Was this yet another form of sisterhood?

"You know, Gigi's the kind of woman who will forget to get you toilet paper when you ask yet she'll walk into your backyard and clink every wind chime that you own, a woman who creates her own wind, look you in the eye and tell you that she loves you," Alex said, thinking she'd been wooed senseless and left wanting.

Kim nodded, keeping quiet.

"What do you like best about Ollie?" Del asked.

"I wish I knew," Kim said, not revealing what she always knew about her relationship with Ollie. It was tasteless and harmful and letting go wasn't going to be as difficult as she envisioned.

What she liked best about Ollie was that she was good looking in a way any woman would like. She was thin, blond, blue eyed. She was a complete contrast to the woman Kim saw in the mirror each morning. To be completely and truly fucked as in Yin fucking Yang, Ollie was her polar opposite. I wanted to fuck the other side. With Ollie I did that, unfortunately I also attached the strings of my heart and like an imprudent spider, I'm reaping the nasty rewards.

"You don't know?" Alex asked, suddenly getting the idea that the situation was worse than it was.

"Ollie is a flirt, like Gigi is a flirt. And we both know this is not the first time either one of them has done this kind of thing," Kim said.

"I'm not ready to face this," Alex said, diplomatically.

"You shouldn't have to," Del said.

"But we do," Kim said.

"I know," Alex replied, thinking this was not how she envisioned love. She wanted Gigi to love her unconditionally with the understanding that their love would have ebbs and tides but ultimately prevail. She thought about making love with Gigi before she left for Yarnell. Gigi had come to her, tail between her legs, apologetic, cute, funny and successful in seducing her. Alex couldn't help feeling worked.

As Alex lay naked and warm in Gigi's arms, she had to suppress the desire to ask the question that nagged at her love like a street urchin, intent on getting a coin. Why can't you behave like my lover and my friend, not my truant teenager in constant need of supervision?

Gigi would be good for a while now but she would fail her again and again. The cost of this love affair was getting too high and Alex began to contemplate the end. Alex hated this part of love, especially now that their love had a past behind them. Letting go of Gigi wasn't going to be as uncomplicated as her other lovers. Lovers she hadn't lived with, lovers with whom she hadn't exchanged more than bodily fluids and a few choice details of her life. Gigi knew everything. Gigi's clothes, books and music, photographs, half finished projects littered the house. Gigi's life was intertwined with her own. Letting go would be painful and evident.

But how do you say goodbye to someone who loves you so hard and so well; who can make you smile and laugh while they break your heart and who tells you things about yourself that you didn't even know. Kissing Gigi on the front porch before she left for Yarnell, Alex felt the hunger of absence and it wasn't about a weekend trip, it was about forever.

Road trips were a new sensation to Mallory who did not stray much past the city limits. Travel seemed like something she had done before but ceased to be part of her life after Caroline left. If Caroline was away, staying within the city limits meant she was safe. She was here, her estranged lover was there and an imaginary line was drawn around the city.

As they reached the outskirts of the city, Mallory felt like she was putting a tentative toe in the steamy waters of the greater world. She waited for the first disaster but it didn't come. They were not harassed in the truck stop. They had a good lunch in a small diner, grilled cheese and fries for Mallory and a burger for Gigi.

Gigi turned up the stereo and drove like one possessed. Mallory plugged in compact discs and neither was concerned with the lack of conversation. They were two exclusive bubbles of reality bumping along together in the cab of a pickup truck. They came over the top of the hill and the small community of Yarnell sprung out of the desert floor. The Airstream trailers looked like great silver beetles assembled in a regiment set for inspection.

Seeing her last chance to talk, Gigi broke the silence.

"Alex is pissed at me," Gigi said.

"About the other night?" Mallory said, offering Gigi a vine of red licorice.

"Yes," Gigi said, turning on Bingham Road and out toward the Horizon Hills Mobile Home Park, domain of the Infamous Lesbian Activists, one of which was her Aunt Lil.

"That was pretty stupid. Don't you think?" Mallory said.

"Very stupid," Gigi replied, eyes straight ahead on the road.

"Losing Alex over someone who can't hope to compare is not prudent and I think you would grow to regret it."

"Gotcha," Gigi said. "And thank you."

"Any time, pal," Mallory said, moving close and swinging her arm around Gigi.

Gigi kissed her cheek. "You're the best."

Mallory blushed but she didn't feel the same buzz, the quiver of excitement that she always felt when she got the chance to touch Gigi. One day she was planning their future and the next her infatuation fluttered limply, a forgotten shear hanging in a deserted window. She saw herself as a cowboy, meandering down a dusty dirt road and not looking back at the old shack, her eyes scanning the horizon for something new. The cowboy that was really a girl was new in the Republic, Mallory thought, startled. The Republic did not usually create characters of its own accord. They were in a new part of the Republic with wide-open vistas and a girl with a horse looking for adventure. Mallory smiled. Maybe getting out of town was a good thing.

They pulled in the driveway of the trailer park and Gigi pointed out the locals, rattling off women's names like an old-time Rotary or garden club. All was wasted on Mallory who was still pondering the intrinsic nature of love. Mallory was thinking about the question she had asked Dr. Kohlrabi earlier that day.

"What question would you ask God if you were granted an audience?" Mallory asked.

"I don't understand," Dr. Kohlrabi replied.

"Let me preface this. You know how everyone wants to have the chance to talk to someone they admire. To some people it's a politician, you know, meet the president, or a musician, a movie star, someone from the past."

"You want to ask God a question?"

"Yes, I want to ask why."

"Why we exist?"

"No, why we insist on asking why?"

"What do you mean?" Dr. Kohlrabi asked, thinking sometimes her crazy clients were more lucid than the so-called normal people.

"Why do we get what we want when we no longer want it? Why do we seek what we already have? What sort of capricious, nasty trick is this?"

"That's what you would ask God," Dr. Kohlrabi replied.

"Yes, got any ideas?"

"Only one. There is a master plan or at least a law looming deep in the crevices of the universe that deems struggle and failure as paramount to one's existence."

"To what purpose?"

"So that we become better people."

"We become better people by getting what we want when we no longer want it and lose what we wanted but didn't realize we had. That is the sign of a bastard universe that seeks only to fuck with the best laid plans. People plan. God laughs."

Dr. Kohlrabi did not have a response. The hour was up and now as Mallory sat with Gigi she knew it was a bastard in charge. Gigi had the jewel in her pocket. She didn't have to search the world over for the one lover she was looking for; she already had it in Alex. But Mallory knew Gigi would lose Alex before she gained this knowledge.

A gray haired woman with immense shoulders and tight Wranglers stepped out of one of the silver Airstream trailers. She nodded as Gigi pulled up next to the trailer. Aunt Lil handed Fran a towel as she got out of the hot tub. Fran was Lil's lover of thirty years. She was as broad hipped as Lil was shouldered. Her wrinkled face was a happy mirror of Lil's more intense lines. Gigi always marveled at the lines on the faces of her aunt and her lover, wondering at the years of sun, wind, emotions, and time that left their traces there.

She had looked at the old pictures when Lil's hair was a brilliant black and Fran had been a blonde, when they had dressed up in suits and skirts and gone out on the town, Lil with a swagger and Fran with a swish of the hips and the click of high heels. Gigi wondered about those days when some girls were girls and some girls were boys. It seemed simpler. Lil assured her it wasn't. She often told Gigi how fortunate lesbians were now, how hard and dangerous life had been in those early days. Now is better, definitely better.

"They have a hot tub," Mallory said, admiring the gazebo decorated with old ship artifacts and wooden beads.

44

"Fran has really bad arthritis in her hips," Gigi said, handing Mallory her cane.

"Well, who have we got here?" Lil asked.

"This is my friend Mallory," Gigi replied.

"What happened to your foot?" Lil asked, taking a good look at Mallory's newly outfitted walking cast.

"I got a vending machine dropped on it by a short, fat man who was fighting with his pregnant girlfriend-soon-to-be-miserable bride at the time and not paying attention to what he was doing," Mallory said, feeling herself get hot just thinking about it.

She was still angry with Jose although she hadn't fired him, because the incident had morphed him into some kind of super worker who prostrated himself whenever he was in her presence. Maybe it takes an accident to cure the bad and create the good.

"You're obviously one of us," Lil said, giving Mallory the conspiratorial wink.

"Gigi doesn't know anyone but PLUs," Mallory replied.

"PLUs?" Fran asked, tying her towel around her waist.

"People like us," Mallory replied.

"I do too!" Gigi said, indignantly.

"Name one," Mallory said.

"Do relatives or grocery store clerks count?"

"No!" everyone said in unison.

"And especially people in *your* family," Fran said, emphatically.

As they sat on the screened in porch of the trailer with the misters and fans going full blast drinking a huge ice cold pitcher of lemonade, Fran and Lil filled Mallory in on the family, the one Gigi never talked about.

Mallory felt like she was sitting in a tropical rain forest with all the hanging, climbing, creeping plants that seemed to be growing out of every niche and corner of the makeshift porch. She was waiting for a snake, monkey, bat or bird to come out of nowhere to complete her illusion.

"But I hate when you tell little Gigi stories," Gigi whined.

"This isn't about you this time, or rather only indirectly about you," Fran replied, leaning over to tuck the rainbow colored umbrella she'd opened behind Mallory and just above her head as she had begun to get dripped on.

"Thank you," Mallory replied.

"You're quite welcome, dear. Now where was I?" Fran said.

"We were talking about Rose, my sister Rose, the Virgin Mary incarnate," Lil said.

"She's found out that you've been coming down here again and she's not happy. We're trying to figure out who her spy is," Fran said.

"You don't think it is someone in the park do you?" Gigi asked, always in awe of her mother's ability to be in every part of the universe simultaneously. Gigi wondered sometimes if her mother could see her having sex. She did have the uncanny ability when Gigi was a child to know almost every move she made and consequently all the trouble she got into.

"Well, not everyone in the park is one of us. The Lesbian Activists is an exclusive group," Fran said, lowering her voice and leaning toward Mallory.

"Why isn't everyone?" Mallory asked.

"We need the others as cover; if we were out here exclusively, people would start to wonder what we were up to," Fran said.

Mallory refrained from asking what they were up to because Gigi had warned her that her aunts were lesbian activists. She had had no real idea what this meant, only that they were engaged in something subversive that they were extremely serious about and that somehow or another it involved Gigi.

"Do you think she knows someone in the trailer park and they're giving her reports?" Gigi asked.

"I'd bet my social security check on it," Fran said, taking a big swig of lemonade.

"I'll be damned if that righteous, overbearing, meddling busy-body is going to foil our plans," Lil said.

46

"It would be unfortunate if something nasty happened to her spy just to get the message across that we know she has penetrated our borders," Fran said.

Gigi could see Fran's brain begin to click on possible tortures for the enemy and she inwardly flinched. Both her aunt and Fran were capable of horrid things. It was Aunt Lil after all that taught Gigi to desecrate shrines of the Virgin Mary when she was a child. They used to go out on late night missions of mercy as Lil referred to them.

Lil would park down the street and wait for Gigi to sneak out her bedroom window. They would drive around town and upset the shrines and free the virgin. Bathtubs and stucco shrines would be overturned and the virgin stolen and buried out in Lil's backyard. They always finished the mission by stealing her mother's precious virgin last.

The next morning her mother would wake up and lament the heathen that would do such a thing. And then she would take Gigi with her to the Lord's Shepherd store and buy another ceramic artifact to replace the one that was stolen.

Gigi had decided that standing in a store full of relics was where she learned to lie. She would pretend to lament her mother's loss while secretly reveling in her nightly deeds. She felt like a double agent and she knew repercussions only came if you got caught. Maybe this kind of an upbringing had something to do with her amoral grown-up behavior. She would ask Aunt Lil later what she thought. Lil knew everything.

Lil and Fran got the girls settled and then the four of them went to the Saturday night barbecue. Every Saturday night the trailer park members got together to share food and family anecdotes and plan future activities under the guise of harmless women having a social evening like women had done for centuries. As the women sat around long tables in the recreation room looking perfectly harmless, Mallory wondered if they had secret rituals, handshakes, and moonlight meetings around a fire, dressed in black and doing strange things to chickens.

It was hard to picture this while these older women sat in lawn chairs and exchanged gossip looking like any other retired people filling in the suddenly long days that no longer contained work. They had the same worries about losing Social Security benefits, the laments for days gone by, and certain animosities for long-lost aspirations. The women looked like other women but every now and again Mallory would see the machinations of the political organization at work.

Fran watched as Mallory observed the group. She knew she had questions but thought it impertinent to ask. Fran took the leap that Mallory could not.

"Trade a question?" Fran asked, snapping a carrot between her perfect white teeth.

"Excuse me?" Mallory asked, holding a spoonful of potato salad and suddenly remembering the last time she had potato salad she fainted. Was she allergic to potato salad or Del's attentions?

"I'll ask you a question, one of those kind that are highly personal and decorum dictates we shouldn't ask and you get to do the same with no repercussions or fear of reprisal," Fran said.

"All right," Mallory said, putting the potato salad down.

"Shall I go first?"

"Please," Mallory said.

"What's with the pajamas?"

Mallory smiled, her mind letting out a giant sigh. This would be easy.

She told Fran the story. Fran thought it was a poetic gesture and liked the idea that it caused most people some concern.

"Kind of like how lesbians cause people concern especially when the bull dykes wore suits because in those days women didn't wear trousers, ride a bike or sit properly in a saddle," Fran said. "The only time a woman could spread her legs was to fuck and birth," Fran said.

"You and Lil have seen a lot and lesbians nowadays take our freedoms lightly, freedoms you fought so diligently for."

48

"I like you. How come Gigi hasn't brought you before?"

"Gigi doesn't like to mix parts of her life. That way if she does something to piss someone off she's got other places to run to. I only got to come because she doesn't want her wife to think she's off with her current infatuation. Alex trusts me, or at least thinks I'm harmless."

"I see. Well, I know how we can remedy that situation," Fran said, with a mischievous glint in her eye.

"How?" Mallory asked, fearing the worst.

"We'll make you a member of the Infamous Lesbian Activists," Fran said, flagging Lil over.

"Are you sure that's a good idea?" Mallory said, envisioning the black robes, bloody chickens, drums and firelight.

"Of course it is. We need smart, insightful, courageous women like you. Anyone who wears pajamas in the middle of the day is a true anarchist in my book. That does it. You're drafted," Fran said.

"I don't think Gigi's going to like this," Mallory said.

Lil leaned over while Fran whispered her the plan. She nodded.

"Don't worry about Gigi. She's going to need your company for a while from the sound of things," Lil said.

"What's wrong with Gigi?" Fran asked, the picture of maternal concern.

"I'll tell you in a bit," Lil said, heading off to resume her conversation with Gigi.

"What was that about?" Gigi asked, perturbed at being interrupted. She never came running when Alex called. Usually, Gigi couldn't tell you where her girlfriend was at a party to save her life. They came together and they left together. It briefly crossed Gigi's mind that perhaps it was her own behavior that was causing the rift between her and Alex. Maybe it wasn't her infatuation with Ollie that made Alex so angry; rather it was Gigi's lack of attention. Was it possible she had grown complacent? The thought of it horrified her. If she was one thing and one thing only she was a good lover. Did being a good lover allow for being inattentive? Gigi wondered.

"Fran wants to make Mallory one of the Activists. Mallory is worried you won't like it," Lil said.

"It's fine. Actually, she'll be a big help. She's very bright," Gigi said.

"And you'll probably need a chaperon for a while," Lil added.

"What I do isn't right, is it?"

"Someday Gigi you'll realize there is more to life than sex and when you do, it would be nice to have the skills necessary to make a decent life with another person. At the rate you're going you won't have a lover and your circle of friends will all be people you've slept with. It makes for bleak company. Believe me."

"Take it from one who knows," Gigi said.

"Yes. My advice to you would be to stay away from Ollie, be extremely nice to Alex and hopefully everything will blow over," Lil said, putting a comforting arm around Gigi.

Three

Mallory sat upright in Dr. Kohlrabi's office looking the picture of sound mental health, not to mention she was sporting a tan from playing badminton all weekend with the Activists in Yarnell.

"So how was your trip?" Dr. Kohlrabi asked.

"It was incredible. I even got past my beyond-the-city-limits-anxiety phobia. I think I might be able to travel again. I have missed traveling. I'm certain the chances of running into Caroline are greatly diminished as long as I stay in the Northern Hemisphere. Right?"

"She went back to Brazil, correct?"

"Yes," Mallory replied, trying to block out the sudden barrage of images she was seeing. Caroline standing on the beach in Rocky Point, her sunglasses sliding down her petite nose. Caroline kissing her beneath the star filled night on North Mountain as she guided

Mallory through the initial courses of making love. Caroline moving in and all those intense joyful days that followed, times when Mallory thought the world was a happy, shiny place. Those were always her first thoughts of Caroline. The downhill moments would come later and they usually cascaded into the moment Mallory realized that Caroline had been lying to her. She didn't know what the deception entailed but Mallory sensed it began and lived in the grip of its terror until the day Caroline announced she was leaving.

"Mallory . . . ?" Dr. Kohlrabi asked, trying to bring her back to the present moment.

"Yes, wonderful weekend. I was practically adopted into the clan and I played topless team badminton with a slew of older women. There were breasts everywhere. It was very liberating as well as enlightening."

"How did you play badminton with your foot?"

"I played back and Gigi ran around a lot. We got a five point handicap. To the Activists nothing is impossible."

"Why topless badminton?" Dr. Kohlrabi asked, trying not to conjure up pornographic images of Playboy bunnies at the mansion engaging every man's fantasy.

"It's a reclamation of our bodies kind of like going back to the matriarchy where women were strong and not simply objects of lust and fancy," Mallory replied, knowing she could only reveal certain facts about her weekend initiation.

She couldn't tell the doctor about standing by firelight in the middle of the desert with her hand jammed in her crotch repeating feminist affirmation statements. At first she had felt like a fool but when she was surrounded by twenty other women doing the same thing she forgot to be scared; instead she was moved by the intense feelings of women coming together in joint purpose. She felt like she was experiencing the kind of moments she had only read about in the early days of the women's movement.

"I see," Dr. Kohlrabi replied, thinking of her daughter's newly installed breast implants whose only purpose were to incite lust and fancy in the opposite sex.

"When I got back I went to see Del," Mallory said, turning the conversation to her present concern.

"Oh," Dr. Kohlrabi prodded.

"I invited her over for dinner," Mallory said.

"That's good, isn't it?"

"I was hoping you could tell me," Mallory replied.

"It's a step forward."

"I had to tell my mother because she wanted me to come over."

"And that worries you?"

"My mother is more scarred from Caroline leaving than I am. She prefers me being celibate and not dating."

"Are you dating Del?"

"I don't know," Mallory said, thinking about the morning. She had put a brilliant pair of blue silk dress pajamas on, and her favorite gold tie. She was looking at herself in the mirror and she undid her hair so it hung long and curly around her neck and fell to her breasts. Mallory hadn't worn her hair down since Caroline left. Caroline adored Mallory's long flowing pelt. She used to comb it lovingly. Was this a sign? Mallory wondered. Was she more interested in Del than she was admitting?

"You're going to have to decide one day."

"I know," Mallory replied.

"If this is something serious between you and Del I would like to meet her. If she was willing of course."

Mallory looked mortified.

"Maybe we should think on this for a short time and discuss it later," Dr. Kohlrabi said.

"Definitely," Mallory said, getting up.

"You still have ten minutes," Dr. Kohlrabi said, looking at the clock.

"I think I'm done for today."

"All right," Dr. Kohlrabi replied, trying not to take affront.

Del was trying to get out of her office early because she wanted
to buy flowers at the gift shop and then get a bottle of good wine at
the Sportsman. She knew it was packaged romance but she couldn't
help herself. Mallory made her feel romance acutely. She felt like
she wanted to take candlelit baths, go for walks in the moonlight,
and picnic on grassy knolls—which in Arizona could only be found
on a golf course. She wanted to experience every romantic fantasy
that came to mind.

She was still marveling at the fact that Mallory had come to the
hospital. She'd stood in the cafeteria and called Del on her cell
phone. The orderlies were threatening to take her to security
because they were certain she was a patient. Del came down to
rescue her.

"I only came to invite you to dinner," Mallory said, trying to
regain her composure and straighten out her pajamas as she scowled
at the departing orderlies.

"You have gorgeous hair and I'd love to come for dinner," Del
said.

"Wonderful," Mallory replied.

"Is this a date?" Del asked before she could stop herself.

"If you wish it to be," Mallory said, blushing.

"I do."

"Seven o'clock okay?"

"Perfect. I missed you," Del blurted, knowing she would kick
herself later. She did her best not to look completely mortified.

"It's not a bad thing . . . missing people. Is it?" Mallory asked.

"I don't think so."

Del had spent the day replaying this scene in her head again and
again trying to recapture every nuance. She was floating in this daze
when she opened her office door and ran smack into Kim.

She nearly flattened her.

"Oh, I'm so sorry," Del said.

"Are you in a hurry?" Kim said, straightening her stethoscope
from its currently askew position.

"Not really. I just have some errands to run."

"Maybe we can talk later," Kim said, backing away.

Del could sense something was wrong. Kim looked tired but she also looked emotionally drained and Del knew she didn't have to look far to discover the cause. She knew that Kim was upset with Ollie but she didn't know how things had been going. Kim wasn't one to open up unless she was under considerable duress.

"Why don't you come in and we'll talk. I've got a couple of iced mochas in my fridge."

"But your errands . . ."

"They can wait. Come on," Del coaxed.

"I'm sorry. I just need someone to talk to, someone with perspective that I can trust," Kim said.

"I'll do my best," Del said, handing Kim her iced coffee and taking a seat on the couch.

"I'm going to break it off with Ollie . . . permanently this time," Kim said, studying her hands and sliding off a gold ring. Ollie had given her the ring as a show of good faith. To show her that she was loved and that she didn't have to worry about lack of commitment, that Ollie loved her, and her exclusively. How stupid and naïve she had been to believe her.

"You two have had trouble before?" Del asked gently.

"Yes, the same kind, always the same kind. Thank god we don't live together. I suppose that's why we don't live together—because she can't keep her hands off other women. Why is it so hard? Other couples manage. She's always played around, or at least flirted with other women but this time it's different. How am I supposed to hold my head up when she's trying to screw Gigi? I shouldn't have to put up with that! " Kim said. Her face tied up in a grimace.

"No, you shouldn't," Del said, taking her hand.

"I haven't called her."

"Has she called you?" Del asked, trying to tread lightly.

"I don't know. I ripped the phone cord out of the wall so I wouldn't be tempted. It's an extreme measure but I can't trust myself not to call, not to let her back in. I wanted to tell someone so I would have to live up to it, really let her go this time. I've got to move on. Right?"

"You should be happy and well loved. If you're not getting it from Ollie . . ."

"I'm not," Kim said.

"Okay then. What are you going to do?" Del asked.

"I'm going to need a shoulder for a while," Kim said.

"I'm here whenever you need me."

"I knew I could count on you," Kim said, squeezing Del's hand. "Why aren't there more women like you out there?"

"You had your chance," Del teased.

"And now you're taken."

"I hope so."

"You know, Mallory is not as strange as I first thought, you know with the pajamas and stuff. I think I'm beginning to understand extreme behavior," Kim said. "She's awfully pretty."

"Yes, and smart, driven, odd and sexy all rolled into one. I can't get her off my mind. She invited me over for dinner. We were only doing lunch before."

"So it's like an official date then," Kim replied.

"I think so."

"Well, no one can say you rushed into this one," Kim said, remembering it had been months since Del had first met Mallory.

"No, but I kind of like that. I've had enough of those 'sleep together the first week and then get to know each other later' sessions. Needless to say, they didn't work out," Del said, instantly reliving a slew of bad love affairs.

That was one of the things she liked about Mallory. She made her feel fresh, like falling in love for the first time. If only she'd known Mallory then. They could have been high school sweethearts, the kind that last.

"I'll testify to that," Kim said wryly.

She had succumbed to Ollie all too quickly and been suffering the consequences ever since. She was now counting the hours in a day and working as much overtime as she could find. At least work kept her mind off Ollie and the insidious blues of losing a lover. It was worse than quitting smoking. This time she was going to do it. This time she wouldn't let Ollie talk her into forgiving and forgetting. How many times could she overlook her playing around?

How many times was she going to fool herself that Ollie didn't sleep with other women? How could she call this a relationship when her partner moved from woman to woman? It wasn't supposed to be this way.

"I should let you go. Thanks for talking," Kim said.

"Are you okay?" Del asked, looking the picture of concern.

"Yes, thank you. Are you sure you don't have any friends just like you?" Kim teased.

"Nope, left them all in Chicago," Del said.

"You go have a good date," Kim said, getting up.

"Do you think it would be corny if I brought flowers and wine? I know it's packaged romance but Mallory makes me feel romantic," Del said.

"I would love it if a woman brought me flowers and wine," Kim said.

Del smiled.

Ollie sat on the hood of Kim's car wondering when the hell her girlfriend was going to show. The roses were starting to look a bit droopy. Ollie gave them a swat to try and freshen them up. Kim was usually punctual and Ollie usually wasn't. She was discovering that waiting wasn't much fun. The connection of course was totally lost on her because Ollie never took the time to analyze her own behavior. The only behavior she was interested in was the ulterior motives and manipulation of others for sexual favors. Quest and conquer were her primary goals. And what was wrong with that, she asked herself. At least I know what I want. And right now I'd like my girlfriend to show up.

Kim finished up her paperwork, read the latest nurse's magazine cover to cover and finally packed it up to go home telling herself she could get through another night of not seeing Ollie. She planned her evening so that every moment was full until bed. Then the long night of counting sheep, which wasn't working, began. Inevitably Smackers, the cat, would jump in the middle of the bed at ninety-nine sheep and she would have to start over.

It would be three o'clock in the morning before mentally exhausted she would doze for a few short hours. She was contemplating asking one of the doctors for a prescription because she couldn't keep working these long shifts and not sleep. And it was all Ollie's fault for being such a wretched little shit, Kim told herself as she trudged across the parking lot to her car.

In her current state of preoccupation she was practically right on top of Ollie before she saw her sitting there, her face hidden behind the bouquet of roses, her eyes looking as pensive and remorseful as she could make them.

"Hi, these are for you," Ollie said, thrusting the roses before her.

"No, thank you," Kim said, opening her car door and throwing her backpack in. She was trying to buy herself some time. This was not what she expected. For this she had no plan. She quickly ran through her mental litany of why she had to stay away from Ollie.

"What do you mean no thank you?" Ollie asked.

"Exactly what I said, now get off my car and out of my life," Kim blurted before she had a chance to censor. Maybe the litany was working.

"Come on, I'm trying to say I'm sorry."

"It's too late. It's over."

"What do you mean it's over? I tried to call but I couldn't get through," Ollie said.

"I ripped the phone out of the wall."

"Why?"

"So I wouldn't call you," Kim said, trying to take deep breaths to keep her composure.

"Why wouldn't you call me?" Ollie said, still not getting the picture.

"Because we're over. I want you out of my life."

"What do you mean?"

"Over as in goodbye," Kim said, gaining momentum. She slid the gold ring Ollie had given her off her finger and handed it to Ollie.

"Here, I believe this is yours. I'll have your stuff sent over," Kim said, feeling a giant wave of fear coupled with exhilaration wash over her, like the thrill one gets from skydiving.

Ollie watched her and despite her usual confidence in being able to win Kim back she was beginning to sense the gravity of the situation. "You can't be serious. We need to talk. Look Kim, I'm really sorry and it won't happen again. I promise. I just got a little out of hand. I love you. I don't want us to be over," Ollie said, grabbing Kim's waist and trying to pull her close.

Kim could smell her fear. She pushed away.

"You've said that before," Kim countered. "Now go."

Ollie stood stunned.

"But I love you. I can't just leave it like this."

"You're the one that desires everyone but me. I'm sure one of your many playmates will console you," Kim said, opening the car door.

"What? So, thanks for the memories and that's it?"

"Exactly," Kim said, closing the car door. She started the car and shoved it in reverse. She left Ollie standing in the parking lot holding the ring in one hand and the limp roses in the other, looking completely confused. Kim took a deep breath and turned out of the parking lot.

As she drove home she kept telling herself she could do it. *I just need something to occupy my time. I need something to do, something big that will keep my mind off her.* Kim took the corner of Indian School and Forty-third too fast, sending her backpack flying and scattering her AJN magazines across the back seat.

At the light she tried to shove them back into the bag, noticing the grotesque cover which featured the human heart in all its ugly brilliancy. She sighed heavily and watched a man painting his house. It was a large ranch style house and it looked like he had years of work ahead of him. *Now there's a project*, she muttered to herself. A big project, something that will take a lot of time and energy, a project that would exhaust a person. She turned into the parking lot of Home Depot and walked straight to the paint department. She dragged two five-gallon drums of white flat exterior to the paint desk.

"Planning on painting something big, I see," said the older gentleman behind the counter.

"My house," Kim said.

"What color would you like?" the man asked.

"The color of the human heart," Kim said.

"Red?"

"Red."

"That's a pretty brave choice," he said, pulling a sampler of various shades of red.

"Right now I need to be brave," Kim said, choosing a swatch.

"Are you sure you want to do this?"

"I do."

One of the stock boys helped her load the paint and Kim didn't give a thought to unloading it until she had backed her Volvo station wagon into the driveway. She unlocked the side gate and stood pondering her dilemma, thinking that at least the paint was keeping her mind off what had just happened, mainly that she'd finally said goodbye to Ollie. In a simultaneous moment the ting and ping of the mail truck could be heard and then the bang of the dog door as Alfalfa came running out of the house and through the backyard to fulfill her daily ritual of barking at the letter carrier. It took Kim a split second to realize the gravity of the situation and by then it was too late.

"Oh, shit," Kim said. All she could imagine was Alfalfa biting the letter carrier but when she got around the car she could see her nightmare had not come true. Instead, Alfalfa was lying on her back while the mail lady stroked her stomach.

"I'm so sorry. I know dogs are a postal worker's nightmare," Kim said.

"It's all right. I've never seen a Chinese Crested before," replied the mail lady.

"Most people don't know what they are. You obviously know your dogs," Kim said.

"I see a lot of them," the woman said, handing Kim her mail. Alfalfa licked her leg.

"Stop that. It's not nice to lick people. She likes sunscreen," Kim said, grabbing her collar.

"That's okay."

"Thanks for being so understanding," said Kim.

The woman smiled. "No problem."

Kim went back to her paint problem and Alfalfa went back in the house, leaving her alone with her dilemma. "You're a lot of help," Kim called after her. She tugged and pulled and got the paint drum to the very edge of the bumper, almost giving herself a hernia in the process.

The mail lady came up behind her, clearing her throat.

"I couldn't help noticing . . . would you like a hand?"

"Maybe I shouldn't have been so zealous in my paint choice," Kim said, glaring at the immovable object that was making her feel completely impotent.

"What you really need is a dolly," the woman advised.

"Or a decent girlfriend," Kim muttered before she could stop herself. She knew better than to assume that women in uniform are dykes.

"Dollies are a lot simpler. You can store them in the garage and take them out when you need them. Girlfriends are definitely more work and they refuse to live in the garage," the woman said, picking up the drum of paint with no problem. "Where would you like it?"

"My goodness you're strong," Kim said. "On the back deck please. I could help."

"Too late."

61

The woman moved both of them for Kim.

"Can I at least offer you a soda or an ice tea?"

"Sure, an ice tea please."

Kim got them both one.

"Thank you," the woman said.

"Thank you. I'm Kim by way," Kim said, extending her hand.

"Angel," the woman replied. "Well, I'd better be off," she said, checking her watch.

Kim watched Angel walk off, admiring her handsome legs. *At least I still have a libido*, Kim told herself.

Dr. Kohlrabi was slowly getting used to Mallory sitting upright. She informed herself in her best professional tone that it was a sign of progress. But it still made her uneasy that Mallory's progress was attached to a woman. It was better for the patient to make peace with their problem and thus find a solution than it was for a placebo effect to occur in its place. Mallory would finally leave her wrecked love affair behind by falling in love with another woman. Dr. Kohlrabi found herself wanting to pray that Del was a wonderful woman who would love Mallory until the end of her days and subsequently cure her. She found this disconcerting because she was an avowed Agnostic.

"How did the date I mean, dinner go?" Dr. Kohlrabi asked.

"I think we can refer to it as a date," Mallory said, rather calmly.

"As you wish. Do you want to talk about it?"

"Yes. Although I don't know where to start."

"The beginning is good," Dr. Kohlrabi prompted.

"But that would take us back to the very first time I laid eyes on her. I think everything stems from that first moment. It must be what people are describing when they talk about love at first sight. It's not really love because I don't think you can love someone without really knowing that person. You know, the other day I was trying to imagine what kind of a place the world would be if there wasn't this strange energy that we call love. Would we have war, rape, and pillage all the time? Less domestic violence? No divorce, and no broken hearts? Would people still live together or would everyone wander homeless in an emotionally void landscape? What would the world be like?" Mallory asked, looking intensely at Dr. Kohlrabi.

"I honestly don't know, having never pondered that particular idea," Dr. Kohlrabi replied, thinking perhaps Mallory should have become a philosopher instead of a vending machine person. Were her talents being wasted? She did seem content in her work. Overly bright patients made her nervous. They were the maladjusted people because they thought about things only her nameless, faceless entity she no longer called God should ponder. Existential questions were best laid buried as they did with most people. Thinking too much never did anyone any good.

"So back to the beginning."

"When I first saw her, when she leaned over to look at me after I fainted, it was like one finger of my soul gently reached out and touched her soul like how you would touch frog eggs, being uncertain of their constitution you would approach them cautiously," Mallory said, holding out her forefinger like something akin to E.T. with his long skinny wrinkled finger.

Dr. Kohlrabi nodded.

"And I think her squishy matter did likewise. That, I think, is the energy a love affair can build on. That is what people are always looking for. They want connection with one special person. When Del looks at me I feel it."

"Do you like that?" Dr. Kohlrabi inquired.

"Yes, but it frightens me," Mallory said, remembering about dinner and the high flush her face had as she sat across the candlelit dinner table, set with flowers and drinking horribly expensive wine. Del had also bought cigars for after dinner.

"Cigars?" Mallory had asked, when Del handed her the neatly wrapped package.

"It's the boy thing. See, after we've survived my overdone attempt at romance then we can congratulate ourselves on a job well done. It's to make you forget these indulgences I'm putting you through."

"I'm not entirely certain I'm the only crazy one here," Mallory said, sticking the flowers in a heavy glass cruet, evening them out so they sat pretty.

"The trappings are nice as are the flowers, and a person striving to regain their tainted innocence should be allowed such indulgences. Don't you agree?" Mallory said.

"Yes, definitely. Shall I open the wine?" Del asked, getting suddenly nervous now that the longed for date was in progress.

Mallory smacked her in the shoulder, hard.

Del looked alarmed. "What was that for?" she said, rubbing her shoulder.

"You're making me nervous because you're nervous. That was to shock you out of it. Just think of this as lunch," Mallory advised, handing her the wooden corkscrew she had stolen from her father's well stocked bar years ago. It was the only thing she took from the house when she moved out that terrible summer her mother found out she was a lesbian.

"I don't want this to be lunch," Del said, trying to rapidly find words for how she was feeling.

"Because you desire a different menu?" Mallory queried, taking the bottle of wine from Del who was botching it up. She neatly extracted the cork.

"How you torment me," Del said, taking a sip of dark burgundy.

"Do you like being tormented?" Mallory asked.

"Only if I shall someday be released," Del replied.

Mallory smiled. "I think you'll like the menu."

And then they had a lovely dinner, Mallory mused as she sunk back into the oversized cushions of Dr. Kohlrabi's couch.

"We sat outside and smoked cigars and looked at the stars because Del has been studying them because she knows I like to do that. I think that's really sweet and it made me feel special and without the accompanying notion that I would have to give something in return. It was a pure altruistic gesture because she knows it will be eons before we go to bed," Mallory said.

"Are you going to go to bed with her?"

"Yes, I think I will," Mallory replied matter-of-factly.

"Just like that?" Dr. Kohlrabi asked, shocked that Mallory would be considering such a thing.

"No, not just like that. What I mean is that I can envision us being in love someday."

"Are you going to wear clothes?"

"Someday."

"What about the thing with Caroline? Are you over her?"

"I'm started to realign myself with it," Mallory replied cautiously.

"I see."

"Do you?"

"I think this is rather sudden. I want you to be careful."

"Because you don't trust Del?"

"I'm concerned that you are using Del as a distraction from the original problem."

"I'm not. I am simply learning to go on with my life. I'm sure Caroline is not sitting around pining over me. Why should I pine for her?"

"You shouldn't," Dr. Kohlrabi replied.

"Exactly."

Mallory stood up and began to take off her pajamas. She had been contemplating this moment since dinner with Del. She had felt funny in her pajamas like she was cheating on Del because she was still mourning her love affair with Caroline. Suddenly, she wanted her tainted innocence to be renewed. She wanted a new life devoid of anything old to remind her of the painful past she had begun to leave behind. It seemed wearing pajamas was holding her back. She saw the cowgirl maverick in the Republic, holding the bridle of the horse that wanted to go free. She let go and they both watched the horse gallop across the golden field. Mallory knew it was time.

"What are you doing?"

"Shedding my former life," Mallory said, stripping down to her underwear. "I think I've had enough for today. We'll talk next week."

She left Dr. Kohlrabi with a pile of pajamas in the middle of her office. Her secretary stood in the hallway, hand on one hip and a quizzical expression on her face.

"What was that?" the secretary asked, motioning to the woman who just left in her underwear.

"I believe that was progress," Dr. Kohlrabi said, picking up the shorn clothing.

"I see."

"Do you?" Dr. Kohlrabi asked, realizing she was slipping into one of Mallory's rhetorical devices.

"No, I will never understand crazy people," her secretary replied, going off to answer the telephone.

Gigi sat in her mother's kitchen listening to a familiar litany of complaints concerning the cares of a mother for her depraved daughter.

"For the love of Christ, topless badminton," her mother ranted.

"You're using the Lord's name in vain."

"Don't quote scripture to me young lady," her mother replied, snapping the top of Gigi's head with a spatula. She then flipped the pork chops.

"Ouch! I hate when you do that," Gigi said, rubbing the top of her head. "You should really wash that spatula before you use it. I have a lot of gel in my hair."

"And I hate when you visit that heathen sister of mine. I strictly forbid it."

"You can't forbid me to do *anything*. I'm a grown-up now, or did you forget?"

"Not one day goes by that I forget anything about you including those acts against God which I'm sure you commit hourly," Rose replied, trying to keep images of her daughter fornicating with another woman out of her head. That was the difficulty of being God-fearing—all of the images of lust that constantly barraged the clean mind of a clean-living person. Why, oh why, did her daughter not grow up to be a nun?

"I wish I had sex that often. Unfortunately I don't have the means, the partner, or the energy to do it. What sort of a thought is that for a good Christian woman to be having anyway?"

"Why couldn't you have become a nun and practiced celibacy if you can't be a normal person like the rest of us?"

"There are lesbian nuns, lots of them. That's what happens when you put a bunch of women together. Then I would have further disgraced you by being a religious pervert. If I were you I would thank my lucky stars that I chose to be a safe sex salesperson at a porn shop," Gigi replied.

Her mother crossed herself three times as giant dildos danced around in her head with accompanying visuals of her daughter selling the batteries.

Gigi's father, Ralph, had the misfortune to smell dinner and wander into his wife's domain.

"*This* is all your doing. This perversion, the pariah of the Lord's words," Rose said, waving the greasy spatula between her daughter and her husband.

Ralph looked at Gigi sympathetically, knowing that once again she had come for dinner but judging from the conversation she would not be staying long enough to get anything to eat. He would always try to slip her cash. Buy a hamburger, he'd tell her. She would gently push the cash back into his hand, telling him she had a girlfriend of means. She wouldn't go hungry. Still the sad look in her eyes mirrored the failure in his. Once she had told him the world wouldn't always be like this; it would get better for her kind, or they'd kill her off; either way, the hate would end, liberating both sides. He never knew how to take this.

"How can it be his fault? You were my supposed role model. I'm your issue," Gigi countered.

"Bad blood, that's what it is," Rose ranted, slapping the pork chops in the middle of the table.

"Your sister is a dyke, the blood is on you," Gigi said.

"Get out of my house right this minute!" Rose screamed.

"Fine. I wasn't hungry anyway," Gigi said, getting up abruptly.

"I'm going to report you and the rest of those perverts in Yarnell. You wait and see, I'm going to foil all their attempts. If I have my way Dr. Jerry Falwell will be leading the crowd of true believers down the streets of Yarnell," Rose screamed, slamming a clenched fist down on the table with the gleam of the righteous in her eyes.

"You do have a spy," Gigi said, smiling.

"Get out of my house!"

"You better warn her before we do," Gigi said.

Fran picked up the phone, sticking a finger in her left ear so she could hear Gigi over the mariachi band that was playing for the salsa lessons.

"You did what?" Fran screamed into the phone.

"I found the spy. It's Ethel Hayes."

"Ethel? Are you sure?"

"I got her number off redial from my mother's phone after an altercation in which she revealed certain information. It has to be Ethel. We should test it first to make sure," Gigi said.

"By goddess, you are a sharp one. I know just the test. Are you coming down this weekend?"

"Sure, if you want to me to."

"I do and bring Mallory. We've got stuff to cover."

"What is all that noise?" Gigi asked.

"We're taking salsa lessons," Fran said.

"That must be quite a sight," Gigi said, laughing.

"All you got to do is pretend you're holding a poop in, which for most of us is always an issue, and shake your hips. We'll give you a demo when you get here."

"I can hardly wait."

Four

The George and Dragon pub was packed for lunch and for the life of her Buffy Simpson could not understand why Mallory insisted they have their weekly lunches here instead of the club. Mallory hadn't set foot in the club since she turned eighteen and now refused to go back because they had fired her tennis instructor for being gay. She would not go back into the club until they added sexual orientation to their employment mission statement.

In the interim Buffy was forced to go to less than reputable places. Once they had gone to Sweet Tomatoes and she had been horrified to discover that she was at a self-serve salad bar. She felt like a pig at the trough. After that debacle, Mallory had agreed that they would go to places that at least had wait staff.

Buffy sipped her martini and watched as an attractive young woman in a well-tailored gabardine suit strolled across the room. Buffy was about to begin her list of woes for wishing Mallory could be like that when the young woman sat at her table. Buffy was about to berate her for being rude by sitting down without so much as asking when she saw it was her daughter. She nearly fainted.

"You have clothes on!"

"They won't let you in here naked," Mallory said, pointing to her mother's drink and signaling she'd desire the same to her favorite waitress, the one with flowing red hair and beautiful breasts.

"Why do you have clothes on?" Buffy asked, beginning to feel panic that the dream she once wished for her daughter was coming true. But at what cost and what was instigating it?

"Because I want to," Mallory said, smiling at the waitress, who winked back.

"You look very nice," the waitress said.

"As do you," Mallory replied, almost flirting.

Her mother noticed. "She's not one of you people is she?"

"Yes, Mother, she is a lesbian just like me."

"How do you know?"

"I've seen her out," Mallory said, taking a sip.

"Out where?" Buffy asked, imagining sex clubs with big metal cages filled with scantily dressed women and chains and whips hanging around, and everything was dark and dirty.

"At the book store, pride rallies, community picnics, and out dancing."

"I see," Buffy said, studying the girl more closely. She didn't look like a lesbian.

"Did Dr. Kohlrabi get you back into clothes?" Buffy asked, starting her line of questioning with her most optimistic thoughts and desires.

"Not exactly. She did make me realize a few things. Actually, she was quite shocked when I removed my pajamas and left her office in my underwear. But it just seemed like the moment of liberation was at hand. I realized that Caroline wasn't giving me a thought so why should I be pining for her. I love Del, not Caroline."

"In love, leaving the shrink in your underwear, have you lost your mind?"

70

"I thought that's why I was going there in the first place. I've never felt more in control and totally normal than I do right now. Thanks Mom. Shall we order? I'm starving," Mallory said, opening her menu. "I think I'll have bangers and mash. How about you?"

"I feel one of my migraines coming on. I'll take a rain check on lunch."

"Sure," Mallory said. "I'll call Del maybe she can come down for lunch. See you."

Buffy Simpson drove home in a complete funk. She had half a mind to rip Dr. Kohlrabi a new rectal orifice. She wanted her daughter cured, not in love with another woman who was going to break her heart. Pajamas this time, what would next time bring? She furiously dialed her cell phone trying to get a hold of Gigi, who of course was not at home. She screeched in front of the Castle Boutique and backed up into the parking lot, causing quite a commotion on Camelback Avenue.

"Hey, lady, can't get your dildo fast enough?" someone screamed from a passing car.

Buffy rolled her eyes at the mere suggestion but nonetheless she took a good look around before she got out of the car and slunk across the parking lot. She did three Hail Mary's and begged God to please let her foray into sex and sin go unnoticed.

"Now this is a sight," Gigi said, nearly falling off the stool she was precariously balancing on as she hung up the latest fashion in leather hardware.

"What is that?" Buffy asked before she could stop herself. She immediately regretted her question when Gigi attached the apparatus to her nether regions and demonstrated the item's purpose.

"Oh, my God," Buffy said, blushing and then as if God was listening Reverend Carlyle came in the door.

The look of panic on his face almost matched the mortified expression on Buffy Simpson's face as clergy met congregation with

Gigi demonstrating the use of a strap-on dildo. Gigi wished she had a camera because it was a truly a Kodak moment. In fact it gave her the idea to create a series of sacrilegious photographs.

"Now this really is a sight. Actually, the good Reverend here has come to help me complete my long neglected course in Catechism," Gigi said. "I'm not entirely sure what Buffy is here about but she wanted a demonstration on this handy little picker-upper," Gigi said, giving the dildo a quick flick of her hand, turning the faces of the Reverend and Buffy immediately crimson.

"Well, I should leave you to your work then, Gigi. Perhaps I can come back tomorrow when you're not so busy," Reverend Carlyle said, backing out door. "Buffy, I'll see you in church on Sunday."

Buffy glared at Gigi. "You could have told him the real reason why I'm here."

"And what is that?"

"Mallory. I'm here because of Mallory. She's wearing clothes."

"That's a good thing," Gigi said, disguising her own sense of panic.

"I want you to tell me about Del," Buffy demanded.

"I don't know anything about her," Gigi replied.

"But you *must*. You're Mallory's best friend."

"All I know is that she works at Phoenix Baptist. Go see for yourself."

"You're not being very helpful," Buffy accused.

"Mallory doesn't talk about it. Maybe she's ashamed. Del is a little different you know," Gigi said, gaining momentum. By the time she was done with Buffy she had her convinced Del was a modern-day version of a lesbian Frankenstein.

Buffy's next stop before going home to dive into a pitcher of martinis was Phoenix Baptist Hospital. She had friends on the Board and if that Del woman was messing around with her daughter she'd see that she was fired just like that slutty little tennis instructor that she got out of Mallory's life.

She marched in to the information desk and demanded to see

Del Farnsworth. Due to the fevered nature of her request, Del was immediately paged.

Del walked down the hall to meet a woman who somehow looked vaguely familiar but she couldn't place her. The receptionist pointed to the woman, who looked most anxious.

"Can I help you?" Del asked.

Buffy read her name tab and screeched, "You're a *doctor*!"

"Are you hurt?" Del asked, thinking the damage might not necessarily be in the physical sense but perhaps mental.

"No, but I don't want you to hurt my daughter," Buffy blurted before she could stop herself.

The vaguely familiar woman instantly registered in Del's mind. She was Mallory's mother.

"I won't hurt your daughter. I love her," Del replied.

"You do? And you are of sound mental health?" Buffy questioned.

"Last time I checked," Del replied.

"Well, they don't just let anybody be a doctor. You are a real doctor," Buffy asked, looking at the receptionist for verification. "She is a real doctor, right?"

The receptionist nodded.

"Perhaps we could go to my office and talk," Del suggested. No wonder Mallory was a little off. She evidently didn't come from real strong stock, judging from the flighty nature of her mother.

"As long as you're a doctor. I didn't know they had lesbian doctors," Buffy said, as Del guided her down the hall.

Mallory fingered the soft white petals of the calla lilies Del had sent her, while she talked on the phone.

"You didn't!"

"I did. I told her they sent us lesbian doctors to a special school because it's a known fact that lesbian people are anatomically different from the rest of the world."

"And she believed you?"

"She thinks we're smarter than most. I don't know. I hope not. But we did have a good talk."

"I'll say. You're practically part of the family. It's pretty scary."

"You're not angry are you that she came to see me?" Del asked, wondering what her heart rate had jumped to.

"No. I just get tired of her making me out to be the victim. I'm not a victim. A martyr maybe, but I chose that. Caroline didn't make me do all those things. I did. My mother needs to realize that I created who I am now and that I'm in control of who l become—regardless of who I sleep with."

"I'm glad you feel that way. You are doing what you do because of you and no one else. I respect that."

"Perhaps over dinner you could explain that to my mother. I'm sure we'll both be invited very soon."

"So what do you look like in clothes?" Del asked.

"Is this like the time you asked me what I slept in because I wear pajamas in the daytime?" Mallory teased, knowing she had mentioned the *sleep together* phrase, something that dangled about both their minds every time they were together.

"I suppose it is," Del replied, remembering the answer was *nothing* and how she had blushed envisioning Mallory without clothing.

"Why don't you come see," Mallory suggested.

"I just might."

"You know where I am."

Mallory went back to work until Gigi strolled in. Mallory looked up from her work and raised an eyebrow.

"To what do I owe this amazing pleasure? It's not often we get you into the pit of blue collar," Mallory teased.

"Your mother came to see me. She wanted to know about Del," Gigi said, studying the flowers. She picked up the card and nodded, thinking *it figures.* Part of her was panicked that Mallory had found someone or rather someone had found her and the other part was jealous that she had once again let Mallory slip through her fingers.

"She went to see her," Mallory replied.

"How did it go?"

"She likes Del."

"Well, that's a good thing isn't it?"

"I think so," Mallory replied, trying to gauge where Gigi was going.

"Do you think Del is interested in you sexually?"

"I don't know," Mallory said, surprised.

"I mean how long and drawn out is this courtship going to be? Or is it really only a friendship that you're pretending is something else?" Gigi asked, sitting on the couch and patting the cushion next to her.

Mallory obeyed like a well trained dog, only this was the first time she noticed it.

"I suppose there is only one way to find out," Mallory replied, studying Gigi's face.

"I suppose so. But do you really want to find out?" Gigi asked, taking Mallory's hand. She gently stuck the forefinger of Mallory's right hand in her mouth.

Mallory blushed. "What are you doing?"

"Presenting other options," Gigi said.

Guadalupe came in. "Excuse me. Mr. Garcia is here to meet with you. Shall I bring him in?"

Mallory stood up and looked at Gigi. "Yes, tell him I'll be right there."

"You look good in clothes," Gigi said.

"Thank you," Mallory replied.

"Alex is making pesto. Come by for dinner if Del has to work," Gigi said.

"I will. Del does have to work. She's pulling a double."

"Great. See you at six," Gigi said.

Del finagled an hour between her back-to-backs. She drove to the warehouse, her heart dancing in her chest. She didn't really know why, only that she had to see Mallory in clothes to fully understand what was happening between them. Guadalupe nodded her in as she was on the telephone.

"You came. I wondered if you would," Mallory said, getting up from her desk.

Del took a seat on the couch. "I must say you look very handsome in your suit."

"Well thank you very much," Mallory said, taking her jacket off and loosening her tie. She went to the door and gave Guadalupe a look indicating that she did not want to be disturbed and shut the door. She walked toward Del.

"Gigi is convinced you don't think of me sexually," Mallory said, taking a deep breath and steeling herself for the next twenty seconds of her life.

She straddled Del on the couch and gave her a most ardent kiss.

"Is that true?" Mallory said.

Del kissed her back, pulling her tighter. She untucked Mallory's shirt and ran her hand up her slender sides and then pulled the small of her back toward her.

"I didn't think so," Mallory said, in between kisses.

"I was waiting for you," Del said. "I wanted you to be ready. I didn't want to push you."

"Are you scared?" Mallory asked.

"Yes, very scared," Del said, kissing Mallory's neck.

"Me too," Mallory said, kissing Del's forehead and eyes.

The door swung open and Mr. and Mrs. Simpson stood in the doorway gaping.

"I tried to stop them," Guadalupe said, doing her best to beg pardon.

"I'm her mother. I will not be trifled with by a mere underling," Buffy said, glaring at Guadalupe.

"This was not how I envisioned our first romantic moment," Mallory whispered to Del.

"Right now I wish I was invisible," Del replied.

"No, you don't. You'd miss meeting Dad."

"Is this really happening?" Del said, trying to untangle herself from Mallory, who had no intentions of moving.

"Well, darling, I see her in clothes and making moves on her girlfriend. Yes siree, I'd say she was healed," Ralph Simpson said, grabbing his wife's arm.

"I'm not leaving until you meet Del and we all go and have a drink," Buffy protested.

"No, honey let's let them be," Ralph replied, taking his wife's arm and physically removing her from the room.

"Actually, I have to go back to work," Del said, sliding out from underneath Mallory.

"I'll go," Mallory said. "I think I could use a drink right now, a really big, cold one."

"Great," Del said, walking over to Ralph, shaking his hand and then exiting the room, with a "Nice to see you" and a nod at Buffy, who smiled warmly which scared her because she'd just been caught in a compromising position with her daughter.

"Call me later," Mallory said, winking lasciviously.

Del blanched, hoping later they could laugh about this moment.

Dr. Kohlrabi was doing her best not to laugh while Mallory told her the story of how she attempted to seduce Del only to be interrupted by her parents. Mallory could tell she was amused by the involuntary curvature of her mouth that was not exactly a smile but rather an attempt to stave one off.

"Has Del recovered from this episode?" Dr. Kohlrabi inquired.

"She's not gone frigid if that's what you're asking, at least not that I'm aware of. But we're not doing it. I think that comes later."

"Why later?"

"Prolong the foreplay I think. We're probably both a little tentative and since we've been ignoring all the other lesbian rules and doing so well we should stick with this new form of lesbian emotional anarchy."

"Perhaps you could explain that particular term."

"It means avoiding the usual trappings of a lesbian love affair," Mallory replied.

"Which are?"

"Eye contact, mutual checking out through secondary parties, talking, first kiss, sex, U-Haul, utopia, followed shortly by disillusion, disappointment, and subsequently break-up. You see the problem with lesbians is that once they've gone to bed they can't get past each other. What should be one-night stands become relationships."

"And you and Del are not doing this?"

"No. I actually like Del as a person first, as an intellectual, as a woman, as a future lover, in that order. For most lesbians the order is reversed."

"I see. Perhaps you could explain this to my daughter one day. I'm sure it is the same for straight people."

"I don't know about straight people," Mallory said.

"What do you mean?" Dr. Kohlrabi asked, stunned by her response.

"How should I know about straight people? I've never been one. Why do you people always assume that straight is correct and dominant in human makeup? Your world looks upside down to me, absolutely incorrect in terms of orientation. I feel like the child that was raised by wolves. I live with them but I am not one of them, nor can I truly understand their way of looking at the world. Just because our straight parents raised us doesn't automatically give us their insight, because we're different from the start."

"So it's an us/them dichotomy?"

"Exactly. I don't consider one side superior to another but distinctly different, and then there are those of us that are different within the perimeters of different."

"And that's what you and Del are?"

"Yes."

"How is the Republic these days?" Dr. Kohlrabi asked.

"Happily unattended. Perhaps my real life has become more interesting."

"Do you miss it?" Dr. Kohlrabi inquired.

"It's not a matter of missing it; rather the images of the Republic do not pop up uninvited in order to cripple the host personality."

"Now that is truly progress."

"I thought your job was to get me dressed."

"That was your mother's desire."

The house being painted the color of the human heart was progressing although Kim was still working on the second story. She'd taken some time off work because she found the task therapeutic, more so than working overtime. Del stood at the bottom of the ladder, concern etched in her face.

"Aren't you sick of doing that yet? Hire someone. This is a big house," Del yelled up at Kim.

"No, I like doing this. It's makes me feel like I'm accomplishing something. In fact, I may just give up nursing and go in for house painting."

"I don't think that's a good idea. Come down and talk to me."

"If you insist," Kim said, tramping down the long steel ladder.

"You obviously don't suffer vertigo," Del said, getting jitters just looking up at the ladder.

"Want some ice tea?" Kim said, refilling her own glass.

"Please."

Kim poured them tea from the giant frosty pitcher on the porch.

"So what do I own the honor of your visit?" Kim said, plopping down on the steps. Painting was hard work but it let her sleep at night due to sheer exhaustion. Her activity was accomplishing her aim.

"I want you to come to a soccer game tonight," Del replied.

"But I don't know anything about soccer," Kim said.

"That's not the point," Del said.

"What's the point then?"

"I want to get you away from the human heart house for a while. It's not good to paint all the time," Del said, handing Kim a wet rag and pointing to her cheek.

Kim missed the spot. Del took the rag and gently rubbed Kim's face. Del smiled and Kim tried to look away. Kim missed being intimate, and run as she might she still thought about Ollie.

"You're holding up well. I thought we could go get a pizza and then see the game. I have a few friends that are playing. They play well and they all have great legs. Will you indulge me?" Del said.

"Where is Mallory?" Kim asked.

"In Yarnell with the activists," Del replied.

"The activists?"

"Gigi's aunts and friends have some sort of secret sisterhood with a plan."

"What sort of a plan?" Kim asked.

"It's a secret but as long as she doesn't get arrested I'm not too concerned. They sound pretty harmless."

"Never underestimate the power of a woman, and get a bunch of them together . . ."

"I know," Del said. "Maybe you could baby-sit me so I won't think of Mallory being abducted by the FBI for questioning."

"Well, if you put it that way," Kim teased. "I just didn't want to be a charity case."

"You're not. If anything you're my benefactor," Del said.

"You are so sweet."

Del shrugged. "I could go get pizza while you showered."

"Sounds good. What time is the game?" Kim asked, getting up and pounding the lid on the paint and gathering up her brushes.

"Seven o'clock at Pioneer Park."

"Rather gay friendly part of town," Kim said.

"What sort of a soccer game do you think we're going to see?" Del said.

"Oh. We're going for the sights then?" Kim said.

"No harm in looking is there?"

"I guess not."

❧

Angel was getting out of her postal uniform, attempting to make a sandwich and talk on the phone all at the same time. She'd been forced to do overtime and now she had all of forty minutes to eat, get dressed and drive to the game. Her friend Sally was giving her a hard time for not responding to Alicia's overtures.

"She's got this huge crush on you and you won't give her the time of day. When are you going to leave all that shit behind?"

"I have left it behind. I don't even think about it anymore. Don't think about her, I don't think about them."

"So when are you going to find someone?" Sally asked.

Angel slapped a slice of turkey and provolone on her sandwich. "When the right someone comes along."

"How will you know that if you don't give anyone a chance? Alicia is a nice girl. Why'd don't you ask her out?"

"I can't try people out. I have to feel something."

"Feel what?"

"I don't know—that feeling you get when you look at her and something happens between you that is different from all others."

"You are grossly romantic and I don't see how you'll ever find a girlfriend."

"I'll find her," Angel said, thinking of Kim. With Kim she felt sparks even though she didn't know her. Something happened every time she saw her even though they didn't exchange more than an afternoon greeting when Angel handed her the mail. There was something between them and perhaps one day something more.

"Whatever. You better hurry. It's almost game time," Sally said.

"Well, if I wasn't yakking at you I'd be ready."

"Can't you just be nice to Alicia?"

"Can't you just stop bugging me?"

"It's not in my nature. I am a natural born matchmaker. I can't help myself," Sally replied.

"Try."

"I'll see you at the game," Sally replied, still thinking of ways to get them together. Sally liked a challenge.

81

Del and Kim sat up in the bleachers eating pizza and drinking beer while the game unfolded below. Del pointed out Celia's niece, Alicia.

"Now isn't this better than painting the house?" Del replied.

"The scenery is definitely better," Kim said, admiring all the leg muscle so prominently displayed before her. Del attempted to explain the mechanics of the game to Kim who was still hopelessly lost.

"Can't I just watch the girls," Kim asked, after frustrating Del again and again by not understanding why they were doing what.

"Yes, you can just watch the girls if that makes you happy," Del said.

"Girl watching does make me happy," Kim said, looking closer at one of the players. She appeared to be the star of the team as she would come out of nowhere, get the ball and charge toward the goal. The woman looked familiar but Kim couldn't quite place her.

"Do you see one you like?" Del asked, noticing Kim's rapt attention on one woman in particular.

"I do see one."

"Which one?" Del asked, leaning in closer.

"You always smell so good," Kim remarked.

Del smiled. "Now which one do you like?" she asked, intent on getting Kim back on track.

"It's not like I can point or anything," Kim replied.

"How about a jersey number," Del suggested.

"Number fifteen."

Del looked closer. "Well, I'll be damned. She didn't tell me she was playing soccer again."

"What?"

"Which one are you talking about?"

"Remember when you asked me if I had any friends that you might like?"

"Yes."

"Well, I do. I know her. She just moved from Chicago."

"I do too I think. But I can't place her," Kim said.

"After the game we'll solve the mystery."

Alicia handed Angel a towel and a Gatorade. She looked overly long at Angel. Angel smiled back, remembering Sally's reproach. Alicia was a nice kid, Angel thought, but then that was the problem. She was a kid with a bad case of puppy love.

"You played a good game," Angel said.

"Thanks. So did you. But you always play well," Alicia said.

"Hey you. You neglected to mention you'd taken up soccer again. I would have come sooner," Del said.

"Like that would happen. I've been here two months and the most I can squeeze in with you is lunch in the hospital cafeteria. How did you manage this?"

"I've been pulling doubles all week and they are afraid I might go off the deep end if I don't get some rest and recreation. Hey, I want you to meet my friend . . ." Del started to say.

"Kim?" Angel said.

"Angel?" Kim replied.

"I thought you said you didn't know her," Del said.

"I didn't recognize you without your uniform on," Kim said. "And you always wear a ball cap and sunglasses. I never really knew what you looked like."

"Going around in disguise these days," Del teased.

"A woman with a past can never be too careful," Angel replied.

Kim made a mental note to pick Del's brains later. Angel was more handsome than Kim had envisioned. Her uniform hid curves, blue eyes and a flattop. Angel made her quiver in ways that even Ollie failed to elicit. She probably has a girlfriend, Kim thought glumly as Alicia and Sally came up.

"We're all going for a beer. Want to come along, Angel?" Sally asked, evidently being an ambassador for Alicia.

"Hi, Alicia, good game," Del said.

"Hey Del, thanks for coming. Celia is going for a beer too. She's right over there," Alicia said, her eyes never leaving Angel's face.

Kim watched, thinking that must be the girlfriend. Alicia and Kim sized each other up.

"I don't know. I've got some work to do," Angel said, feeling the encroaching pressure of being social thrust upon her.

"Come on, Angel. We'll catch up," Del said.

"Are you going?" Angel asked Kim, surprising everyone.

"If you are," Kim replied, trying not to blush.

"All right then. My Jeep is right over there we could ride together. The bar's just down the street," Angel said.

"Sure, that sounds great," Del replied.

"So we'll see you there, right Angel?" Alicia said, trying to be enthused to cover her frustration.

"Yeah, we'll be there. Come on," Angel said, leading Del and Kim off.

Angel threw her bag in the back of the jeep and pulled a clean T-shirt out of it. Kim tried not to look when she changed. Del stared without shame.

"Still the nicest torso west of the Mississippi," Del teased.

"Stop it. If you remember it was the torso that got me into all that trouble in the first place."

"Her torso and other sundry parts of her body are famous, you know," Del told Kim.

"Don't," Angel said, getting into the Jeep.

"Can't I tell?" Del asked.

"They're not around much anymore, thank God," Angel replied.

"She was the model for all those J. Haley erotic photographs," Del explained.

Kim laughed.

"What's so funny?" Angel asked as she backed the Jeep out of the parking space. She waited until Sally's car pulled out into traffic.

"I have one of those in my bedroom no less," Kim replied, blushing profusely as was Angel.

"You don't," Angel said, pulling out into traffic.

84

"I do," Kim said.

"I thought we were going to the bar," Del screamed from the back seat.

"We are," Angel said.

"But everyone else is going that way," Del replied.

"Look, you wanted to go have a drink, right?" Angel said.

"Yes," Del replied.

"So do I. But I don't want to go to the same place as Alicia and Sally because Sally is trying to fix me up with Alicia who is yet another nice, young, typical blond soccer player who doesn't really turn my crank," Angel explained.

"Who does turn your crank these days?" Del teased.

"Wouldn't you like to know," Angel replied, taking a quick look at Kim.

"So is Mallory turning your crank these days?" Angel asked.

"Oh, yes. I met her parents the other day," Del replied.

"Really?" Angel replied.

"They are madly in love. It's really rather disgusting," Kim replied.

"Why disgusting?" Angel asked, pulling into the parking lot of Nasty Habits.

"Because I'm jealous," Kim said.

"Because you wanted Del?" Angel teased.

"Is that why? I never knew," Del said, hopping out the back of the bright red Jeep.

"You were long smitten before I ever got a chance," Kim retorted. "No, it's disgusting because you two are going to be happy and you're going to make it and that's something I want. But I always pick the wrong woman."

"You're not alone there. I'm always with the wrong woman, huh, Del," Angel said.

"It was just a bad patch, Angel. You got out in one piece and that's a blessing," Del said.

"Maybe you can inspire Kim and me by telling us the wonders of true love over a pitcher of beer."

"I'll try," Del said.

Angel bought them several pitchers of beer and drank half a beer the whole night while they got rather sloshed.

"Are you going to be in trouble with your friends?" Kim asked as Angel beat her at yet another game of pool.

"A better question would be do I care," Angel replied.

"Do you?"

"If Alicia was here I'd have to feel bad for not reciprocating her feelings. I can't make myself feel something I don't. Besides I wouldn't get to play pool with you," Angel said.

"Why not?" Kim asked.

"They don't have pool tables at the other bar," Angel replied.

"You're a smartass," Kim said.

"Is that bad?" Angel teased.

"No, I kind of like it," Kim replied.

Del came in from outside with a huge smile on her face.

"How is the activist doing?" Kim asked.

"She's fine," Del said, putting her cell phone away. Mallory had called her every day since she'd been gone. Technology was a beautiful thing, Del thought.

Later as Kim lay in bed she looked at her J. Haley print with a whole new perspective. Tomorrow she'd go to the bookstore and get Dykeland and a compilation of J. Haley prints. There had to be one. Suddenly she wanted to know everything about Angel and tomorrow afternoon couldn't come soon enough. She had the day off and she knew she'd spend it painting and thinking about Angel, knowing she was beginning to exist for those three minutes at the end of the day when the mail came.

Is that how you cure a heartache, trade your brokenhearted vision for yet another illusion, pulling love like a rabbit from your empty hat, praying this time the illusion will solidify into something warm, fuzzy and real? It didn't matter. For the first night in weeks she fell asleep not thinking about Ollie but dreaming of lovely torsos.

The phone jangled Kim awake. She rolled over to answer it before she could stop herself. As a habit she let the answering machine pick it up because Ollie kept calling.

"Hello?" Kim said, sleepily.

"Is your hair messy and your lovely breasts soft and warm?" the caller asked.

"Excuse me," Kim said, getting vertical immediately.

"I can't believe I finally got a hold of you. I was beginning to feel like I was having an affair with your answering machine. I was starting to call it sweetie," Ollie said.

"Ollie . . . I don't want to talk to you," Kim said, getting out of bed and going to the coffee machine. Now that she was awake she felt the damage of last night slowly creeping across her brain like the waves slipping across the sand and hitting the rock barrier. The barrier was her headache.

"But maybe I need to talk to you. I don't know what you heard about me but I want another chance. No playing around, just you and me. I've realized some things about myself since you've been gone. I know I can do better. We'll get a house together, you know, be like a real couple."

"Ollie, go away," Kim said, hanging up the phone. She should have never got it reconnected but her father had insisted that a young woman living alone must have a phone in case an intruder or sociopath had designs on her. She told him he watched too much television. He told her that when she got old she'd watch a lot of television as well. It baby-sits the mind and deadens the soul, he told her. *I'm glad I have something to look forward to.*

The phone rang again and Kim figured it was Ollie but she scrambled for it as Del started to leave a message.

"Ollie still calling?" Del asked.

"As a matter of fact," Kim replied, getting coffee, "I just talked to her. She wants us to buy a house together and be like a real couple."

"Wow, that's certainly a turnabout," Del replied, suddenly hoping Kim wasn't going to consider it, because she'd only seen Angel look at one other woman like she looked at Kim. Now *they* would be good for each other.

"You know, if I'd been smart I should have just stuck it out," Kim replied.

"Why?" Del asked, instantly mortified that her old college buddy had once again set her sights on the wrong woman.

"Because if I let her break up with me then she wouldn't be obsessed with getting back together. Women like Ollie cannot comprehend rejection," Kim replied, pouring orange juice and popping three aspirin.

"But what were you supposed to do, wait until she fell madly in love with one of her fuckmates and then get a divorce?"

"We were never married. No, I think I should have let her fuck around with Gigi. Those two deserve each other. They could have fallen madly in love and then spent the rest of their relationship trying to outdo each other in the on-the-side girlfriend department. Now that's poetic justice," Kim replied, feeling better.

"That would have been beautiful," Del replied. She had known women like that before and things usually ended up totally miserable because once you're a dog you're always a dog.

"But unfortunately, I obviously have too much self-esteem and couldn't wait out the degradation, so alas I'm stuck with Ollie's pathological tantrums until she finds a new girlfriend. Maybe I should run an ad for her. Speed things up a bit," Kim said, studying the contents of the fridge looking for edible matter.

"I can only imagine what it would read like," Del said.

"It's all in the word choice. You can make the worst slime sound practically lovable," Kim replied.

"True. Did you have fun last night?" Del said, trying to gently steer the conversation toward her intended goal.

"A little too much fun. My head is throbbing," Kim replied.

"I'm not much better myself," Del said, glad she was working the night shift because she wasn't in any shape to play doctor this morning.

"I really liked Angel. She's fun. Can you believe she's my mailman? It's like the best coincidence. Or perhaps the Astral Goddess is finally doing me a favor."

"You should have seen her in Chicago. She had the gay mecca section of town. Women waited with anticipation for the post every day. It was funny to see."

"She's got the body to die for," Kim said, her thoughts floating back to the soccer game.

"Do you wait in anticipation?" Del asked.

"Del! You're pumping me," Kim replied.

"I just wondered if you like her?" Del asked. Forced to show her hand, she might as well get it out in the open.

"Who wouldn't like her? She's smart, talented, athletically inclined, and cute."

"You know what I mean," Del replied.

"Do I have the hots for her?"

"Well, yes."

"It's a known lesbian faux pas to date anyone who is rebounding, especially if the ex-girlfriend is still hanging around," Kim replied.

"Angel's not your average lesbian," Del replied.

"Meaning?" Kim asked.

"It's not about time and place, it's about . . ." Del replied.

"What?"

"I don't know, true love or something," Del muttered, feeling stupid for getting mushy when Kim obviously wasn't entertaining those notions.

"Del, you are so sweet, but as much as I'd like to think about Angel she doesn't go for women like me," Kim said.

"Why not?" Del said, absolutely flabbergasted.

"I'm not flashy enough, rich enough, good looking enough," Kim replied, remembering that her first attraction to Ollie was that Ollie had all those things and was actively pursuing her. She had let flattery lead her heart.

89

"You have definitely got her pegged wrong. She's not like that at all."

"Look at her last girlfriend."

"Jennifer was a shithead among other things."

"But she was also talented, famous, and a babe," Kim replied.

"Angel got dragged into that," Del said.

"Anyway, I can look and long and be a pal if she wants."

"So you like her?"

"Yes, I like her," Kim said, feeling blue suddenly because sobriety and morning light had brought all her dreams of last night crashing down. There would be no going to the bookstore to learn about her new fancy.

"Good," Del said.

Angel handed Mrs. Jacobs her mail. Her cell phone rang.

"So I talked to our friend," Del said.

"Yes," Angel replied, fingering the mail for the next house and dodging a sprinkler.

"She's got a bit of a headache," Del replied.

"Stop teasing me and get to the point," Angel demanded, dumping the mail into the box with precision and force.

"She likes you but she doesn't think you like women like her," Del replied.

"What is that supposed to mean?" Angel replied.

"She thinks you like flashy girls."

"Oh, for fuck sake. Where'd she get that idea?"

"Your last girlfriend," Del replied.

"How long is that shit going to follow me around," Angel said, unlocking the Jeep and taking a seat.

"Your entire life I would imagine. But I think with diligence, hard work, and emotional finesse, she could be won over," Del replied.

"I hope so. I think she's incredibly sexy. I haven't stopped thinking about her since the day we met. That doesn't usually happen to me."

"I know. Maybe I could put that buzz in her ear," Del offered.

"No, someday I'll tell her myself."

"Okay," Del replied.

Kim lugged another can of red paint up the ladder. She was close to finishing the second story. She plugged her CD in and her mind lulled itself into the task at hand and the music. She tried not to think about why Del had been pumping her. She did like Angel but as she thought about last night she saw herself reading things into a harmless night of pool and drinks. Angel was new in town and looking for friends. Looking for friends did not a romance make. She needed to remind herself of that fact daily. Suddenly the ladder started to shake. Kim pulled out her headphones. She figured it was Angel.

"I want you to know I hold you personally responsible for my hangover," Kim said.

"And why is that?" Ollie asked. "Been out playing around, have you?"

"Ollie! What are you doing here?"

"I want to talk to you. I figured if I showed up in the flesh you would be forced to talk to me."

"I don't want to talk. We don't have anything left to say."

"I have things to say."

"Your actions speak for you."

"Come down here and talk to me. I know we can work things out. Please," Ollie said.

"No, I want you to go away. Ollie, I can't do this anymore. I'm trying to get over you. Right now I need space. I'm done talking. You had two years to straighten things out and you were always too busy looking over my shoulder for someone else. Now you have the chance to find them. Why don't you go fuck Gigi? That's what you want isn't it?"

"No, I want you. I want our relationship back."

"We didn't have a relationship. We had mutual friends, mutual sex and mutual fights. That's not a relationship."

"What if I want to make it a relationship?"

"It's too late," Kim said, turning back around to resume painting.

"How can it be too late if we never tried?"

"Ollie, go away," Kim said, making nice even strokes.

"I'm not going away until you come down and talk to me. This is ridiculous. I love you. I'm not going until you hear me out," Ollie said, grabbing the sides of the ladder. "Now come down right this minute."

"Go away!"

Ollie gave the ladder a good shake.

"Stop that! This isn't funny," Kim said, trying to stay calm and keep her mind from calculating what a fall from two stories would do to her body.

"I want to talk."

"I don't see the point. Now I'm busy."

"Look, you can either come down and talk to me, or you'll have to talk to me when you're laid up in traction," Ollie yelled, giving the ladder a serious shake.

The paint bucket went rolling down the roof and spattered across the lawn and all adjoining shrubbery. Kim grabbed the gutter for support.

"If I fall and you kill me you still won't be able to talk to me, not to mention you'll be in prison."

"I'll take my chances," Ollie said, giving the ladder another shake.

Kim held on tight and said a prayer for the radical enlightenment of her ex-girlfriend. One more shake of the ladder and she and the gutter would come clean off the roof.

Ollie was getting ready for another good rattle when she felt someone grab her collar. The next thing she knew she was flat on her back with the breath knocked out of her. She looked up to find a boot on her chest and a woman in uniform peering down at her.

"Now the way I see it you've got a few options here. Number one I can kick your ass, number two, I can call the police and get you nailed for aggravated assault if not attempted murder, or three, I let you go and you leave her alone forever."

"What if I don't like any of those?" Ollie said.

"I'll go for number one first," Angel said, putting pressure on her boot.

"Number three," Ollie squeaked out.

"I thought so," Angel said.

Ollie got up and scrambled away.

"I mean it. You lay a hand on her again and I'll kick your ass."

Kim let out a deep breath and came creeping down the ladder. She was shaking.

"Are you okay?" Angel asked.

"I think so," Kim replied, feeling weak in the knees and tears start.

Angel took her in her arms and held her. Kim started to cry and Angel held her tight, whispering reassuring words.

"I'm sorry," Kim muttered.

"Don't," Angel said, brushing her tears away. She held her again until she stopped shaking.

"Thank you for saving me," Kim said, when she had calmed down.

"I take it that was your ex," Angel said, going to pick up the paint bucket and the brush.

"Yes," Kim said, sitting down on the porch.

Angel sat next to her.

"It does get better, you know," Angel said softly.

"I don't understand it. When we were together she never exhibited this much interest in me. I try to walk away and she hounds me. I can't make myself forgive her and I can't make myself love her again. She's done too much damage."

"Did she play around?" Angel asked.

Kim nodded.

"That's the hardest thing to overlook. When I was with Jennifer I overlooked a lot of things but after a while you've got to draw the line. I shared her with alcohol and drugs, which were hard enough, but it finally ended when she started sleeping with my best friend. She chose the person who meant the most to me and deliberately wrecked that. I had to let go."

"How did you get away?"

"I moved here."

"So I've got to move away?" Kim said, looking despondent.

"I hope not," Angel replied.

Kim smiled. "Where did you come from?"

"Chicago," Angel replied.

They both laughed knowing what she really meant.

"I always wanted to be a knight in shining armor," Angel said.

"Well, you are. How will this fair damsel ever repay you?"

"I do have a favor to ask."

"Name it," Kim said.

"Next Saturday is the postal gay and lesbian picnic. I want to go but I don't want to go alone because then everyone takes pity on you and next thing you know they are all trying to set you up with one of their single friends. But if I took someone . . ."

"Is that an invite?"

"Please . . ."

"Sure, I'll be your escort," Kim teased.

Angel wrinkled her brow. "No, I want to take *you*."

"Angel . . ." Kim started to explain.

"Look, I know you've got stuff to deal with. But I really like you. I'm a patient woman. I'll wait," Angel said, getting up to leave.

"Then I'd love to go," Kim said, blushing.

"Good. Are you sure you're okay?"

"Yes, thank you."

"Will you stay off the ladder, just for today?" Angel said, staring up at it and thinking how lucky Kim was to not be lying flat on the ground right now. "She wouldn't have let you fall, right?"

"I don't know."

"Can I call you later?" Angel asked.

"Please."

Five

Gigi lay in bed thinking. Mallory was taking a shower after a full day of lawn darts and barbecuing. She was replaying the afternoon Ollie came to see her at the store. She'd just made a big sale of a vibrator and a strap-on setup to a very attractive older woman who was a little tentative about the whole thing. Gigi had done her best to reassure her, flirt, offer suggestions and generally be her best salesperson self. She was sitting back, figuring her commission, and enjoying another day in the sex shop when Ollie walked in.

"Ollie, how are you?" Gigi asked, feeling her pulse jump.

"Yeah, long time no see, stranger," Ollie said. "Where have you been keeping yourself?"

"Oh, you know, out and about," Gigi replied, nervously straightening the *Curve* magazine display. She wished someone would come in the store so she'd have a reason not to talk to Ollie. Ever since the night Kim threw her out of the house Gigi had steered clear of

Ollie, not wanting any further repercussions. She'd come to realize she didn't want to lose Alex over a roll in the hay or in their case a quick fuck in the back of a van. Gigi had sufficiently chastised herself for letting things get that far. They hadn't even taken their clothes off. It was like bad teenage sex and now Ollie was on the loose. Gigi was more than apprehensive.

"So I'm not part of the group anymore and now I don't get to see you?" Ollie said.

"I just figured it was best to lay low for a while, you know, until things clear up."

"Well, things aren't going to clear up. Kim won't even speak to me anymore. I think we are really done this time."

"I'm sorry," Gigi said, feeling immediately odd for apologizing for something she had nothing to do with.

"You should be. If I hadn't fucked around with you I'd still have a girlfriend."

"Listen, you cruised me. If you're so in love with Kim why the hell were you fucking around with me? You're the one that took harmless flirtation to new heights."

"Oh yeah, and you were protesting the whole time you were coming," Ollie replied.

Gigi refrained from saying she hadn't come because she was too nervous and freaked out to enjoy the moment of illicit passion. She kept worrying that Alex was going to come looking for her, open the van door and find her between the legs of another woman.

"You got what you wanted. Don't blame me because your girl-friend finally saw the light. Maybe she got tired of you fucking around on her all the time. I'm sure I wasn't the first," Gigi retorted.

"Someone must have told her things, enlightened her. A hand job in the car is hardly grounds for dismissal," Ollie said, picking up one of the display vibrators on the counter.

"I certainly didn't tell anyone. Maybe you were too out in the open for her tastes," Gigi replied, thinking a hand job would be grounds for dismissal if Alex ever found out and right now Ollie was a loose cannon. Gigi would have to do her best to placate her and hope Ollie found another girlfriend quick so her failure with Kim would quickly become a footnote in the journal of a seductress.

"I've always been like that. What makes this time any different? Are you sure you didn't tell Mallory anything?"

"Ollie, I don't want anyone to know about it. I would just like to forget the whole thing ever happened. I'm sorry you lost Kim in the process but I don't really think you can blame me for that. It was half an hour at a party. It's not like we had some torrid affair going on. Maybe Kim just wants more out of her love life."

"Yeah, like the fucking postman, woman, whatever."

"What are you talking about?"

"They sit and talk every day and the mail lady is a looker and she's looking at my girlfriend," Ollie replied, not bothering to mention the altercation she had with Angel the other day.

"How do you know that?"

"I've watched them."

"You're not stalking Kim are you?" Gigi said, thinking her life was getting more complicated by the second.

"I was just checking up on her."

"You need to stay away from her. There are tons of women out there," Gigi suggested.

"There's only one that I want."

The door opened and Reverend Carlyle came in. Gigi let out a sigh of relief.

"I best let you go. Call me if you ever want another tumble out back," Ollie said, facetiously.

Reverend Carlyle raised an eyebrow. Ollie smiled at him and did three Hail Mary's. The good Reverend blushed. Gigi took his arm and made ready to lead him away from the heathen.

"Sure, Ollie, take care now," Gigi said.

"Maybe you should do confession while there's a priest in the house. Perhaps he can absolve you of your sins," Ollie suggested.

"That's a very good idea," Gigi said.

"Interesting young woman," Reverend Carlyle said, as he and Gigi made their way to the erotic video department.

"Did you like your latest addition?" Gigi asked.

"Yes, very much thank you. I can help you with the confession if you like."

"Oh, I'm afraid it's too late for that. But thanks anyway."

The good Reverend nodded. Sometimes he missed the old days when people would share their juicy details and he could make them feel better by acting as a human eraser on the blackboard of humanity.

"We all do bad things. It's getting caught that makes us feel the error acutely," the Reverend said.

"I don't want to get caught. I don't ever want to do it again. If I could undo it I would."

"Hindsight is a beautiful thing."

"And worthless."

"Not if it shapes future behavior," Reverend Carlyle advised.

Mallory softly padded into the bedroom thinking Gigi would be asleep. It was a full moon and it flooded their bedroom. Mallory dug around in her duffel bag for a T-shirt. Gigi leaned up on her elbow and watched.

"Has anyone ever told you that you have an incredible body?"

"I thought you were asleep," Mallory said, sliding the shirt on, feeling suddenly shy in Gigi's presence, which was absolutely stupid since they'd seen each other naked since they were ten. Mallory had been privy to the sprouting of Gigi's first pubic hair and they had gone to get their first bras together, giggling and laughing in the changing room.

"No, as a matter of fact, no one has," Mallory said, beginning to think about how Del might perceive her body.

"Well, just for the record, I'd say it's gorgeous," Gigi said, opening the covers for Mallory to get in. Mallory slid into the crook of Gigi's neck like they always did. Maybe they were the sisters each didn't have. Whatever it was, Gigi always felt safest here. She pulled Mallory tight.

"How come we were never lovers?" Gigi asked.

"Dr. Kohlrabi says because we've been friends for too long."

"Do you think that's true?"

"No."

"I would have been so good with you. You would have made me good," Gigi said.

"That's why we're not lovers. I shouldn't have to be your parent. I need a partner."

"And Del's going to be that partner?" Gigi asked, feeling suddenly, inexplicably sad.

"Yes, she is. We'll take care of each other."

"So I missed my chance?" Gigi asked.

"Yes, but I still love you," Mallory said, kissing Gigi's cheek. "And this way we'll never have to break up. You need to be nicer to Alex. She loves you."

"I know. I love her too but . . . I just don't know."

"Good, then treat her better."

They lay in silence, each wrapped up in her own thoughts. Mallory was thinking about Del and trying to envision their future moments, complete with sex. Gigi was trying to decide if she should confess her indiscretion with Ollie to Mallory to see what she thought she should do. Keeping the secret was giving her daily anxiety attacks especially now that Ollie wasn't giving up her pathological desire to get her girlfriend back or at minimum extract some form of retribution. The desire for retribution scared the shit out of Gigi. She could only imagine what Ollie was capable of doing. Gigi needed to figure out how best to do damage control. She needed Mallory's help.

"I have to tell you something, something that Alex doesn't know and shouldn't know," Gigi started. "Remember the party where Kim got really angry with Ollie and threw her out, well earlier that night something happened between Ollie and I, something . . .

sexual, something more than a kiss. We were getting high in the van and next thing I know we were *doing* it. I was so nervous but I still did it and now I'm really scared that Alex is going to find out. It only happened that once and I regret it but I can't undo the fact that I fucked another woman and that was what it was—fucking, pure and simple lust incarnate and now . . . now I don't know what to do. What do you think I should do?"

Silence.

"It's not like we were having an affair. It's more like an isolated incident and believe me I'm not proud of it. Mallory?"

Mallory rolled over and made murmuring noises. She'd been asleep the whole time.

Shit! Gigi thought, *like I'm going to be able to muster up the courage to do that again.* She couldn't even bring herself to tell Aunt Lil because she was too ashamed. It appeared she would have to bear the burden of her own guilt, as her mother would say. What a sad state of affairs when she found herself quoting her mother, Gigi thought, rolling over.

Maybe Alex would never find out and she could spend the rest of her life trying to make it up to her. Ever since the thing with Ollie, Gigi hadn't even looked at another woman and her desire to flirt had become nonexistent. Alex noticed the change. Gigi told her she was growing up. Alex looked at her uneasily. Gigi tried to brush it off, telling her she finally realized what a wonderful woman her partner was. Alex gave her an even odder look and went off to load the dishwasher.

Gigi could hear the phrase echoing in her head, once a dog always a dog. Could she change the inevitable? Lesbians need a patron saint. We could call her Saint Vulva. She was having thoughts like her mother's. How disgusting. Gigi groaned and tried to fall asleep.

Del sat across the table from Mallory at the Orbit Cafe. She was covering shifts for Dr. Lee and so her days and nights were full. Lunch was the most she and Mallory could squeeze in. Mallory was telling her stories about Yarnell.

100

"So they know for sure who the spy is," Mallory said, in between bites of her grilled mushroom sandwich.

"How did they do that?" Del asked, seriously wondering if having the tuna sandwich was such a good idea after all.

"Aunt Lil leaked the idea to the spy, telling her that there was to be a ritual goddesslike mass held at the old grange hall up on the hill behind the trailer court where everyone would consort in utter nakedness in worship of the goddess. The spy then relayed the information to Gigi's mother, Rose, who called the police. When the squad cars got there they found Aunt Lil and her cronies holding a bake sale."

Del was laughing so hard she nearly choked on her tuna sandwich.

"Are you all right?" Mallory asked in alarm as Del gulped water and tried to get her breath back.

Del nodded, wiping the tears out of her eyes. "I can just see the look on those police officers' faces when they raided the bake sale."

"Aunt Lil says the local police have been trying to figure out what all those old ladies at the trailer court are up to but aside from a few misdemeanors here and there they can't get them on much," Mallory said.

"What kind of misdemeanors?"

"They sent Anita Bryant a rainbow colored set of dildos, the President a box of cigars with pubic hair attached, Jerry Falwell a leatherman Billy doll, Senator Jesse Helms twenty-five ten-gallon drums of urine just for starters," Mallory replied, matter-of-factly. "And that was only their mailing campaign."

"Holy shit!" Del said. "You're not going to get thrown in jail are you?"

"Will you post bail?" Mallory asked, getting the check.

Del smiled. "I'd do anything for you."

"Good, let's go," Mallory said, getting up.

"I still have some time before I have to go back to work," Del said, taking a last bite of her sandwich as Mallory pulled her out of her chair.

"I know."

Mallory parked back by the loading dock of the hospital. She turned the car off and looked at Del expectantly.

"What's up?" Del asked.

"Can I kiss you?" Mallory asked.

"I just had a fish sandwich," Del replied, wishing she had taken the time to grab a mint at the restaurant but Mallory had been in such a hurry to get out of there.

"Open wide," Mallory said, shooting Del with Binaca.

"You think of everything."

"Not everything. I should have told you not to order the tuna."

"True," Del said, feeling Mallory draw her close, her lips and tongue against her own.

Kim walked out the employee entrance just as Del was getting out of Mallory's car. She was tucking in her shirt and she had a generally disheveled look about her. Kim smiled. At least somebody was getting some action.

"You need some time off," Kim teased, doing up one of Del's buttons.

"I need a cold shower," Del said.

"There is nothing quite like the early days of love," Kim said.

"Speaking of that how are you and Angel doing?" Del asked, attempting to appear nonchalant.

"There is no Angel and I. There is Angel who delivers my mail and there is Angel I played pool with once."

"And there's Angel who is taking you to the postal picnic," Del said.

"It's a buddy-date," Kim replied.

"That's what you say," Del said.

"What? You know better," Kim said, trying not to blush.

"I just think you two would make a cute couple, that's all," Del said.

"We'll see."

At the post office Sally peeked around Angel's case. Angel was putting Advo cards up and listening to Barry White on her headphones. Sally swatted her hard on the head with a rolled up magazine.

Angel yanked her one of her earplugs out. "That hurt!"

"It was supposed to," Sally said, putting the magazine back.

"Not to mention that was blatant disregard of postal property," Angel said, picking the magazine back up and trying to smooth out the cover. Mr. Earl was extremely particular about the shape his mail was in when it arrived. Angel discovered that her second day on the route when he ripped her a new asshole for cramming the mail into his wall slot. They had since come to an understanding and now she put his magazines neatly in a wooden box by the front door.

"Are you going to the picnic?" Sally asked.

"Why do you want to know?" Angel countered.

"Because Alicia wants to know."

"Did it ever occur to either one of you that I don't want to date fellow postal workers or anyone I play soccer with. Those are two no-no's in my book because when things go wrong, it's hard to go to work and I have to switch soccer leagues."

"So you're not going to the picnic," Sally said.

"As a matter of fact I am going," Angel said, smiling.

"Why bother if you don't date postal workers?"

"Because I'm bringing a date," Angel replied.

"You are? Who?" Sally said, curiosity lighting up her face.

"You'll just have to wait and see," Angel teased.

Sally went to grab a magazine when Dick the supervisor came by and growled at her to get back to her case. Angel smiled sweetly at him. He loved her because she ran her ass off and did more relays than anyone else. She could do no wrong.

"If I could get that mouth of hers to deliver mail we could get rid of five PTF's," Dick said.

They both laughed.

"Imagine if we could harness it as a power source," Angel replied.

"Like a windmill, jaws flapping in wind," Dick said. "Hey, thanks for helping out the other day. We need more people like you and less like her. Keep up the good work."

"Thanks," Angel said, watching him limp off to retrieve the salami sandwich he'd left at his desk.

The pile on the bed looked like something at a rummage sale as Kim tried on yet another outfit. She looked at herself in the mirror and then looked at her print of Angel's torso on her wall. What was this perfectly darling woman doing being interested in her? She walked into the living room and sat dejected on the couch. How did she ever think she could date someone like Angel. Ollie had always made her feel so unattractive, so less cute, darling, stunning than all the other women. And now Angel—model, artist, fame-and-fortune woman —was hanging around and Kim knew she wasn't up to another relationship that made her feel so inadequate. It was hopeless.

Kim jumped when the doorbell rang. She looked at the clock. Holy shit! It was one o'clock and the front door was open with only a screen between Angel and herself, and she was only wearing shorts and a sports bra. It wasn't like she could slink by Angel to grab a shirt. She stood up and answered the door.

"You look lovely," Angel said, coming in.

Kim smiled, her shoulders drooping. "I can't figure out what to wear, so needless to say I'm not dressed."

"You could wear what you have on," Angel offered, "with a liberal dose of sunscreen."

"This isn't funny. I'm having a crisis here."

"Why?"

"Because it always seems like everyone else is so fucking beautiful and then there's me," Kim said, walking off toward the bedroom and her heap of discarded clothing. Angel grabbed her arm.

"Wait a minute. Who made you think you're not beautiful?"

"Every white girl in the world, every ad, every blond-haired, blue-eyed, big-breasted woman, every stunning supermodel, every cover of *Curve*, *Out*, and *Cosmo*, and my last blond-haired, blue-eyed girlfriend, that's who," Kim said, slumping down on the bed.

"Just for the record, Latinos aren't exactly icons of beauty either according to mass culture," Angel said, picking up shirts and looking at them.

"But look at *that*," Kim said, pointing to the print of Angel's torso.

"*That* is good photography," Angel said, choosing a shirt.

"Next you'll be telling me it's been airbrushed."

"No, but have you ever seen that ad in *Curve* with Melissa Etheridge and her girlfriend . . . the one for PETA. Now that one has been airbrushed. So you see the old cliché is true. Beauty is in the eye of the beholder and lesbians are just as fucked up as everyone else. Why didn't they leave Melissa with her big, old, fat butt? Because everyone wants that magazine kind of look but it doesn't truly exist. We are what we are. And you are the picture of beauty. It's all in the presentation and the belief."

"Are you fucking with me?"

"No. Here. Wear this one. It's a nice color. I have a passion for azure so humor me," Angel said, pulling Kim up from the bed and slipping it over her head.

"So this shirt is going to make me beautiful?"

"No, our combined faith does. Now come on. We don't want to miss the sack race do we?"

"The one I wear over my head," Kim muttered.

Angel gave her a disapproving look.

"It's not vanity you know. It's about how the world treats people who are pretty," Kim continued.

"Only while they are young and beautiful. When they get old they are tedious and vain and no one gives them the time of day anymore."

"It's lookism you know."

"Are you always this freaky before you go to a picnic?"

"Only if it's a gay and lesbian event."

"Which is most of what we do," Angel said.

"I know. I must have an ugly personality disorder," Kim said, locking the front door.

"I'll cure you of it," Angel said.

"How are you going to do that?" Kim said, getting in the doorless Jeep and suddenly wondering if anyone had ever fallen out of the extremely high four-wheel-drive vehicle with large, knobby tires.

"Tell you you're beautiful every day and if I ever get the chance to do something really nasty to that ex-girlfriend of yours I won't hesitate because I'm inclined to think she's the one behind this."

"You're probably right. I'm sorry. I don't mean to be such a twit, it's just that it's hard to know where you fit in an alternate culture because the rules are not clearly defined."

"And that's what makes it fun, confusing, liquid, empowering and destructive. We are what we make ourselves. Did it ever occur to you that women don't approach you because they think you're too good for them?"

"No, way!"

"Someday I'll give you lessons on cruising women and we'll try it out. I'll prove it to you. We can't do it at the picnic because you're my date, but some other time."

"Some other buddy date?"

"Yeah," Angel said, stopping at the light and suddenly wondering if she was making a mistake. She didn't want Kim to think they were just friends. She only wanted to go slow so Kim would have time to get over Ollie and not feel rushed into another relationship.

"I don't have to go home with them do I?" Kim asked.

"No, it would just be a test. You have to leave with the teacher."

"Because I'm the teacher's pet?" Kim said, arching an eyebrow.

"Yes," Angel said.

Sally was sitting with Alicia, whose shoulders were slumped in dejection. All around them the balloons and banners were flying, the barbecue grills filled the air with the smell of roasting flesh and one keg had gone dry already.

"She really did bring a date," Alicia said, as they watched Kim and Angel approaching.

Kim saw Alicia first and neatly took Angel's hand. Angel was surprised but then understood why.

"I'm your date, right?"

"My *beautiful* date."

"Oh, yeah, silly me," Kim said, smartly.

Angel grabbed her waist and pulled her in close. "If you don't behave I'll make you write it on the blackboard a zillion times."

Kim smiled. "Yes, ma'am."

"Where did she meet her?" Alicia asked Sally.

"She lives on her route," Sally said, putting her arm around Alicia. "Come on, let's go get a beer. We can talk to them later."

Alicia allowed herself to be dragged off but she watched Angel out of the corner of her eye until Sally suggested they go watch them in the sack race.

"If you continue to crane your neck like that trying to stare at them you're going to have to go to the chiropractor by the end of tonight."

Alicia brightened a little as they sat on the sidelines.

Angel waved at them as she stood, legs in a burlap bag, waiting for the starting gun.

"Her girlfriend is pretty," Alicia said, sizing Kim up. "She kind of looks like that bitchy lady Ling on *Ally McBeal*."

"Hmm . . ." Sally replied, watching everyone taking the first tentative hops.

Angel, of course, won but did help to drag Kim in as second. They didn't have a lot of competition; between the flaming, the fat, and the uncoordinated players they were certain to win. Kim was laughing so hard she tripped herself and brought Angel down with her. They lay in a hysterical heap.

"See, I told you that would be fun. It was the only reason I wanted to come," Angel said, pulling off her sack.

Kim sat up and tried to compose herself. "Well, I admit that was fun but I'm still looking forward to butt darts myself."

"I am not doing butt darts," Angel said, pulling Kim up.

"I did the sack race. You're doing butt darts, besides with an ass like that you'll surely win," Kim said, giving it a swift pat.

"Hey!" Angel said, pretending to be offended.

Kim didn't get her wish because Angel got drafted into the volleyball game that was a challenge between rival stations. Kim declined because she was non-postal. She sat up in the bleachers. Alicia sat next to her. She smiled.

"How come you're not playing?" Kim asked diplomatically even though her adrenal glands experienced an instant rush.

"I don't like volleyball," Alicia replied. "How about you?"

"I don't work for the post office," Kim replied.

"They wouldn't have cared."

"I know but I always seem to get run over by an overzealous, buxom woman. I'm not into pain."

"You don't play soccer then."

"No," Kim replied, "and for that very reason. I do, however, admire the sport."

"Are you sure it's not the players you like?" Alicia inquired, gathering momentum. Maybe it wasn't so hard talking to cute women, you just had to have guts or a cocky attitude, Alicia thought.

"You caught me," Kim said, laughing. "You all are a rather stunning bunch. It's better than watching big hairs at the bar."

"So you like athletic looking women?" Alicia asked, smirking.

"I think it depends on the person in their entirety. You could have great legs and a shitty personality and it would be hard to fall in love. At best it would be lust for a body part."

108

"I've lusted for a body part, but you're right, it's the whole woman that matters."

"What part was that?" Kim asked.

"It'll sound stupid," Alicia replied.

"Tell me anyway."

"It was this woman's forearms. You know that muscle between your wrist and your elbow," Alicia said, flexing her own to demonstrate.

Kim ran her finger along her arm. Alicia looked over at her and blushed.

"Yes, that's very nice," replied Kim, smiling.

Angel was busy watching them when she got nailed in the head with the ball.

"Stop girl watching and pay attention," Sally chided.

"I was," Angel replied.

"So how long have you been going out with Angel," Alicia asked, summoning up her last reserves of bravado to ask the things she really wanted to know.

"Not long. She's helped me out of a jam with my ex, who was giving me some trouble. Angel's been very supportive," Kim replied, not lying but not being overly truthful either.

"She's an incredible woman," Alicia replied, her gaze turning to the game.

"Good women are hard to find, and I always seemed to set my sights on bad women until now," Kim replied, talking more to herself than Alicia.

"I guess it's your turn then," Alicia said, wistfully.

"Date enough bad ones and suddenly the woman of your dreams comes walking in when you least expect it," Kim said.

"Think so?" Alicia replied absently, wondering if she tried too hard. No one is interested in a grappler. That was what her camp counselor had told her when she was sixteen, madly in love, and about to be left. Even now she couldn't fathom how someone could touch you like that and still walk away.

"Can I get you another beer?" Kim asked.

"Sure, thanks," Alicia said, finding it more and more difficult to not like Kim. Perhaps she should find someone more like Kim who was tired of bad relationships instead of setting her sights on people like Angel who were already accustomed to being loved and adored.

Kim stood waiting in the beer line that always ran longer than the food line. She half contemplated getting a snack and then waiting for beer. Ollie snuck up behind her.

"What are you doing here?" Kim said, looking over her shoulder to the volleyball court. She scooted Ollie out of plain view.

"I wanted to see if it was true that you're dating the postal worker," Ollie said.

"How did you find out about this?" Kim whispered savagely.

"I saw it advertised in the Women's Community paper. I wanted to see if you would be here."

"Why?"

"Then I'd know you were going out with *her*."

"You can't be here," Kim said, looking over her shoulder. She wasn't entirely sure Angel wouldn't back up her threat to pummel Ollie if she ever saw her again.

"I want to know if you were dating her before we broke up."

"Why?" Kim asked, getting tenser by the moment.

"Because it matters," Ollie said.

"It's none of your business and it has nothing to do with you anyway," Kim said, handing the bartender her and Alicia's cups.

"That's for me to decide. It's my right," Ollie said.

"You forfeited your rights when you slept with Gigi and god-knows-how-many others."

"Can I get one of those?" Ollie asked the bartender.

"Bud or Bud Light?" the bartender asked.

"Bud Light," Ollie replied. "How do you know I slept with Gigi?"

Kim looked away. "I don't want to talk about it." She took her beers and walked off.

"I want to know what makes you so certain I played around on you. It's not like you haven't flirted with other women before," Ollie said, trying to remember such a moment.

Kim rolled her eyes. "No, that was you."

"Flirting isn't fucking."

"I heard you in the van with Gigi that night at the party." She hadn't been proud of standing there listening to her girlfriend fucking someone else in the back of a van. She had gone out to see what Ollie was up to. She'd found out all right. It was standing there listening and faced with the physical truth that pushed her away, that finally allowed her to leave.

A number of lies, excuses, and manipulations ran through Ollie's head. Suddenly, looking at Kim's stern face none of them seemed plausible.

"I'm sorry," Ollie said.

"Me too," Kim replied, walking off.

Angel kept scanning the bleachers waiting for Kim to return. When she arrived with beers for herself and Alicia, Angel breathed easier. She was amazed at Kim's social skills as she watched them talking. Angel was sure by the end of the night Alicia would harbor no hard feelings and Kim would have another admirer. Angel smiled to herself. She felt certain that together they could make themselves better. Today was only the beginning.

Six

Del and Mallory drove at a leisurely pace down Central Avenue admiring the skyline and the Sunday morning lack of traffic. Del finally had a day off and she was taking Mallory out for brunch, then to the museum for a display of Spanish art and finally dinner with the family. Del was delighted, albeit nervous. Mallory was mortified.

"I still can't believe we got roped into dinner," Mallory said, looking at the Dial tower and thinking how it always reminded her of a bar of soap. She wondered if that had been an intentional architectural whim or a designer faux pas.

Del laughed. "You make us sound like cattle being hauled into the stockade."

"We are. Dinner will be tedious, trite, pretentious and ultimately unappetizing and at the end of it you will be wishing you had been mercifully put out of your misery."

"Well, let's have a big breakfast," Del suggested, hoping dinner was not going to be as bad as Mallory described.

They drove past the warehouse district on their way to First Watch.

"Doesn't your friend from Chicago live down here?" Mallory asked, looking up at the dull gray exteriors of the buildings with their windows like gaping holes staring out across the railroad tracks and junkyards.

"She does. Right over there as a matter of fact," Del said, pointing to a large aluminum gray building.

"I would like to meet her someday," Mallory said, cautiously. She was curious to see other parts of Del's life because there was so little of it to see. Her father lived in Chicago, her mother was dead and she was an only child. Now with Angel in town Mallory could learn more.

"Would you like to see if she wants to have brunch?" Del asked, sensing Mallory's interest. She was getting better about reading her and she liked the sensation it gave her. It made her feel like she was getting closer to Mallory and that the once unfathomable depths were starting to have dimension.

"If you want," Mallory said, handing Del the cell phone.

Del smiled. "She might play soccer on Sundays. I'm not sure."

One portion of Angel's brain briefly gathered that it was the phone ringing. On the fifth ring her hand reached for the phone and without opening her eyes she answered it.

"Planet Claire, how may I direct your call?"

Del laughed hysterically, "That is by far the most original opening line I've ever heard."

Angel opened her eyes, registered the caller and replied, "Sometimes I get mistaken for a night club. What's up?"

"Come for brunch?" Del asked, going around the block.

Mallory watched with anticipation.

Angel leaned over and looked at the clock. "I just had breakfast three hours ago."

113

"Some date!"

"We talked all night," Angel replied.

"Better date," Del said.

"I think so," Angel said, starting to replay the evening's events.

"So does that mean you aren't hungry?" Del asked.

"I don't know," Angel said.

"There's someone I want you to meet," Del said.

"Mallory?" Angel said, sitting up.

"Yes," Del replied.

"I'm awake now. I need to take a shower."

"We could pick you up."

"Where are you?" Angel said, figuring she had some time.

"First Street and Washington."

"Oh."

"We could drive around the block a couple of times," Del offered.

"No, come up. I'll leave the door unlocked and take a shower," Angel said, getting up and weaving toward the coffee maker.

"You're wonderful," Del said.

"I'm not in good shape," Angel replied, still bleary from sleep deprivation.

"I won't make you explain the theory of relativity," Del replied.

"Okay then. See you soon," Angel said, taking a quick look around the loft. At least it wasn't a pig pen at the moment. That was one benefit of not having Jennifer around, Angel thought wryly. I won't have to hide the drugs and sex toys or try to pick up a zillion empty liquor bottles. There is something to this clean living stuff.

Del gingerly opened the door to the loft. She didn't hear the shower. She shrugged her shoulders and went in. Mallory followed.

"Where is she?" Mallory asked.

Del smiled. "On the couch. Want a coffee?"

Mallory sat down in the overstuffed chair next to the couch and looked upon Angel for the first time. She lay on the couch with her hand in her huge cup of coffee.

Del handed Mallory her own cup of coffee.

114

"She's dreaming," Del said.

"How can you tell?" Mallory asked, feeling half guilty for gazing on someone in such a vulnerable state.

"Look at her REM movements."

"Will she pee like at slumber parties when you stuck someone's hand in water?" Mallory asked, thinking of her days of being shoved off by her mother to spend time with friends she didn't trust.

"I guess we'll see. I think that is a myth."

Angel was dreaming the same thing she often dreamed since leaving Jennifer. She was always running and trying to hide and she didn't see her until the last minute when she thought she had escaped and Jennifer popped up and caught her. She would wake up in a fright.

Angel awoke screaming "No!" and spilling her coffee as did Mallory, who was totally unprepared for this moment.

Mallory stood up, looking at the pool of coffee at her feet and the cup still spinning. Angel sat up and felt the coffee soaking into her socks. She looked at Mallory, who stared back.

"You must be Mallory," Angel said, still trying to get oriented to the present moment.

"I am. I'm awfully sorry about the mess," Mallory said, taking the towel from Del.

"I'm the responsible party. I must have fallen asleep. Del, it's time for the method," Angel said, going to the kitchen.

Del grabbed the ice cube trays while Angel filled the sink with cold water.

"How long?" Del asked, checking her watch.

"Fifteen seconds."

"And then she stuck her face in the sink with ice cubes and cold water. It was the most extreme awake mechanism I've ever seen," Mallory told Dr. Kohlrabi.

"She hadn't got much sleep."

"True, they said they used to do it all the time when they were in college after partying all night."

115

"So you found out things about Del," Dr. Kohlrabi queried, comprehending that Mallory had been fretting about not knowing about Del's past.

"Yes."

"And were you disappointed?"

"No, actually I feel better. They both went out with a lot of women and then Angel got involved with Jennifer and Del went to med school. That put an end to the playing days. Now it appears they are both ready to settle down with the woman they love."

"Which would be you?"

"Del says so."

"Do you trust her?" Dr. Kohlrabi asked.

"I do. It's taken me a long time to say that but I trust her. I don't think she would put up with me if she wasn't in love."

"Don't shortchange yourself," Dr. Kohlrabi cautioned.

"I'm not. I asked her if she would come see you."

"What did she say?"

"She agreed."

"I'll make time at your next session."

"Deal. There is this other issue I need to discuss."

"Yes," Dr. Kohlrabi asked, marveling over Mallory's response, thinking proudly *She is getting better*.

"Angel went to take a shower and I was sitting at her desk looking at her new book of cartoons. She's a cartoonist. Then she was changing and it's a loft apartment and I could see her in the reflection on the window."

"And?"

"And she is beautiful. I felt bad like I shouldn't be thinking that. She *is* Del's best friend."

"Do you love Del?"

"Of course I love Del. Do you think I would put myself in such a precarious situation if I wasn't in love?"

"I'm not saying that."

"What are you saying?" Mallory said, getting freaked by the

minute. Therapists are supposed to sort things out not create muddles.

"I'm saying that finding another woman attractive doesn't mean you don't love Del and it doesn't mean you've desecrated that love."

"You mean it's not like what Gigi does? *That* is my greatest concern."

"What does Gigi do?" Dr. Kohlrabi asked.

"She lives with one woman and cruises other women."

"How does that work?"

Mallory rolled her eyes. "It's a boundary thing. As lesbians, our lines are not as clearly drawn, meaning that women are friends and lovers and lovers and friends and sometimes everything gets all yanked around. Does that make sense?"

"Meaning your friends can potentially be your lovers rather than with straight people who have friends and then husbands."

"Yes," Mallory said.

"Okay, back to your original question. It's not like what Gigi does, rather you are opening yourself up sexually for the first time in several years and finding women attractive is simply a by-product," counseled Dr. Kohlrabi, wondering if perhaps Gigi was the one in need of therapy rather than Mallory.

"All right."

"How was the rest of breakfast?"

"Fun. The two of them together is hilarious."

"You're getting better you know," Dr. Kohlrabi said.

"I know."

"Are you okay with that?"

"I'm kind of scared but I can't depend on you forever. One day you'll retire."

"I will. You'll be long better by then," Dr. Kohlrabi replied.

Angel was putting herself through the paces of yoga followed by weight training. She had been to see her chiropractor. He had advised more stretching exercises. She tried to tell him that all she needed to last was seven more years and she could retire. She thought of Jennifer calling her a coward for not getting out and doing the cartooning for a living.

It was a constant source of annoyance for Jennifer that her artistic lover was also a blue-collar worker. Angel kept trying to explain the reasons behind this kind of employment. "I have a retirement plan, health insurance, and a monthly income." These were unfathomable entities to her happy-go-lucky girlfriend. Thinking of Jennifer always frightened her because she was trying to eliminate her presence from her life. Thinking of Jennifer made her think of how she felt about Kim.

Kim made her think of falling in love. Falling fast, maybe too fast, and she wasn't entirely sure she was ready. She looked forward to delivering the mail each day because Kim would be there at the end of the route. She spent the nights figuring out yet another way of seeing her, of going to the art museum for the South Western display or the long drive to hike in the Preserve, how they hugged at the end of an evening, of how Kim touched her thigh, or smiled, or dancing, all those things that implied closeness but didn't entail sleeping together. Angel thought of how Jennifer had courted her.

Or rather stalked her, Angel thought wryly. It wasn't like Angel hadn't had girlfriends before but none so deep and all encompassing as Jennifer. Jennifer saw her at the gym while she was looking for bodies for her photo shoots. She chose Angel, who refused. She pestered her until she became a permanent fixture in Angel's life. Jennifer knew how to get to her, to find those places that Angel thought well hidden and once discovered she exploited them, right up to the day Angel left.

Angel would not have gotten free if Jennifer hadn't been stuck in rehab. She remembered the frantic call she'd gotten from Skyler saying Jennifer was in the hospital having her stomach pumped and her system flushed of a myriad of drugs and alcohol. Angel went out of a sense of duty. She wasn't speaking to Skyler, who was her best friend until she slept with Jennifer. She nodded at Skyler as she went in to see Jennifer. She was hooked up to tubes. She smiled weakly at Angel, who looked at her with a mixture of sadness and disgust.

"They're going to put you in rehab you know," Angel said.

"I know. It's probably a good thing."

"Why do you do this?"

"Because I have no self-control," Jennifer ventured.

"Exactly," Angel replied, reliving all the other times she'd held her head while she puked, pulling her out of cars when she was too drunk and high to walk, of cleaning up the loft of all the empty bottles after parties that seemed to happen every night.

"Angel . . ."

"Yes."

"I love you."

"Yeah. I got to go."

"I'll see later."

"Yeah," Angel said, walking out knowing it was the last time.

"She's your problem now," Angel told Skyler.

By the time Jennifer was released, Angel was gone.

Angel tried putting all those memories behind her but falling in love somehow dredged them up again. It made her compare now with then. Maybe that was why she had shied away from love. Being in love meant dealing with the past and she wasn't sure she was ready for that. She went to take a shower. The phone rang.

"Do you like to camp?" Kim asked.

"I don't know. I've never been camping," Angel replied.

"You've never been camping?" Kim asked incredulously.

"I admit my education has been lacking," Angel replied.

"Can we go camping?"

"If you'd like," Angel said.

"I would. I was cleaning out my garage and found my camping stuff and I thought I missed doing that. I figured since we hike together well, that camping might be fun," Kim said.

"What are you doing tonight?" Angel asked, suddenly missing her immensely.

"Wondering what you're doing," Kim replied, blushing because she'd spent all day thinking about Angel. Sometime it scared her how attached she found herself to this woman and worrying about rebound action and all the advice columns she'd read that voiced caution but she couldn't help herself. She felt like she was on a roller -coaster ride of high emotion.

"Can I take you out to dinner?"

"I'd like that."

"Me too," Angel said.

"Is this a buddy date?" Kim asked, feeling shy and tentative but suddenly needing to know where they stood.

"Do you want it to be?"

"No."

"Me either."

"I'm going to kiss you tonight," Kim said, her whole body filling with adrenaline.

"Okay," Angel said, her heart pounding in her chest.

"Are you scared?" Angel asked.

"Petrified," Angel said.

Kim laughed. "So am I."

"Are you all right with this?"

"Angel, you're not taking me anywhere I don't want to go."

"I'll pick you up in an hour," Angel said.

"Perfect."

Del was trying to track Mallory down. She wanted to see how Mallory's physical therapy session went. Dr. Van Dyke was not happy. It appeared after fifteen minutes of physical therapy Mallory had called him a savage butcher, informing him that she was never coming back and he could go fuck himself. Del found her at Gigi's.

Gigi and Mallory were sitting on the couch out back, fishing with their play rods in the canal. Gigi smiled at Mallory.

"We haven't done this in a while," Mallory said, suddenly feeling guilty for not spending time with her best friend because she was in love.

"Yes, I've been ditched."

"I'm sorry," Mallory said.

"You love her."

"I do, more than I ever thought possible. It kind of makes me wonder about how I felt about Caroline."

"You were young. We were all young then. I thought she was the one for you. Maybe I was wrong," Gigi said, thinking of a past she did not relish. She was starting to reevaluate some of her past indiscretions and wishing they hadn't occurred.

"I thought she was too. That scares me. I just don't understand what I did to turn her away."

"It's hard to tell," Gigi said, looking away.

"I don't want that to happen with Del."

"It won't," Gigi assured her.

"How do you know?" Mallory asked.

"I just know," Gigi said.

Mallory's cell phone rang. She handed it to Gigi, who was well versed in pretending to be her secretary.

"No, I'm sorry she's not available."

"Gigi, it's Del, tell her I need to talk to her," Del said.

"It's Del," Gigi said, handing her the phone. "Are you in trouble?"

"Maybe a little," Mallory said, covering the phone.

"What did you do?"

"I told the physical therapist to fuck off," Mallory said.

Gigi laughed.

"Mallory," Del said.

"He was a butcher," Mallory said.

"He is the best PT we have."

"I don't like him," Mallory replied.

"He might be lacking in the people skills department but you have to work with him."

"I don't *have* to do anything. I'm not going back," Mallory replied.

"Can we talk?" Del said.

"I'll take you to dinner. When are you off?" Mallory asked, feeling guilty for causing Del grief.

"Six-thirty."

"I'll pick you up."

"Mallory, you're not angry with me are you?"

"Because you're one of them?"

"Yes," Del said.

"No, I love you," Mallory said, turning instantly crimson.

There was a pause.

"Del?"

"You are an incredible woman," Del said.

Del called Angel because she understood women better than most from their old days of cruising women together.

"What's up?" Angel asked, trying to pick out an outfit.

"It's Mallory. She had physical therapy today. She told the PT to fuck off and left abruptly."

"The girl has spunk," Angel laughed. "I've felt like that a time or two myself."

"This guy is the best."

"Her foot was badly broken, right?"

"Yes," Del said, remembering removing the cast and surveying the damage, hoping Mallory wasn't going to have a permanent limp.

"Give her some time."

"I don't think that is going to make a difference. She's really angry."

"But she's not angry with you?" Angel asked, beginning to grasp the reason Del called.

"No, she loves me, even if I am one of them."

"So what's the problem?" Angel asked, picking out her one and only tailored suit, thinking tonight would be appropriate. She wanted to take Kim to the Bistro.

"When she left the hospital she went to see Gigi," Del said.

"Instead of coming to see to you."

"Yes."

"Like she said, you are one of them and Gigi is her oldest friend. It's a natural reflex. Are you jealous?" Angel asked.

"Yes," Del said, embarrassed to admit it. "I know I shouldn't be but I can't help myself."

Angel laughed. "It's perfectly understandable. It's part of the loving-lesbian-syndrome."

"What?"

"Meaning you love her and want to be all things to her, lover, parent, best friend, confidante, soul mate, advisor, and your feelings are hurt because you're not there yet. But you will be. And you don't like Gigi."

"No, I don't."

"Why?"

"Because I don't trust her."

"She plays around?"

"From what I've seen she does."

"Why does that worry you?" Angel asked.

"Because she's in love with Mallory, always has been. Neither one of them will admit it, but it's there."

"Where do you think that's going to go?" Angel asked.

"Nowhere I hope," Del said.

"Del, I've seen her look at you and if love can be written across a face it was. I wouldn't worry about it."

"Okay, it was reflex."

"A bad reflex. She loves you."

"Okay. How are you doing?" Del asked, feeling guilty for not even inquiring.

"I am outstanding. Kim and I are going out to dinner and she said she's going to kiss me tonight."

"Are you ready?"

"Yes. I know it's not prudent but I can't help myself," Angel said.

"She let you know, which means she's ready. Oh, Angel, if you only knew how badly Ollie treated her. You are a saint."

"I hope so. I am there. We get along so well and I can't get through a day without seeing her," Angel said.

"That's good."

"It is."

"Call me tomorrow."

"Del, if you get a list of what Mallory can do with her foot from the PT I'll work with her. I've been through enough of them and maybe she can work back into it."

"I don't know if she'll go for it."

"Oh, she will," replied Angel.

"How can you be so sure?"

"Because I will tell her stories about you."

Del laughed. "It's worth a try."

At ten o'clock Del was carrying Mallory up the stairs to her house. Mallory was celebrating not having a cast on her foot anymore and the subsequent pain of learning to deal with her newly repaired limb as well as telling the PT to fuck off. She told Del this as she finished her fourth glass of wine and Del took her car keys away.

"I always kind of wondered what it was like to be carried over the threshold," Mallory said, gazing into Del's eyes.

"Now you know," Del said.

"I think it's the idea of promising to take care of someone for the rest of their lives no matter what, even though that promise is broken almost as often as it is spoken. I'd like it to mean something," Mallory replied, continuing on her philosophical loquaciousness fueled by the four glasses of wine.

Del set her down, took her shoulders and looked straight into her eyes. "With us it will mean something. I will always take care of you. I will love you always."

Mallory was about to kiss her when her cell phone went off. They both searched for their phones out of habit.

"It's you," Del said, suddenly cursing technology.

"Mallory, I'm at the 12th Precinct. Will you come get me?" Gigi screamed into the phone.

"What are you doing there?"

"I'll tell you later. And bring a credit card. I need bail."

"You got caught smashing shrines? Gigi!"

"I got to go."

"Gigi got arrested. I have to go get her," Mallory said.

"I'll drive," Del said.

"Good idea. We don't need both of us in prison," Mallory agreed.

"No, we don't."

"Do you suppose we shall always be interrupted?"

"Interrupted from what?" Del asked, opening the car door for Mallory.

"From that moment when we are about to fall into each other's arms and into bed," Mallory said, leaning on Del's shoulder and sighing.

Del kissed her cheek while she put Mallory's seatbelt on.

"No, one day everything will be right and we will spend the whole day in bed. I promise."

The police station lighting made the place look even dingier, and aside from motivational posters and duty rosters, Gigi could not find one redeemable quality about this kind of public space. The detective sat down and slipped his report in the typewriter.

He looked at Gigi and swallowed his bile once again that he had slept with the Chief's wife and was now demoted to the Domestic Violence squad which reminded him only of his divorced wife, his own violent upbringing, and the piss-poor state of the human condition as he now knew it to be.

"You guys really need to hire a better interior decorator."

"Yeah, like put a lavender wall and then some nice chintz pillows and a lovely bowl of fruit," Detective Gonzalez replied.

"Perfect," Gigi replied. *Finally*, she thought, *someone to talk to in this hell-hole.*

"So why don't you tell me what happened tonight?" Gonzalez asked.

125

"From the beginning?"

"That would be a good place to start."

"It goes way back," Gigi replied.

"How about you start with telling me how it was that we found you tied to a chair in your mother's kitchen, broken dishes everywhere and you screaming you were going to kill her while she was snapping photographs of you and quoting scripture," Gonzalez said, thinking it was one of the more bizarre crime scenes he'd come upon. Not to mention they had to run her into Emergency first to get her stitched up and cleaned up enough to arrest her.

"She lassoed me while I was taking a sledgehammer to her Virgin Mary shrine."

"She lassoed you, like the cowboys?" Detective Gonzalez asked, adding this to his list of mental pictures, none of which entirely made sense.

"My mother was in 4H most of her junior years. She used to rope calves in exhibitions. She won a lot of medals," Gigi explained.

"So roping you in the front yard is not that unusual?"

"For my mother it's not. Catching me is."

"You're usually quicker?"

"Much," replied Gigi proudly.

"Not tonight obviously."

"I think she got a tip that we'd be around," Gigi said.

"We?"

"I mean me, the royal we, I always refer to myself in the plural. I don't feel lonely that way. It's like a trinity of self, me, myself and I," Gigi said, scrambling, knowing that Aunt Lil and Fran were out desecrating other shrines across the city. Hopefully, they hadn't been apprehended. Gigi was worried. The police had confiscated her cell phone so she couldn't warn them.

Gigi tried to send Mallory telepathic messages.

"Is there any particular reason you smash Virgin Mary shrines, including your mother's?" Detective Gonzalez inquired.

"Because I'm rebelling," Gigi replied.

"Against religion or your mother?"

"Both," Gigi said. "She loves the shrine more than me and it's nothing more than idolatry but of course I am an abomination against her religion so the way I figured it I might as well live up to her worst nightmares."

"You don't look like a pedophile," Detective Gonzalez replied.

"I'm the next best thing. I'm a lesbian."

"I think I'm beginning to get it now," said Detective Gonzalez.

"Funny, isn't it. You tell people you're gay and suddenly everything makes sense," said Gigi.

"Yes, so why'd she tie you to the kitchen chair and then take photographs?"

"For the *Catholic Herald*. It will make front-page news. They've been looking for us, I mean me, for a long time."

Detective Gonzalez shook his head. There was a commotion down the hall as Mrs. Dupont was screaming prophet curses at the police officers that were taking her back to her cell.

"Boy, I don't know what we're going to do with this one," Detective Gonzalez muttered.

"Technically speaking the damaging of private property is only a misdemeanor," Gigi said, looking at him with her wounded and abused child eyes.

He fell for it. His own childhood had these unkind moments. The kid could use a break.

"It's not you I'm concerned with. In fact, if you want, you can file charges against your mother for assault."

"I don't want to get her in trouble," Gigi said, laughing.

"She's already in trouble. She decked one of my officers with her purse. You got a friend coming?"

"Yeah," Gigi said.

"I'd stay away from your mom for a couple of days."

"Good advice."

Mallory sat up straight in her seat. "Aunt Lil!"

"What?" Del said, turning left on Adam Street.

"Aunt Lil and her fellow crones are out doing the same thing," Mallory said, scrolling through her cell phone for Aunt Lil's number.

Lil picked up. "Hello?"

"Lil, this is Mallory. Where are you? They got Gigi."

"Who got Gigi?" Lil said, shushing the party behind her.

"The police," Mallory said. "We're going to get her right now. You're not out smashing shrines are you?"

"Goodness no, we don't do that until the witching hour. Gigi was supposed to meet us here at Valerie's and then we were going to head out. Did she start with her mother's?"

"I think so."

"Bring her here when you get her."

"Okay."

"Is Del with you?" Lil asked.

"Yes," Mallory replied, puzzled.

"Bring her too. I'd like to meet her."

Mallory smiled queerly at Del.

"What?" Del said, pulling into the parking lot of the police station.

"The Ladies of Yarnell would like to meet you," Mallory replied.

"Should I be nervous?"

"No, I'll protect you."

When they got in the police station to rescue Gigi there was a ruckus down the hall as some crazed woman was screaming biblical curses upon the heathens in her cell as well as her captors.

"Is that your mother I hear screaming?" Mallory asked Gigi as they signed her release papers.

"Yes, she assaulted a police officer with her purse."

"I can hardly wait for the whole story. Have you called Alex yet?" Mallory asked.

"She's not home. I tried her first. Hey Del, thanks for coming," Gigi said.

"I called Lil, we're supposed to meet her at Valerie's."

"So everything is fine there?" Gigi asked, taking a quick look around.

"All is well," Mallory said, in a conspiratorial tone.

"Should we bail your mother out?" Del asked, listening to another wail of insults.

"No," Gigi said, walking out.

Del looked at Mallory, who shrugged her shoulders.

There were two lights on at Koontz and Koontz Public Accountants. Alex looked up from her desk to find Taylor Koontz, hand on hip, shaking her head.

"You're making me look bad," Taylor said.

"Excuse me?" Alex said, rubbing her burning eyes.

"I thought I was the quintessential workaholic around here, aside from Daddy of course, but you're burning more midnight oil than we are. Not that I'm not grateful, mind you."

"Thanks," Alex said, leaning back in her chair.

"I don't know about you, but I'm starved. Let me take you to dinner," Taylor said.

Alex faltered.

"I'm not taking no for an answer," Taylor said, pulling Alex's blazer off the coat rack. She wrapped it gently around Alex's shoulders.

Alex smelled her perfume and when she met her gaze Alex felt the chemistry of two women coming together. For the first time since Taylor had come to work for her father, she realized that maybe the favorite daughter was not the straight girl Alex had automatically assumed. Gigi was always telling her that everyone was a lesbian until proven otherwise.

"I have to make a phone call," Alex said.

"Sure. I'll get the car and meet you out front," Taylor said.

Alex called Gigi but didn't bother leaving a message, since her girlfriend was out why shouldn't she do the same? Alex, being a conscientious lover, felt a pang of guilt for going out to dinner with an attractive woman.

Taylor pulled up front and leaned over to open the door of an old Volvo.

"I was wondering if this was your car," Alex said, getting in.

"It's not the most aesthetically pleasing of cars, but I can't make myself part with her. She has one hundred and forty-two thousand miles on her."

"Shouldn't the junior partner have a Jaguar or something?" Alex teased.

"Like you should talk," Taylor said, pointing at the 1974 Volkswagen beetle that Alex couldn't bring herself to part with.

"At least we have something in common," Taylor said.

"Old cars."

"And no car payments. We have something else in common," Taylor said.

"What's that?" Alex said, trying to unwind her seatbelt from the knot at its base.

"We're both gay," Taylor said, leaning over and releasing Alex's seatbelt.

Alex blushed.

"Did you know that?" Taylor said.

"No, I didn't. I'm not very good at things like that."

"So I shouldn't take it personally that you've said approximately four sentences to me since I came to work here."

"No," Alex said. "You shouldn't."

"I thought maybe you were in the closet and didn't want anyone to know and befriending me would definitely bring it out in the open."

"It would?" Alex said.

"Dad knows. He's known since I was twelve. He keeps hoping I'll find a nice woman and settle down."

"And you haven't?"

"Not until now. Do you like Thai food?"

130

"I do," Alex said.

"Another thing in common. Relax, I promise to be lighter for the rest of the evening . . . oh, and I know you have a girlfriend but that doesn't mean we can't be friends."

"Actually, I don't have a very attentive girlfriend."

"That's what Dad says," Taylor replied.

"He knows everything doesn't he?" Alex said, blushing again.

"He's a sharp guy," Taylor said, pulling out of the parking lot and heading downtown.

At midnight, Alex stumbled into the living room, tripping over a pile of books that had mysteriously been stuck in the middle of the foray.

Gigi switched on a light. "I can account for my whereabouts this evening. How about you?"

Alex's pupils instantly dilated and for a moment she felt like she was in the interrogation room. She quickly gathered her wits about her and then reeled again when she saw Gigi, who was wrapped up like a mummy.

"What happened?" Alex asked, tripping over another stack of books that had been set as another trap in case the first set failed. She pushed the books aside and sat next to Gigi.

"My mother got ahold of me," Gigi said, rather sullenly.

"With what, her Mixmaster?" Alex said, trying to peek under the gauze bandage on Gigi's forehead.

Gigi pulled away. "It's a long story. Where were you?"

"I worked late and then I got dinner out. I tried to call but you weren't home."

"With whom?"

"How do you know it was with someone?" Alex asked, feeling like she was being interrogated.

"Because you'd rather eat cold macaroni and cheese than eat out by yourself."

"I went with a woman from work," Alex replied, acutely aware of Gigi's gaze.

"A straight woman?"

"What does it matter? I went to dinner with her. I didn't have sex with her."

"But the question is did you want to?" Gigi said.

"That's your game remember. Not mine," Alex said, getting up abruptly. She went to the kitchen to get an antacid, thinking she shouldn't have lied and said she liked Thai food when it always played havoc with her stomach.

"I'm sorry. I just needed you and when you weren't here I freaked," Gigi said.

"I'll tell you about dinner, if you tell me what happened," Alex said.

"Like I said it's a long story. Maybe we could eat ice cream in bed and I'll tell you, like the old days," Gigi said, remembering the times when they would stay up late talking to each other, having ice cream and then making love.

"Is this going to be one of those times when I end up all sticky?" Alex teased.

"Could be," Gigi said, taking her hand.

Later Alex laid awake and thought about dinner with Taylor and dessert with Gigi and the differences aside from food between them. It had occurred to her before that she and Gigi had a mostly sexual relationship. It was how they ended fights, discussions, and tedium. They seldom changed things, they just tried to fuck them away. Talking with Taylor, Alex began to realize some things and they made her more than a little uneasy. She tried to cross them off to flirtation and the intrigue of newness. She looked over at Gigi and knew that she loved her but for all her trying she didn't really know her and probably never would. Funny thing was she felt like she knew more about Taylor from one dinner than three years of sleeping in the same bed with Gigi. Alex wondered who was really the emotional cripple in their relationship—herself or Gigi? Perhaps it was both of them.

Seven

The front porch steps were piled high with camping gear and Kim was concerned that all this stuff wasn't going to fit in the back of Angel's Jeep. She added the ice chest to the stack and stood back to take stock. It had been a long time since she'd been camping. She didn't want to forget anything. Kim went over her mental checklist. She was busy checking the tent stakes when Ollie pulled up. Kim heard a car but assumed it was Angel. She wasn't prepared for Ollie.

"Where are you going?" Ollie asked nonchalantly.

Kim was always amazed that she could walk up like nothing was wrong, no harsh words, no lying and no cheating.

"What are you doing here?" Kim asked.

"Coming to see you," Ollie said. "I didn't know you liked to camp."

"There were a lot of things you didn't know about me," Kim replied.

"Maybe I'd like the chance," Ollie said.

"Ollie, there is no chance," Kim said, studying her ex-girlfriend and wondering at her stamina in beating this dead horse.

"Why? Are you in love with the postal worker?" Ollie asked.

"Ollie, just let it go, okay? We had our time and it's over now. We both need to move on. Find another girlfriend and you'll forget all about me," Kim said, refraining from saying *just like you used to when we were going out*.

"The funny thing is the harder I try to forget about you the more obsessed I become. I just want another chance. I know we can be good together. It doesn't have to end like this."

"Ollie, I can't."

"Because you love her?" Ollie asked, feeling her stomach start to cramp, and tears well up.

"You need to go home," Kim said.

"I just can't believe we're over," Ollie mumbled.

Kim walked her to her car and for the first time since they broke up she felt sorry for Ollie.

Ollie got in her car. "Was I really that bad?"

Kim sighed. "There were times in the beginning when I thought we could do the long-term thing, but Ollie you wrecked any trust we had by playing around, that kills love faster than anything."

"And you don't think the postal worker will do the same?"

"No, she won't. She's not like that."

"But I am?"

"You don't have to be. Take care, Ollie," Kim said, trying to be kind.

On the way to Copper Creek, Kim told Angel about Ollie coming to see her.

"She wanted to know if I was in love with you. I guess that truly signifies the end. Maybe that's why lesbians always line up girlfriend number two as soon as they get rid of girlfriend number one, so there will be no turning back," Kim said.

"I suppose it helps," Angel said, pulling off the highway and onto the dirt road up to Copper Creek. She smiled mischievously.

"Is this going to be one of your road trips where my kidney's hurt from all the bumping around?" Kim asked.

"You wanted to go camping," Angel replied.

"I didn't mean that's what we were doing when I was talking about lining up girlfriends," Kim said, suddenly alarmed that she might have offended Angel.

"I know. We didn't do that. But I am curious about the love part," Angel said, taking Kim's hand.

Kim leaned on her shoulder. "What do you think?"

"I know how I feel," Angel replied.

"So do I," Kim teased back.

"Tell me," Angel pleaded.

"Not while you're driving," Kim said, gripping the roll bar as they wound through the first of a series of hairpin turns. By the time they got to the tiny town of Copper Creek, Angel had had to pull over three times to let Kim throw up. She left Kim in the Jeep with a wet bandanna over her forehead and went into the general store to get Dramamine. The old guy behind the counter chuckled.

"The road got to her eh? She's a nasty one. You should see her in the rainy season. Slick as snot she is," he told her.

Angel tried not to think about the metaphor. Instead, she hopped in the Jeep and drove to the first campsite she could find that was far enough from the road to give them some privacy.

She got a sleeping bag out and laid it down for Kim.

"I'm sorry," Kim murmured, as she got out of the Jeep.

"Don't be. Here, take these. I'll set up the tent. You'll feel better soon," Angel said, stroking her forehead, and then kissed it gently.

Kim lay down under a tall pine and tried to look up at the clouds. Motion sickness set everything reeling, so she closed her eyes and tried to concentrate on thinking still, very still, thoughts.

Angel looked at the tent and considered her upbringing as an urban girl with no training whatsoever in the outdoor arts. Images in movies and the cover of magazines comprised her knowledge. It's all in acting like you know what you're doing that allows one to conquer the fear of the unknown until you get a chance to know it, after which it is no longer a threat, Angel told herself as she unpacked the mystery tube that was the tent. She played with the poles and figured out how they snapped together but after that she felt like the first architect creating the first building in the history of humankind. She attempted several shapes only to understand their limitations.

This tent thing wasn't as easy as in the brochure. Finally, she came upon something that resembled shelter and got Kim inside to take a nap. Next would be the camp stove and dinner. Angel could only imagine the rest of her evening. She looked in at Kim asleep in the tent and realized that in doing this they were utterly alone and without any artifice to conceal their true selves. She was certain she gained the spirit of camping in that moment.

Angel took a good look around at the pines, the sky, the brilliant white clouds and the scenery void of any skyscraper. She felt overwhelmed and yet more comfortable than ever before in her life. She imagined the cartoon strip where she could have the character Detroit experience this moment, of the noblesse oblige of the universe as she wrapped her large warm arms around you and you basked in the golden light of her benevolent willingness. She always kept a sketch pad in the Jeep. She retrieved it from the glove box. Looking in at Kim again she sat down and boxed out the page. It was sitting there in the pines that she conceived of a new character inspired by her restored faith in love. Suddenly she experienced a new, fresher feel to the strip, and she made herself laugh at the endless possibilities as they careened through her brain.

She remembered the beginning of the cartoon and how she had worried when she got out of school how she would find her voice. There were tons of books on writing and how to get started but the cartoon strip was different. Angel used to sit in the lesbian coffee shop and listen to conversations with her eyes closed so she would listen intently to the tone, cadence and word choice of the women around her as they discussed their lives. Then she would turn around to see what they looked like. She was often surprised.

As she did this she began to envision what lesbians would look like in a cartoon strip going less by actuality and more by compilation. As a career move everyone told her that a lesbian cartoon strip would never make her big money, to which she replied that she was old fashioned in her belief that true art was created despite funding and hype. It was Jennifer that believed the two could be combined and Angel's would be the first syndicated lesbian comic strip. It was mostly through Jennifer's diligent public relations methods that Angel became famous. For that Jennifer would always have a corner of her heart despite the carnage she created in the aftermath. Jennifer was the first one to believe in her.

Angel finished the preliminary sketch and then set about dinner preparations. Sticking chicken on the hibachi was something she could handle. Kim woke up groggy but hungry. Angel was sipping a margarita and feeling no pain; she explained the moment of benevolent willingness brought on by the wilderness. Kim laughed and gave her a big hug. Angel smiled happily and told her they should go camping more often.

Ollie sat at the bar and contemplated her situation. Old love could not hope to compare to new love. She knew by the look on Kim's face that she had fallen in love. At first, Ollie thought she could dig up some dirt on Angel and prove her an unfit mate or at least plant doubt into Kim's mind. Unfortunately, this was not an option. It seemed Angel had lived quietly with her fucked-up girlfriend and worked diligently to make a career for herself. The postal worker, it seemed, was famous, good looking, and talented. Ollie was stuck.

An attractive dark-haired woman sat next to her at the bar and ordered a martini. Ollie got herself another Long Island iced tea. The woman looked at Ollie for a moment.

"You look familiar," the woman said, idly taking a sip, like she didn't really care if Ollie responded either way.

Ollie was instantly intrigued. She gave the woman her full attention.

"Could be the light," Ollie teased. "One woman can look like any woman."

"No, I think I saw you once at a party or something. Do you know Gigi Dupont?"

Ollie smiled. "As a matter of fact I do."

Caroline Jimenez raised an eyebrow. "She still gets around, I see."

"She's got a girlfriend."

"That never stopped her."

"How do you know Gigi?" Ollie asked, feeling the quivering of a plan moving about in the back of her mind.

"I went out with her best friend Mallory," Caroline stated, evenly and with practiced poise as she referred to a period that still did strange things to her emotional landscape. Of course, that was her mission for coming back, to right some old wrongs and to experience firsthand the damage she had done. She was hoping the aftermath was going to be a delightful surprise and she could assuage the guilt she felt. Having been rudely dumped herself in the past few years she was hoping to correct the karmic wrong that seemed to plague her relationships since the war zone she had left five years ago.

"Wow, you must be the one she wore pajamas for all that time, pining the morning you left her holding the coffee pot and flabbergasted that you were leaving . . . the country no less. Welcome back," Ollie said.

"Thanks," Caroline said, signaling the bartender.

"I used to go out with a friend of hers until my girlfriend found me in a compromising position with Gigi one night at a party. Gigi has fled the scene and is consequently suffering very little."

"Some things never change. She did the same thing to me. That was why I left the country. Only we had an ongoing relationship and I thought it was love. Gigi didn't," Caroline said, carefully measuring Ollie's response.

"While you were going out with Mallory?" Ollie inquired.

"Yes," Caroline replied, remembering the ease of confession in those dark closets in the golden churches of South America.

"Well, what a tangled web we weave, when first we practice to deceive," Ollie said.

"You're a well-read woman, I see. An English major perhaps?" Caroline commented.

"Not exactly, Mallory told me that one," Ollie said, remembering a soiree that Mallory attended and how she pointedly repeated those words at Gigi when they were in the early days of lust.

"Yes, Mallory is definitely well read, always felt a little less than adequate in the academic department when I was with her. People who read seem to know everything."

"Except how to keep a girlfriend," Ollie said, finishing her drink.

"Can I buy another?" Caroline offered.

"Sure, we can tell tales," Ollie said, knowing exactly how she was going to use this contact.

The wind whistled through the pines and Kim lay in Angel's arms. Her even breathing made Kim feel restful. They hadn't made love but she could feel it coming, that Angel was moving toward it slowly and Kim knew she would have to be patient. Angel probably thought she was waiting for Kim but Kim knew better.

Angel was the one who needed courting. Angel was the one who believed making love was the combining of two souls and the act required the utmost sanctity. Angel was waiting for the right moment, the time when she knew they were both cleansed of all the bad memories, the furtive emotions that still plagued a new relationship. Kim smiled in the darkness. She wanted this love to work, this relationship to last. She wanted to do it right.

Kim's ponderings on the alchemy of love was rudely interrupted. Someone or thing was rattling the cooler and a strange snuffling noise. She sat straight up. She gently nudged Angel.

"What?" Angel said, rolling up on her elbow.

"There's something outside," Kim said, trying to find the flashlight.

"What kind of something?" Angel said, also rummaging around.

"I don't know," Kim said, clutching the flashlight to her breast and trying to summon up her courage.

"I'll go," Angel said, taking the flashlight and brandishing her can of pepper spray.

"What's that?"

"Dog spray."

"I don't think it's a dog," Kim said.

"I know. But animals are animals. I'll be right back," Angel said, slowly unzipping the tent.

She flashed the light. Something large caught the light. All Angel saw was the flash of its eyes and then a quick retreat as it stumbled over the cooler. Angel stopped in her tracks and flashed the light around. Whatever it was took off. Angel collected the contents of the cooler and then put it in the back of the Jeep.

"Are you all right?" Kim said, poking her head tentatively out of the tent.

"Yes."

"What was it?"

"Something big, like a dog, kind of looked like a potbelly pig," Angel said, suddenly remembering Arvis the potbelly pig on her route and feeling less frightened. She liked Arvis.

"Oh, my God, it must have been a javelina," Kim said, getting out of the tent.

"What's a javelina?" Angel asked.

"It's a wild boar," Kim said, taking a good look around. The moon was full and gave the forest an eerie glow.

"Oh, my. Are they fierce?" Angel asked.

"I don't know," Kim said, moving closer to the tent.

"I think it was just looking for a midnight snack," Angel said, pushing the lid down tight on the cooler and then snapping the canvas top tight on the back of the Jeep.

"Well, maybe now that the food is out of the way, he or she won't be back," Kim said, tying the trash bag up in the tree.

"Let's hope so," Angel said, flashing the light around. She took the lid of a pot and picked up a piece of kindling. She played the little drummer boy.

"They probably don't like loud noises," Kim said, trying to reassure them both.

"I'm sure not," Angel said, coming over to give Kim a hug.

"Back to bed," Kim said.

"Yes."

They rolled into each other's arms and hoped for a quiet evening.

In the morning, Angel slipped out of the tent to go pee and hoped their uninvited guest from last night had found other distractions. The campsite was quiet and the sun was just starting to rise. Angel stretched and tried to get the kinks out of her back and neck. She crawled back in the tent so she could gaze at Kim and imagine what it would be like to wake up to her every morning. She thought back to the night they first kissed. Love, she decided, brought out the best in people.

After dinner, Angel drove Kim up to the Mountain Preserve for a dance, telling Kim that when she discovered this place—a concrete slab at the base of the mountains meant to be a picnic area—only it must have been forgotten as only the slab remained, she thought it would make a wonderful dance floor. At the time she never thought she would find a dancing partner. But that night they had danced beneath the moon and stars, no longer obscured by the city glare, and they kissed. And it was a perfect kiss, as if their tongues and lips had touched a thousand times before, and Angel knew then that she had found the right partner.

Kim woke up and pulled Angel toward her. Angel smiled.

"I was just thinking about you," Angel said.

"What were you thinking?" Kim asked.

"About the night we went dancing," Angel said.

"I liked that night," Kim said, starting to get up. Her bladder was calling. She bent to kiss Angel. Something caught the corner of her eye.

"What's for breakfast?" Angel asked, nibbling at Kim's chin.

"I think it might be javelina," Kim said, staring into the pink eyes of a large pig.

"What!" Angel said, rolling over. Involuntarily she screamed. The javelina went running and Kim nearly peed her pants laughing.

"For a tomboy, you sure have a funny high pitched little scream," Kim said.

Angel grimaced. "It was effective wasn't it?"

"I'll say," Kim said, getting up. "The poor thing is probably in the next county by now."

"I certainly hope so."

"Do you still like camping?" Kim asked, kissing Angel's neck.

"Yes, but I'm not that fond of the neighbors."

"Wait until we see the ruins. You'll forget about them and fall in love with the neighborhood," Kim said, running her hand up Angel's shirt and finding her nipple. She traced its outline and watched Angel's face to see if it was all right. Angel smiled and pulled Kim on top of her. Kim took her shirt off. Angel touched her breasts and ran her hands down Kim's slim waist, making her quiver.

Angel turned the Coleman stove on with the flair of a seasoned professional and thought maybe there was something to this facing one's fears thing. It gave her a charge and she liked that. Suddenly, she was the tightly clad mercenary in her own emotional landscape, just like Mallory had explained to her the other day as they went for a walk. The dark woman in an eerie white landscape looking for elusive emotions that created knots in your life, that kept you from doing the things that make you a larger person, a well balanced being, that could get you off the Ferris wheel once and for all.

There are no better people to be therapists than psychiatric patients, Angel had decided after two weeks of physical therapy with Mallory. Her foot got better and Angel was starting to feel a lot lighter. It was time to let go and start over. But those brave words were so difficult to achieve. She didn't want to hang on to all that stuff with Jennifer, but being in love again seemed to dredge up old lovers and one in particular.

Telling Mallory old stories was serving as process, saying it out loud made life back then seem more comical and less dangerous. Mallory made her laugh and in the process was healing her. Angel was certain she was doing the same for Mallory. They were the wounded caring for the maimed.

Kim kissed her neck and handed her the coffee. She didn't really know where Angel had been traveling but it must have been nice judging from the look on her face.

"Welcome back to Planet Earth. We hoped your journey was a pleasant one," Kim teased.

"Why thank you," Angel replied.

"I'm having a really good time. I don't get those often," Kim said.

"Me either, I'm glad it was with you."

"Could this be an epiphany of fun?"

"I'd like to think so," Angel said, thinking that Kim was going to do nice things for her comic strip in terms of verbal repartee.

Taylor Combs sat across from her father as they discussed future business strategy. She had gone to six years of college and through a lot of women to be sitting here contemplating the rest of her life. She was trying to pay attention to the conversation but wondering at the same time what Alex was doing right now. Ever since they had dinner, Taylor had begun noticing things about Alex in particular. Before she was interested, today she was contemplating acts of embarrassing degrees none of which she could honestly entertain.

"Mr. Combs, I'd like to ask you a personal question," Taylor said, addressing her father, the senior partner of the firm.

"Yes," Dallas Combs replied.

"Dad, why do you have so many gay and lesbian people working for you? In fact, I'm almost certain you are the only straight person on these premises," Taylor replied.

Her father brought his finger to his lips. "Shhh, you'll blow my cover."

"What?"

"They all think I'm an old queen. I never told them your mother's name. I just always called her my partner."

"You're passing as queer?" Taylor said.

"Well, kind of."

"Why?"

"You're going to run this firm some day and I wanted you to be comfortable. So, when the old employees from Grandpa's time started to retire I simply replaced them with *family*. And it's worked out great ever since. We're talking better than ever before. Your lot is an overachieving bunch. And the stink over domestic partnership benefits is entirely incorrect. The firm only has to insure one partner without children thus no maternity leave, and less sick time, it's simply amazing. The firm's numbers have never looked better. I'm sold," Dallas Combs said, smiling benevolently at his daughter.

"Exactly how did you find all these gay and lesbians," Taylor asked.

"I placed an ads in all the gay and lesbian papers and then I recruited from within."

"What about this passing thing?"

"I started out by always referring to your mother, God rest her soul, as my partner. Then I watched *The Birdcage* several times until I got the moves right. Haven't you seen me do my fag act? It's a beautiful thing," Dallas said, getting up and doing a little strut and then an elaborate hand gesture.

"See, it's easy to be an old queen," Dallas said, as Alex walked into the room.

Taylor blushed.

"I'm sorry I'm late. MacAllister was on the phone," Alex said, taking a seat.

"Quite all right. Dad was just giving me lessons on how to be a queen," Taylor said.

"I see," Alex said, trying not to look at Dallas, who was watching her acutely.

Dallas would never tell his daughter that he hired Alex because she would be the perfect mate for Taylor. He remembered the day he introduced Taylor to Alex and how both of them had pretended not to notice the other. But he had seen how they looked at each other and he knew he'd figured right. He kept harping on Taylor to be more assertive and Taylor kept telling him to mind his own business.

One day, Dallas knew, they would figure out that they were perfect for each other, just like he had the first time he met Helda. Taylor told him that Alex had a girlfriend and she didn't want to compromise either one of their integrity's. Dallas reminded her that Helda was on the verge of getting married when he met her and they fell in love. "I know, I know but Dad . . ." "Don't but Dad me, do something. You can be friends at least, get to know one another. And then we'll hire someone to bump off her girlfriend," Taylor replied. "Not exactly, but things have a way of working themselves out," her father had advised.

After the meeting, Taylor said, "So what's for lunch?" hoping she could once again convince Alex to have lunch. She remembered being surprised that Alex didn't go for lunch. "I don't like to eat alone." "Then eat with me" Taylor suggested.

"There's a new bistro that just opened up down the street," Alex replied, trying not to wonder why she found herself shopping around for new places to have lunch. She was becoming fond of lunch.

Every day Alex became more relaxed in Taylor's company as they slowly discovered that they had a lot in common. They made fast friends, although some of the energy between them was definitely sexual. Alex was always acutely aware whenever she was close to Taylor, and she had caught Taylor looking at her in that way. Taylor was always respectful of her relationship with Gigi, which served as a pleasantly refreshing attitude considering how everyone else they knew either ignored the perimeter or saw it as a tantalizing line to be crossed if given the chance. Taylor treated it like a fortress complete with a moat.

"Anything big and exciting happening this weekend?" Taylor asked as she smothered her pastrami and rye sandwich with a horseradish condiment.

Alex tried not to wince at the sight of so much horseradish in such a small amount of territory.

"No, it's Gigi's weekend with the activists," Alex said, doctoring her ice tea with sugar. Sometimes she wondered why she automatically ordered ice tea when she didn't really like it. Habit, she supposed. It seemed she did a lot of things out of habit except having lunch with Taylor, which for all practical purposes was completely spontaneous. Even living with Gigi was more habit than desire these days. She could see that in both their eyes sometimes. Although lately, Gigi was making more of an effort to be around and to spend time that had the look of quality to it.

"The activists?" Taylor asked.

"I haven't told you about them. They are Gigi's aunts and friends. They have an agenda against the Patriarchy in general, social mores in particular and a running family feud over sexual orientation and certain religious beliefs."

"Wow, that's a mouthful. You're not one of the activists?"

"No, Gigi doesn't like to mix the personal with the political. She has serious boundary issues and keeps most things separate."

"She must be quite the woman," Taylor replied, feeling suddenly ordinary and mundane.

"Not really, she's more like a giant pain in the ass that I still can't begin to fathom," Alex said, before she could stop herself.

Taylor laughed.

"I can't believe I just said that. What I mean is that she is really intense, hard to read, has mood swings like a pendulum and she makes me really tired sometimes," Alex said.

"So it's your weekend off then?" Taylor asked, trying to steer the conversation away from Gigi. She didn't want Alex to think she would harbor any ill will toward Gigi and it seemed not talking about her was best.

"It is."

"Do you golf?" Taylor asked, hoping she might steal a couple hours of Alex's time away from work.

"I used to. But Gigi isn't exactly your golfing type."

"I love to golf but I haven't found a partner as of yet. Maybe we could go when you've got some free time."

"Like this weekend maybe," Alex teased.

"Well, yes," Taylor said, straightening up her discarded horse-radish packets. Alex reached over and stopped her.

"Taylor, I want us to be friends. We like to do the same things and we can do them together without having to feel weird. Gigi has her own life. It's high time I have one as well."

"I don't want to cause strife," Taylor said, feeling certain her flesh was on fire as Alex still held her hand.

"You won't, because you would never do anything unethical," Alex said, removing her hand and marveling at her candor.

"Do you still have clubs?" Taylor asked.

"I'll dust them off tonight," Alex replied, picking up the check. Taylor started to protest but Alex gave her the look. They took turns paying. It was Alex's turn.

"You know one day I want you to tell me how it is that you don't have a girlfriend," Alex said.

"With eighteen holes ahead of us, I'll weave the whole yarn for you."

"I'm holding you to it."

"I can't wait."

Mallory kissed Del goodbye as Gigi rolled her eyes and waited patiently in the truck. Gigi was going through the CD collection to find something uplifting for the drive. She briefly contemplated Nine Inch Nails so she could crank up the song "I want to fuck you like an animal" just to serve as a metaphor for Mallory and Del.

"Gigi, you never thanked Del for driving me the other night," Mallory said.

"Yes, well, thank you Del for driving Mallory to post bail. What are friends for," Gigi replied, finding the song and turning it up.

Mallory blushed and hugged Del goodbye, giving Gigi a stern look over her shoulder.

"I'll call you later," Mallory said.

"I miss you already," Del said, starting to feel like a football widow.

As soon as Gigi pulled out onto the freeway she broke the silence, and Mallory's blissful meditation on the beauty of the Arizona desert on a fine October day came to a screeching halt.

"So have you two done it yet?" Gigi asked.

"That is a rude thing to ask," Mallory replied.

"One not dignified with a response. It makes you look guilty," Gigi said, reaching over and pinching Mallory's inner thigh.

"I hate when you do that."

"Which is why I do it," Gigi replied.

"We haven't had time."

"What a crock of shit!"

"Bugger off," Mallory said, looking out the window and thinking again.

The ride to Yarnell was quiet until they hit Wickenburg. Gigi looked over at Mallory and suffered a pang of guilt.

"I'm sorry about what I said," Gigi offered.

Mallory turned to Gigi with an almost bored look on her face.

"I didn't give it a second thought," Mallory replied.

"I thought you were mad," Gigi replied, indignant.

"No, I've learned to expect that kind of behavior from you."

"Why?"

"Because I consider you crude and insensitive," Mallory replied, pining over an antique shop they passed that she knew Gigi would never take her to. She wondered if Del would.

"I am?"

"Yes," Mallory replied.

"If you weren't mad then what were you doing all this time?"

"Daydreaming."

"About what?"

"Making love with Del."

Gigi pinched her again.

"What was that for?" Mallory asked, rubbing the sore spot.

"For not spending quality time with me. What am I, some minor distraction in the otherwise glorious ramblings of your imagination?"

"What is wrong with you? I used to spend most of my time in the Republic and you knew that."

"That was different. You used to share those stories with me."

"You're saying I'm not sharing Del stories."

"I don't necessarily want Del stories. I know those are private but I feel like I'm losing you," Gigi said, feeling her eyes getting moist. She was thankful for her sunglasses.

Mallory took her hand. "You're not losing me. I'm just not as accessible which doesn't mean I love you any less."

"I know. I shouldn't be so needy but you having a girlfriend is really a new experience for me."

"I'll be patient," Mallory teased.

"I knew I could count on you. And I guess I still get some of your weekends."

"That's right."

When they pulled into the Yarnell Grange Hall the place was already buzzing with activity. The perfunctory bake sale was going on to cover up the real meeting. Mallory barely had time to snag a piece of strudel before they were ushered into the back room of the grange hall. Aunt Lil immediately called the meeting to order and Fran put Mallory and Gigi up front as they were the reason behind the emergency meeting. Mallory sat munching her strudel, hoping she was going to get to finish before the inquisition started. It was unique and unusual punishment to be this close to such good food and not get to sample.

"Gigi, I want you to describe in detail your travails of the last week at the hands of the overzealous," Aunt Lil said, handing her the bright pink plastic vulva that each speaker held indicating that the floor was hers.

Gigi hated the pink vulva. She felt stupid holding it but nonetheless she respected the tradition. On more than one occasion she had mentioned her discomfort to her aunt only to be told she needed to get in touch with her femaleness. Holding the vulva was the first step. Gigi didn't see how holding a disgusting pink replica had anything to do with her femaleness.

Mallory tried not to giggle as Gigi held the dreaded vulva and relayed her story to the others, who murmured their discontent at the situation.

"Tied her to a chair, that's just not right!" Fran screeched, drawing the rest in with her. The energy in the room was filled with indignation. Mallory listened and watched as a plate of brownies started to make its way down the row. She counted the pieces left. They could make it to her. She only had to be patient.

"But what are we going to do about it?" Lil said, whipping the crowd to a fevered pitch.

The brownie plate was two away from her and Mallory could almost taste them.

"There has got to be a way to retaliate in such a manner as to assault like we've been assaulted," Lil said.

The brownie tray reached Mallory at the exact same instant as the idea, which seemingly came out of nowhere.

"Why don't you put on an exhibition of defaced Virgin Mary statues? That would send them into an absolute frenzy and with a little doing we could probably implicate Gigi's mother, Rose, and thus extract revenge as well as make a statement."

Everyone in the room stared at Mallory. Lil snatched the plate of brownies from her and pulled her up on the stage to further enunciate her plan. By the end of the evening Mallory was starving and her brains had been picked clean.

"You're a fucking genius!" Gigi said, as they sat across the kitchen table from each other and ate a huge bowl of chili complete with cinnamon roll.

"A hungry genius," Mallory said, getting up for seconds.

"I can't believe I'm finally going to have an outlet for my socially unacceptable artwork. This is great," Gigi said, beaming with excitement.

"We could hold the exhibit in my warehouse," Mallory suggested.

"Yes, perfect. Will you let me drive the forklift?"

"No, I'll get it cleaned up. You are a hazard with a forklift. I don't want any more industrial accidents."

"I just need to get the hang of it."

"No."

"I should call Alex and tell her the news. I'm really charged about this," Gigi said.

"I know," Mallory replied, handing Gigi her cell phone.

Gigi dialed and let it ring. The machine picked up but she didn't leave a message.

"Where would she be at eleven o'clock at night?" Gigi said, her brow furrowed in consternation.

"Out having fun," Mallory replied, harmlessly.

"What kind of fun?"

"Fun, the kind we all have. What makes you think anything different?"

"I don't know," Gigi said, sulking.

"Alex is entitled to have fun while you're gone. You're having fun."

"This is work," Gigi said.

"Well, it's still her weekend. I don't expect Del to sit home while I'm gone."

"I would wager that Del is at work," Gigi countered.

Mallory looked cagey. "All right she's working."

"I don't get it. Alex didn't mention anything about going out," Gigi said, trying to wrack her brains for clues.

151

Mallory refrained from asking *were you listening to her or did you blow out of the house like you usually do?*

"I'm sure everything is fine. Alex is the most trustworthy and loyal person I know, aside from Del of course."

"Of course," Gigi said. "Bed time?"

"Please, I'm exhausted. Who would think direct action to be so physically stimulating," Mallory said.

"What are you sleeping in these days if you've given up pajamas?" Gigi asked.

"Silk negligees," Mallory teased.

"Really?" Gigi said, her eyes big as saucers.

"You'll have to wait and see," Mallory replied.

The full moon sat high atop the mountains and Alex marveled at the complexity of its surface and the degree of force that created its various features. She remembered how Beatrice told the poet Dante that those craters, then thought to be seas, which accounted for their names, were the virtues of the heavens.

"What are you thinking?" Taylor asked.

Alex smiled. "It's silly really."

"Tell me anyway," Taylor said, feeling immensely fortunate to be sitting on her deck with Alex on a Saturday night. She had hardly let herself think about what it would be like. Perhaps her father was right. They could be friends and they could do things together. Taylor had told herself this all afternoon while they golfed—even as she knew she was falling in love. She could love her best friend and still practice celibacy with a pure heart. Taylor leaned on the arm of the chair to be closer to Alex, who sat in a matching chair facing the Four Peaks.

Taylor remembering buying the chairs because oak went well with the red brick patio, something she vaguely recalled from her school days when she wanted to be an interior designer and not an accountant. She set the chairs up together seeking perfect placement and when she got the aesthetics right Taylor wondered if she would ever sit with her soul mate watching the sun drop into the crest of the mountains.

"I was thinking about how Beatrice told Dante that the craters of the moon were virtues."

"In the *Divine Comedy*," Taylor said.

Alex was surprised. Taylor noticed.

"I even read *Vita Nuova*."

"I'm sorry. I wasn't underestimating you. I'm not used to having someone that would even entertain the thought of reading Dante."

"I liked it."

"So did I," Alex replied, her delighted face dancing in the candle-light.

"I really had fun today," Taylor said.

Alex smiled. "Yeah, I think that's what triggered the virtues."

"Having fun?"

"No, being with someone virtuous."

"How do you know I'm virtuous?" Taylor asked.

"Because you have a soul that desires purity in thought and action," Alex replied.

"I do, but it does not mean I was not once a complete rogue."

"But you must have been young," Alex prodded, hoping Taylor would find now the right moment to tell her story.

"I was. When I was eighteen and before college I wanted to see Europe but I also wanted to live there so I went as an English tutor to a wealthy Parisian family. They had a little boy. The father was an Ambassador and he had a lovely wife."

"Sounds like a fairy tale," Alex teased.

"Until the lovely wife opened my sexual vistas."

"She seduced you?" Alex asked.

"Suffice it to say she was the more knowledgeable one. I fell hard for her and not that I would trade the experience but for two years we lived together and loved one another without a thought to the future. Her husband was much older and often away. But he figured us out and had me deported. I begged her to come with me but she

153

couldn't. I came back to the states and thought one day I might make her change her mind, not understanding the power of husband and child."

"That was definitely the epitome of an ill-fated love affair."

"What comes next is almost better. I go to college and hope I can repair my broken heart, only the girls I meet are just that—girls— and I suddenly seem much older than I should be. Then I meet and fall in love with my art history T.A. and we start a relationship that ends just as badly. She gets a job teaching in Iowa and I'm finishing my degree. She has to take it, as teaching jobs are not easy to get at the collegiate level. We agree to conduct a nine-month separation until I graduate. She moves. We call, fly out on holiday and everything seems fine. It's hard to adjust at first but I'm willing to wait. I love her. Until one day I call her and another woman answers the phone."

"Not good," Alex replied, seeing old ghosts and old hurts surfacing in Taylor's eyes.

"No, and since then I haven't had the zest for dating, or even looking for that special someone. So does my track record support your theory?"

"Actually, it does."

"How?"

"Because you deeply loved those women and because they were forced to choose or chose another doesn't make you any less virtuous. You were true to love and cheated by fate."

"I think perhaps you have a bad case of rose-tinted glasses," Taylor teased.

"As do all true romantics," Alex replied. "Of which I consider you one."

"I guess you caught me," Taylor said.

Alex groped around in her dark house, not having left a light on because she was only going golfing. She hadn't anticipated going for a barbecue and a hot tub at Taylor's but after golf they were hungry and Taylor offered to cook and then Alex found herself not wanting to end the day. As she brushed her teeth, she ran the night over in her head. The look on Taylor's face when she slipped into the hot tub in her swim suit and how nice that felt.

"What?" Alex had asked.

"Nothing. I was just having a teenage boy moment. Your nicely tailored business suits do not do you justice," Taylor said, blushing.

Alex had laughed. It was nice to feel sexy for someone. She knew she shouldn't be having these thoughts but still they were there and as she gave Taylor a hug goodnight she was acutely aware of holding her, of feeling her smooth skin next to her own, of inhaling her scent. She petted the cat and turned off the light and began to wonder what life in a parallel universe might hold. The phone rang and broke her dream.

"Where have you been? It's two-thirty in the morning," Gigi said.

"I was golfing," Alex replied, shocked. Gigi never called her from Yarnell. "Is anything wrong?"

"Yes, you've been out all night. I've been trying since eleven. Who did you go midnight golfing with?" Gigi asked, her heart pounding like an angry drum her chest.

"I was with Taylor. We had dinner," Alex said.

"The boss's daughter?" Gigi asked.

"Yes."

"Until two-thirty in the morning."

"We were talking. Gigi, with your track record, you are not in the position to accuse me of anything," Alex countered.

"I wasn't accusing. I was just curious because I was worried. You don't usually do anything on the weekend."

"That's because I don't usually have anyone to do it with."

"And now you do."

"We both like to golf, so what? It doesn't mean we're fucking."

"I wasn't saying that," Gigi said. "You're awfully defensive."

"I don't like what you're implying," Alex said, realizing Gigi was right. She was defensive but she was also innocent in deed if not thought. Maybe she did have feelings for Taylor that she was denying. Nonetheless, Gigi the flirt had no room to accuse her of anything.

"I was worried, Alex. I had good news I wanted to share with you, and when you weren't home I got scared. I'm sorry," Gigi said.

"I understand. I didn't check in because you never call, so it was just a misunderstanding. What did you want to tell me?"

"It can wait. We'll talk when I get home," Gigi said.

"All right."

"Alex?"

"Yes?"

"I love you."

"I love you too. Sweet dreams," Alex said, feeling a sudden sharp pang in her heart. Something was very wrong here.

Gigi knew when she set the phone down that Alex had found someone else; her fears would be well founded, she knew. She always knew when she was losing her lover. She was always the interim lover. Alex had been the longest, and the most patient, but the good women she loved always found someone else. She crawled into bed and wrapped herself around Mallory. It was her own cowardice that had brought her to this.

Eight

The dark street was splattered with the lights from lofts. Angel stared out into the night. It was nice being a day person when most of the artists around her were nocturnal; however, tonight she couldn't sleep and found herself up with them creating works of art in the middle of the night.

Ever since the camping trip with Kim she'd been contemplating her new character. Each time a new character came into the strip Angel was reminded how she got started in the comic strip. After her parents found out she was gay and threw her out of the house, she lived with various women and men and learned about the culture that would become her life.

Somewhere in that discovering of self and of art she found the strip or rather it found her. She drew up her imaginary world that had what she liked and didn't like about the gay community. She studied cartooning and was given the grim reproofs from her professors that she would be wasting her talents on a lesbian strip. But her muse was a dyke with an opinion and Angel followed her lead.

It wasn't until Jennifer came along that the strip really got its start, aside from a few local papers that for want of anything better stuck her strip in between the sex ads and the personals. Angel found it disheartening that the gay and lesbian community ached for an art of its own but did little to support or even acknowledge the gay and lesbian artists.

Still, Angel plugged away and continued to hone her skills. But it was Jennifer with her amazing business acumen that put Angel out there and got the strip a place in the world. For all the fucked-up things Jennifer had done, Angel felt an immense gratitude for her work and her belief that Angel was artist and one who deserved to be recognized.

Angel tried to convince herself that she had paid that debt by putting up with Jennifer's wayward behavior. She always came up short. She would never get past being angry and saddened that they hadn't come to a better end. Life is not like that, she told herself as she tried to shrug off those old feelings. She drew her new character and carefully inked her in.

Her new character was named Bethesda. She was an Asian woman with long dark hair and a black leather mini skirt. She was smart, witty and the perfect mate for her strip's protagonist Detroit. She hoped Kim wouldn't find offense in any of it but Angel lived her life and its moments through her art. To love the artist was to live with her product. She knew Kim would be one of the few people in her life to understand that. This was a good thing, but the cobwebs of her past life started to flutter about again and she wondered.

A year had gone by and she had successfully avoided any contact with Jennifer, but she feared that creating a new character in the strip might complicate things. Maybe she flattered herself into thinking that Jennifer followed the strip. Maybe she wouldn't even notice. Somehow, Angel doubted that but she held this moment as her Declaration of Independence. Lesbians shouldn't have divorces since they couldn't actually be married; instead they should have a Declaration of Independence. Someday, the world would understand itself through its art and Angel was afraid that Jennifer, in her love of anarchy, would get what Angel was saying. The future would tell and Angel, for the first time ever, felt strong enough to withstand what her nemesis had to offer.

The office complex was dark when Alex pulled in. She was the first one in. She turned on the lights and got the coffee going. Shirley, the receptionist, would be grateful. Alex sat down at her computer and set it humming. She felt bad for sneaking out on Gigi but she couldn't quite face her after they'd made love last night. Alex had given in so easily in body so she could float in mind, and she felt guilty because her mind had wandered and it wasn't right. It was hard to know what was right anymore. Alex went to work so she wouldn't have to think.

An hour later Taylor stood in the doorway looking surprised.

"It's kind of early. I was sort of planning on you not being here. It's six-thirty," Taylor said, holding a putter with a red bow around it.

"I couldn't sleep," Alex replied.

"I see. Well, this is for you," Taylor said, giving her the putter.

"Thank you," Alex said, blushing. "Maybe we should try it out sometime."

"Like now, maybe. I'm sure we can get a tee time."

"Taylor," Alex said, her eyes never leaving Taylor's face.

"I'm the boss's daughter. He'll understand. Let's go to breakfast and then golfing," Taylor said.

"We can't," Alex said.

"We can, come on," Taylor said.

"This is bad."

"No, this is really good," replied Taylor, taking Alex's hand.

Alex didn't let go.

159

The warehouse at Kokopeli Was An Alien Vending Company was already buzzing with activity when Del pulled up in the parking lot. She was just contemplating how nice life would be when she switched back to days and could slow down a little. Del had landed a job with a private practice and was beginning to imagine a life beyond residency. She would be an honorary citizen who had normal hours and maybe a home life, one she was hoping Mallory would want to share with her.

Every day it seemed they got closer, but Del could not quell her apprehension that one day Mallory would wake up from her dream of normalcy and exit the scene. A small voice in the back of Del's head kept telling her that life with Mallory was not going to be the smooth sailing of the present. Del believed that if you thought things were going too well, beware the crash just around the corner. She almost dreaded the good times because she could not stop anticipating the bad. Not a good system when one should adopt the philosophy of water—when you can't overcome, go around.

She had met Dr. Kohlrabi and been quizzed and examined. The good doctor was impressed with her diligence and did not doubt her sincerity but added a note of caution. She told her that overly bright people like Mallory grew to understand the mysteries of the universe that the rest of us in our belief in the importance of banal activities managed to overlook. These people are never happy, experiencing moments of calm only to succumb to the path of enlightenment that affords ultimate freedom of mind but is far removed from the rest of the world—including the one you love.

"In other words," Del had told Dr. Kohlrabi, "she's not the best partner."

"Yes, but suffice to say you will never be bored and she'll probably love you for the rest of your days—in that wonderfully old-fashioned way where you stick by your promise and accept all that it entails."

"I think that will do just fine for me," Del said.

Dr. Kohlrabi shook her hand and wished her well, thinking Mallory the luckiest girl on the planet.

Mallory stood in the doorway of the warehouse like she had been mysteriously summoned. "I thought you might be out here."

"Did you feel my presence?" Del said, taking Mallory in her arms and kissing her ardently.

"I must have," Mallory replied, thinking one day they would fondly remember the days of longing before they made love for the first time. "I should tell you that this has been the most perfect courtship."

Del held her tighter, murmured her consent and said, "I love the way you smell," taking a deep breath.

Fran came out to smoke a cigarette. "Ah, nothing quite like young love. Is this the fabulous woman you've been telling me about?" Fran teased.

Mallory smiled. "Yes, this is my beloved. Del, this is the illustrious lesbian activist, Fran Rolmen."

"Pleased to meet you," Del said, extending her hand.

"You are very lucky girls," Fran said, standing back, taking a drag off her cigarette and surveying them.

"And just why do you say that?" Mallory said.

Fran smiled and shook her head. "You know."

"Come inside and see what we're up to. She has clearance, right Fran?"

"Of course, we might need a physician on hand. Consider yourself hired," Fran replied. "But no cancer talks," Fran added, looking at her cigarette. "I get enough of that these days. My Marlboro and I go back a long way."

Del nodded, trying to remove the clinical image of black lung from her mind.

Inside the radio was blaring the daily rosary on AM channel 1010. Long tables were set up across the warehouse and lesbian activists everywhere were painting ceramic Virgin Marys in a variety of sizes and colors. Jars of paint and white ceramic dust covered the tops of tables and the floor. As Mallory continued the tour, Del saw other women making long rosary chains, and others were moving the completed works to another room. Inside this room there were still more women poring over sketches laid out across two huge drafting tables with Gigi at the center of the discussion. She nodded at Del.

"What's going on?" Del asked as they stepped into the quiet of Mallory's office and got a cup of tea from one of the vending machines now parked in Mallory's office.

"We're making a bad art show starring our fair lady with a twist, of course," Mallory said.

"You aren't going to get arrested?" Del asked.

"We're looking into legalities right now," Mallory said. "I'm betting the First Amendment covers us."

"What are you going do to the blessed virgin?" Del asked, fearing the worst.

"The exact same thing that men have done to women all along."

"Meaning?"

"Desecrate her," Mallory replied without compunction.

"To what purpose?"

"To make the adoring public realize the damage that has been done in the blessed virgin's name."

"Are they going to see it like that?" Del asked.

"Probably not, but the press will be good and it's really going to piss Gigi's mother off. In fact, we are planning on implicating her."

"Is she out of jail yet?"

"Yes," Mallory said, wrapping her legs around Del and rubbing her shoulders.

"You seem a little tense," Mallory said, pressing hard on the knot in Del's left shoulder blade.

"Activism makes me nervous," Del replied, wincing.

"It gives me a stomachache sometimes too."

"Whose idea was this anyway?" Del asked, wishing the genius

162

behind this scheme hadn't been so intellectually active. She supposed it was Gigi's idea. Del had seen some of her Anti-Art and the words *tasteless* and *profane* didn't begin to describe it.

"Actually, it was mine," Mallory said, softly.

"Oh, my God."

"I think God is with us now. Can't you almost feel the spiritual energy here? He wants us to correct the wrongs. I'm sure of it," Mallory said, getting flushed.

Del abstained from saying that studying the fossil record in college showed that the likelihood of God was nothing more than ancient fertility cults bleached to the lily whiteness of Christianity. If Mallory chose to see collective human effort as spirituality she was fortunate. As a doctor Del was forced to rely too much on science to be capable of the necessary mysticism to worship and believe.

There was an ecstatic cry from the workroom floor. Mallory and Del got up to see about the commotion. Del assumed the worst, thinking that Christian Activists had discovered the plan and infiltrated the perimeter. Instead, it was Aunt Lil dancing around with her prizewinning Virgin Mary. The ceramic sculpture was painted in horribly garish colors and thus Lil had won the "Make the Worst Virgin Mary" contest.

"See, I told you I'd win," Lil said.

Fran put her hand on her hip. "You did honey."

Del rolled her eyes. Mallory beamed at the group of crones.

"This is incredible," Mallory said.

"It is definitely different," Del replied.

Del, Kim, Angel and Mallory stood on the front lawn and admired Kim's red house. She'd finally finished painting the house and was marveling at the therapeutic nature of having started painting it as a gesture of protest and how she had come to heal herself as well as fall in love during the course of labor.

"It looks nice," Mallory said.

"The trim definitely toned it down a bit," Kim said. "I was worried I had created an eyesore but I think it's okay."

"A job well done," Angel said, taking her hand. "Is everyone perfectly starving?"

"Yes," Del said, thinking lunch was an old memory.

"I'll get the grill going," Angel said, heading out back, much to the dog's excitement.

"She just loves Angel," Kim said, getting Del and Mallory a cocktail before going in to get the steaks.

"I'll go in and see if she needs help," Mallory said, leaving Del and Angel to talk. She could sense they needed to for some reason—maybe it was the way Angel kept beginning to say something and then seemed to think better of it.

"Can I help?" Mallory asked, as Kim pulled sundry items from the crisper. "I make a good salad."

"That would great. Then I can start the potatoes," Kim said.

"I'm glad you're not with Ollie," Mallory said, as she washed the produce. "She wasn't good for you."

"But you like Angel?"

"Very much. I think there is something special about Midwestern girls."

"You know, I owe you an apology," Kim replied.

"How so?" Mallory said, looking quizzical.

"I always thought you were crazy. I even tried to warn Del about you."

"I am crazy."

"No more than the rest of us. But after painting the house because of my breakup with Ollie, I understand why we do extreme things. Everyone thought I was crazy for doing it."

"You were."

"I know. But I feel better."

"Craziness can be a positive outlet for grief, loss and the mending of a broken heart. It's sad that the rest of the world is so afraid of being crazy. That's why there are so many miserable people out there. No one heals anymore; they just move on to make the same mistakes again and again."

"I think you're right."

"Hey, I saw the new character in Dykeland. She's beautiful and funny, just like someone we know," Mallory said.

"I was kind of concerned at first but I'm getting used to the idea," Kim replied.

"It's a gesture of love."

"Yes, it is."

Angel finished getting the grill started. She sat next to Del.

"So what's up?" Del asked.

"What makes you think something is up?" Angel asked, trying to look unflustered.

"You have that look."

"What look?"

"The one where you want to talk but you can't seem to get it out."

"Jennifer found me," Angel said.

"When?" Del said, sitting straight up in her chair.

"Today. I was waiting for Kim and Jennifer came instead."

"Did you freak?" Del asked.

"Of course. I was going over my proofs for the next strip and voilá, she came strolling in the loft all ready to get close again," Angel said, instantly reliving the horror.

She had left the door open because Kim was on her way. Angel was sitting at her drafting table. She heard someone knock softly.

"Come in," Angel said, as she put the finishing touches on. She looked up to witness her worst nightmare come to life.

"What are you doing here?" she said, standing up.

"Hello to you too," Jennifer said. "Boy, some things never change, always trying to squeeze your artwork around your daytime job."

"How did you find me?"

165

"Angel, you can relax. I just wanted to see you. You cut your hair. It suits you," Jennifer said, reaching out to touch her. Angel stepped back.

"I don't want to see you. I never wanted to see you again. Now go," Angel said, pointing to the door.

"I'm here. Can't we at least talk?" Jennifer said.

"We don't have anything to say. You made your choices a long time ago. How is Jody, by the way?" Angel said, anger tracing a path across her face.

"I really don't know. I haven't seen her since rehab."

"Well, that's just fucking perfect," Angel replied, getting that losing-control sensation she experienced every time she was in Jennifer's presence, even vicariously. It was like she had planned for this moment only to be left forgetting her lines at the crucial moment.

"What do you mean?" Jennifer replied calmly.

"Meaning, I lose my girlfriend to my best friend and get to keep neither. Commonly referred to as a woman-oriented dream gone awry. The least you could do is live happily ever after; it should be a requirement," Angel said.

"I admit it wasn't a smart move on my part. But I thought about a lot of things in rehab. I'm clean now."

"Congratulations."

"It would have been nice if you'd hung around. I didn't expect you to bail," Jennifer said.

"You taught me how to expect the unexpected. Should I have waited around? I needed to get on with my life."

"You call this getting on. You're still selling yourself short."

"Don't go there. I like how I live. I'm not the fuckup here."

"I still love you," Jennifer said, moving closer. Angel moved back, abruptly knocking over her inkwell and spilling it on her shirt.

Angel looked at her shirt. She was angry with herself for being upset, not to mention she had obviously ruined her favorite shirt.

"Well, I suggest you stop immediately," Angel said, moving to the sink and looking hopelessly at Jennifer.

"Can't we try again?" Jennifer said, moving with her.

"Have you lost your fucking mind? You've done enough damage," Angel said, taking off her shirt and running cold water over it, suddenly grateful she had a distraction from the apocalypse that was occurring before her very eyes.

"But I'm better now. If you hadn't disappeared we could have patched things up then."

"I didn't disappear. I left because I was sick of all your shit. I left because you were a drunk and when you weren't drunk you were high and when you weren't fucking me you were fucking someone else. Now I want you to leave," Angel said.

"I've changed," Jennifer replied.

"So have I. I'm in love with someone else," Angel said, as Kim walked into the open doorway with a tentative glance. She had heard arguing as she came down the hall and now stood mortified.

Kim walked in to find Angel cornered in the kitchen half undressed with her ex-wife.

"I hope I'm not interrupting anything," she said, instantly alarmed that the open door wasn't an invitation and a welcome. She hadn't given it a thought as she stood there. Angel could tell by the look on her face.

"Hi," Angel said, looking completely horrified, immediately sensing what this looked like. "I've got ink on my shirt," she said, holding up the shirt .

"I was just leaving," Jennifer said, enjoying the confusion. Jennifer strutted by Kim and turning around said, "I have a show downtown. Why don't you come by?"

"Not in *this* lifetime," Angel said, almost savagely.

Jennifer left. Angel threw the shirt in the trash bin.

"It's not what you think."

"I don't think anything," Kim said, leaning on the kitchen bar.

"That was Jennifer-who-in-her-own-twisted-mind-thinks-we-can-get-back-together-psycho-bitch," Angel said.

"Well, in that case," Kim said, going over to wrap her arms around Angel and kiss her ardently.

"Are you all right?" Kim asked.

"I am now," Angel said, pulling her so tight she could feel Kim breathing against her.

"Wow," Del said, as she tried to envision what Angel had told her.

"It wasn't pretty," Angel said.

"At least your relationship with Kim is going strong. The comic strip probably tipped Jennifer off that it was time to step back in," Del said.

"I was hoping that wouldn't happen," Angel said.

"Well, it obviously has."

Kim and Mallory came out of the kitchen. Their girlfriends smiled at them.

"Had a good talk?" Mallory asked.

"It's hard having a telepathic girlfriend," Del replied.

Rose Dupont walked out of the Bishop's office glowing with the light of the righteous. She was sure she had brought her daughter around to the Lord our Savior. Gigi had come by to apologize and inform her mother that she was putting on an art show featuring the Virgin Mary in all her gloriousness in penance for her desecration of the shrines. She had invited her mother to come and even suffered a warm embrace as Rose uttered words of forgiveness.

Gigi hadn't flinched, and reconciliation was spinning about in the air. They had a family dinner and Rose felt warm and motherly in the blossoming light of resurrection and enlightenment. Her daughter had been saved. Rose arranged for the Bishop to come see the show and Gigi had smiled the smile of the redeemed. It was a beautiful thing. The Bishop had agreed to attend the show as well as speak with the Catholic press afterward. Rose was ecstatic.

Gigi went to inform the activists of her success. They deemed her the lesbian manipulator of the century. She basked in the light of triumph with her peers. Only a smidgen of guilt clung about her brain. She talked to Aunt Lil.

"You know I feel a slight pang of guilt," Gigi said, shoving a potato chip filled lasciviously full of onion dip from her overfilled snack plate courtesy of the pre-art show potluck.

"About Mother Rose?" Lil inquired.

"Well, yes."

"Don't. That woman deserves a little Old Testament judgment. She's shunned more than her share of folks in her life. It's time she got the other end of the stick," Lil advised.

"And that's what this is about, right?" Gigi asked.

"Yes. If you're worried about still having a family in the aftermath, you will, only it will be the kind you deserve, one without reservations, hesitations, or manipulations. Gigi, I know it's hard to let go of your mother, but she will only cause you more pain and grief than any small amount of her acceptance will ever give you. You will never be what she wants in a child. So don't bother trying. You'll only hurt yourself in the process. Understand?" Lil said, taking Gigi by the shoulders and staring deep into her eyes as if burning her words upon Gigi's brain.

"Yes, ma'am," Gigi said, trying to tie her aunt's words to a mantra she would need to repeat every day. She knew that her mother had birthed her but tormented her ever since. She needed to let go, to leave their relationship as it was—a never-ending battle of wills in which neither would ever prove the victor.

Alex showed up late but hungry. Gigi didn't inquire where she had been. When Gigi was the one showing up late, Alex had the decency not to ask; perhaps she hadn't wanted to know. Gigi, on the other hand, wanted to know but was afraid to ask. She got Alex a plate of leftovers and deduced where her wife had been.

Alex smelled like the outdoors, had a small grass stain on her knee and was in an extremely good mood, meaning she'd been golfing with Taylor. She smelled ever so slightly of scotch, meaning they'd had drinks in the clubhouse afterwards, and judging from Alex's rushed demeanor she had had to pull herself away in order to make this appearance.

169

Gigi knew all these things because she used to see them in herself. She hoped that if she were patient and kind, Alex would leave off her infatuation with Taylor.

They had only talked about Taylor once. Alex had firmly stated that they weren't sleeping together. They were friends who happened to like to do some of the same things. Alex told Gigi that she didn't sleep with her friends but if she did it would be as a single woman. Gigi let it go at that because she was worried that Ollie was hovering about getting ready to bring her world tumbling down with a few quick sentences. Having no room to talk, Gigi didn't question Alex any further. She knew that her wife wouldn't cheat. She'd end it first. Gigi didn't know which one she dreaded more.

Instead, she tried to find comfort in the fact that Alex was throwing her a birthday party in a few weeks and surely that was a sign of love.

As Alex told her, Mother Rose certainly wasn't going to be giving her one. Alex had laughed nervously saying, "I'm hoping she doesn't show up with a shotgun to end her creation after she finds out what you have planned for the Christian Exhibition."

"Maybe we should rent bullet proof vests," Gigi said.

"Might not be a bad idea," Alex said.

Thinking back on that Gigi felt better. She stayed close to Alex the rest of the night, looking for clues that she still loved her.

The next morning Gigi was up early. Pre-show jitters had kept her up most of the night. The old cliché *This is the first day of the rest of your life* kept dancing around her brain. Gigi couldn't decide if this was a good thing or a bad thing.

Alex stumbled into the kitchen and looked at the clock on the stove. She was a morning person but this seemed like the middle of the night. It was four in the morning.

"You're up early. What time does the show start?" Alex said, shuffling toward the coffee maker and thinking that religious people must get up really early.

"It starts at noon, high noon, you know like when shootouts used

170

to start in the old west. I'll meet you at high noon and blow your brains out," Gigi said, pulling a mock pistol out of her mock holster and aiming it at an imaginary opponent.

"Gigi, are you all right?" Alex asked.

"I'm fine. I'm fucking wonderful. I am going to go down in Catholic history as the righter of all wrongs," Gigi said, with more enthusiasm than was necessary.

"You don't have to do this. You could call the whole thing off," Alex advised.

"No way," Gigi said staunchly. "This is a war and there can be no truce. I'm going to the warehouse. You'll come by later, right?"

"Sure," Alex said.

The Kokopeli Was An Alien Vending Company was ready and waiting for Rose and the Bishop. The activists stood around twittering with excitement. Avid art goers had come to view the exhibition as the activists had advertised the show in the local papers. Serious young women dressed in black with a variety of eyewear strolled around the exhibit. A reporter from the City Pages interviewed Gigi on intent and execution of the various pieces. Gigi watched his goatee as it bobbed up and down on his chin as he uttered lugubrious phrases on what he thought the show meant. Usually, Gigi despised these parasites of the art world but today he gave her a distraction from the wait. All she could think about was the look on her mother's face when she saw the show. Rose was late and Gigi was anxious.

Lil came up and whispered in her ear, "Where is she?"

"I don't know. She is not usually late. I hope she didn't get in an accident," Gigi replied, thinking what a waste that would be.

As if summoned, her mother, the Bishop and the elders from the church came strolling in with Rose at the head and the rest of the entourage like a flowing red carpet behind her. Rose beamed with pride and excitement. Gigi felt her stomach drop. Given a moment longer before all hell broke loose she probably would have puked.

Alex came in behind them and even she was unprepared for what happened next. Perhaps it was the image of good and evil juxtaposed that took her back. Rose stood in the middle of room, looking at the hideous garish figures of her blessed virgin, and her face crumpled. Alex stood watching as Gigi was frozen at the sight of her mother.

"Rose, what is the meaning of this?" the Bishop said, his face getting red.

"I . . . I don't know. It wasn't supposed to be like this," Rose said, scanning the crowd for Gigi. "It's a mistake. It has to be a mistake."

The holy entourage flocked about like a bunch of startled crows scanning the room for some semblance of the sanctity they were expecting.

Lil and Fran grabbed Gigi who for the first time in her life felt trepidation. It was like she was experiencing a fear enema, the gravity of her actions was suddenly being shoved up her ass and all she wanted was a toilet.

"Rose, Bishop, and members of the congregation, welcome to the show. So glad you could come. The Virgin as you can see is being portrayed as a metaphor for the misogyny that the patriarchy has perpetrated upon womankind for the last zillion years," Lil said, putting her black spectacles that hung from a gold chain on and peering over them to look at her sister.

Rose lurched at her and luckily was restrained by larger members of the congregation.

"I should have known you were behind this. You are an abomination against God and you have brainwashed my daughter."

"I beg to differ. God made all things and thus God made us, your daughter included. In fact, if you were a more accepting, gentle, mother your daughter would not have to resort to terrorist tactics in order to get your attention. I suggest you mend your own wicked ways before you start casting stones," Lil advised.

Rose broke loose and floored her sister. The battle ensued and was not ended until the police arrived.

Del, Mallory and Alex sat in the rafters of the warehouse and watched as food, artwork, slinging purses and obscenities were hurled between supposed Christians and radical Heathens who waged war on the floor below.

"Do you think this is what Armageddon will look like?" Mallory asked as she snacked on finger food rescued from the buffet table.

"How can you eat at a time like this?" Del asked, wondering if and when Emergency Services were going to be called.

"It's easy. I'm starving," Mallory said, thinking she used to see this kind of behavior at Gigi's house all the time. Gigi usually walked away with a lot less hair. Perhaps that was why as an adult she chose to wear it short.

"Should we be doing something?" Del asked, wondering what that something would be.

"Not unless you want to lose your two front teeth," Mallory advised.

"It won't last long," Alex said, putting her cell phone away.

"How do you know that?" Del asked.

"I called 911. I was the tenth caller," Alex said, watching as Rose tried to deck Gigi with ceramic incarnation of the virgin.

There was a package sitting propped up by the front door of the loft with no return address. Angel picked it up and tried to figure out if it was dangerous or not. No telling with Jennifer in town. She knew from the postmark that it was local so it wasn't anything from her editor. She brought it inside and sat it rather unceremoniously on the floor. She had a deadline to meet with the comic strip so she set to work and forgot about it until bedtime.

Kim called from work to wish her good night, another one of their rituals. If they couldn't see each other every day then they called. Kim listened to her about the strip. Angel picked up the box and absentmindedly opened it while they talked. It was a blue shirt identical to the one she had ruined with ink when Jennifer had surprised her that day in the loft. Pinned to the shirt was a quick note of apology and an invite to the gallery show as well as Jennifer's telephone number.

"Angel, what's up?" Kim asked, noticing the queer silence that had come over their conversation.

"I can't fucking believe it!" Angel said, wadding up the note and pitching it across the room.

"What?"

For a split second, Angel considered not telling but her conscience got the better of her. Start omitting things now and it looks like a coverup later, she told herself.

"Jennifer sent me a shirt for the one she helped ruin," Angel said.

"I see," Kim said, feeling her adrenal glands kicking in.

"I'm not letting her back in my life," Angel declared.

"There is always the restraining order," Kim said.

"I don't want anything to do with her."

"And you don't have to. Why don't you come for a cup of tea? I've got my half an hour break coming up."

"Would you mind?"

"No, I'd really like to wrap my arms around you and kiss you all better," Kim replied.

"I'll be there in a flash," Angel said.

Over tea in the hospital cafeteria Angel and Kim discussed the latest predicament. Kim was glad that Angel was sharing her fears with her about Jennifer rather than hiding them.

"Maybe we should go to the show," Kim suggested.

"Why?" Angel said, immediately horrified.

"Because we could let her know we're together in love and together, and that might put a stop to her putrid and insane thoughts of getting you back," Kim said.

Angel laughed. "I do love you."

"Then let's make it known to Jennifer. It's got to be better than hiding out," Kim said, trying not to blush.

"Can we bring Mallory and Del?"

"As reinforcements?" Kim teased.

"Yes," Angel said, taking Kim's hand across the table.

"All right," Kim said, trying to envision the outfit she would wear to let Jennifer know she had some serious competition.

174

"I don't deserve you," Angel said.

"No, you do. I deserve you and you deserve me. We've done our time in lesbian hell. It's time we showed the rest of the world that as well. Agreed?"

"All the way. I'm off tomorrow. Can I take you to breakfast before you crash?"

"I'd like that," Kim said.

At the Obelisk Bookstore the line of women waiting to get their copies of *Adventures in Dykeland* was rather formidable, not that Kim was surprised. But she was kind of nervous as she passed the line to see Angel, who was busy being charming and signing books. Kim sidled up next to her.

"I had no idea you were so popular," Kim whispered as she took the chair Angel offered her.

"Neither did I," Angel said, squeezing her hand.

"How are you doing?"

"Fine, I can't believe I got talked into this," Angel said.

"It's good PR," Kim said.

"You sound like my publicist," Angel said.

"We're just looking out for your career. I've got the night off, want to come for dinner?" Kim asked.

"I'd love to. I'm done at eight."

"I'll be waiting."

Angel kissed her. "I'll see you then."

Kim made her way past the line. Outside someone grabbed her arm.

"Long time no see," Ollie said.

Kim tried not to bristle.

"What are you doing here?" Kim asked.

"I'm coming to buy a book," Ollie said.

"Not the best day," Kim said.

"Why? Because the mail lady gone famous is here," Ollie said.

"Well, at least she's got a dream," Kim said, wishing there wasn't animosity between them every time they met. It was sad thinking that the woman she once loved and shared her life with was now such a thorn in her side.

Angel excused herself from her fans. "I'll be right back," she told them.

"Are you okay?" Angel said, sidling up to Kim.

"Yes," Kim said, taking her hand.

"I told you to leave her alone," Angel told Ollie.

"It's a free country," Ollie taunted.

"Not if you hurt people," Angel said, taking a step closer to Ollie.

"What, do you have special rights because you're rich and famous now?" Ollie said.

"No, I don't. I have special rights because I love her," Angel replied.

Ollie stepped closer.

"Come on, buy a book later," Kim advised.

Babe, the bookstore manager, came out.

"Is there a problem here?" she asked, puffing up her already formidable frame.

"No, she was just leaving," Angel replied.

"We're not done," Ollie said, pointing a finger at Angel.

"Leave her alone," Angel said, taking a step forward.

"Fuck you," Ollie said.

Babe stepped in between them.

"Look, Angel is supposed to be here. So I think you better leave," Babe advised Ollie.

"Until next time, sweetheart," Ollie said, blowing Kim a kiss.

"Thanks, Babe," Angel said. She took Kim in her arms. "Are you all right?"

"Now I am," Kim said, watching Ollie's car screech out of the parking lot.

"I hope you got what you wanted," Ollie said, looking over at Caroline, who was holding her autographed copy of *Adventures in Dykeland*.

"Yes, thank you. Did you know we'd run into her?" Caroline asked.

"Kind of figured I would. Half thought I might see some of my other old buddies. I hear they all hang together now. Mallory goes out with Del who is friends with Kim who is dating Del's best friend Angel who is getting famous because of women like you who think a comic strip means something," Ollie said, giving Caroline a snide look.

"It does mean something but I won't waste any of my philosophical thoughts on the unappreciative," Caroline said, thinking the only reason she suffered hanging around Ollie was that she had promised to get her in to see Mallory.

"I did, however, find out that Alex is throwing Gigi a birthday party at the house in two weeks and guess who shall be crashing it. I think surprise will be our best friend," Ollie said, with a perfectly evil glint in her eye.

Nine

Gigi awoke with a start. She was sweating profusely and her bad dream clung to her like a wet T-shirt. It was always the same dream or a subtle variation on the theme. Ever since the Christian Exhibition had gone public and her mother had been excommunicated from the church, what should have been a day of triumph had turned nasty, and now guilt swirled around Gigi's brain at night and gave her wicked visions of her mother. She'd taken to staying up late and watching bad television just so she wouldn't see her mother in those nasty apparitions.

The show was a great success and Gigi and the Lesbian Activists were now famous anti-art artists. Gigi had gotten several offers from galleries to show more of her stuff, including the photographic montage of life on the canals. She should have been happy but all she thought about was her mother screaming at the Bishop and his entourage as they did an about-face and walked out of Mother Rose's life forever. Her mother crumbled into a sobbing pile in the middle of the exhibition. It would have been a stunning scene if it hadn't been so sad and disheartening. Lil told her that Rose having her faith taken away would be the best thing anyone had ever done for her, but Gigi had her doubts.

Even Gigi's father would not speak to her. This time she had gone too far. She'd finally gotten her wish to be truly free of her family. Somehow her expatriate status did not sit well with her. Her dreams, the tarot card reader told her, were a manifestation of her remorse and guilt. She must work through all the bad she had caused before she would be a clean woman again. Gigi didn't have the heart to tell Sister Rita that she had never been a clean woman . . . only now all her misgivings had taken shape and were haunting her. There was no worse punishment for an amoral person than to suddenly infuse them with conscience. Gigi was on the verge of going to see Dr. Kohlrabi.

All she had to do was get through her birthday party this weekend and then she would seriously consider therapy. She couldn't keep on like this. Gigi looked over at Alex sleeping soundly. Oh, to sleep like that again, Gigi thought wistfully as she snuck out of the bed to lie on the couch and watch old movies. Maybe God is punishing me, Gigi mused, or the Virgin Mary. If I said a thousand Hail Mary's would I sleep again? Gigi poured herself a brandy and suffered through another night of penance.

Mallory sat sprawled out on the couch with a huge bowl of popcorn balanced on her stomach. Del was in the kitchen making root beer floats. They were watching movies. It was Del's first weekend off since she entered private practice. She and Mallory almost didn't know how to behave with such a chunk of time to spend. Mallory opted for home life, a quiet dinner and then a flick.

Del just wanted to be anywhere in the vicinity of Mallory. She always felt like she could never get enough of Mallory's company, like she was forever being teased with snitches of time between both their schedules. She just wanted to hold Mallory in her arms for an entire evening with neither of them having to rush off somewhere. Kim teased her that she need not worry about becoming suffocated with codependence. "But I want to be suffocated," Del had whined, thinking she could hardly imagine what that was like.

Suddenly, Mallory clicked the movie off and looked at Del.

"What are we doing?" Mallory asked.

"I thought we were watching a movie?" Del ventured.

"No, tonight we have the whole night together, alone, without interruption, and what are we thinking," Mallory said, moving closer to Del and pushing her back on the couch. "What's wrong?" Mallory asked as Del looked suddenly alarmed and confused.

"You're making me kind of nervous."

"Don't you want to?" Mallory said, starting to pull away.

"No, I do. Come here. It's just so sudden. I need to switch gears, that's all," Del said, pulling her in closer.

Mallory kissed her softly and then more ardently. "I have been waiting for this moment for so long," she said.

"And you're not scared?" Del asked.

"No," Mallory said, taking off her shirt and gently lowering her nipple into Del's eager mouth while she deftly unbuttoned Del's shirt.

This was nothing like Del had imagined making love would be, slow and sensuous, with the two of them leisurely exploring each other's bodies, rather it was like an explosion of hormones, lust whipped up into a fervor like a whirling dervish. Clothes coming off, half off, in a singleminded attempt to get inside one another and closer to that diligently sought-after moment of release. Mallory felt Del wrapping closer around her, feeling Del inside and being inside Del and somewhere between the rocking and thrusting a falling sensation took hold.

At first Mallory thought it was just the beauty of making love until she was brought suddenly back to reality as her back hit the edge of the coffee table and she was flat on her back with the wind knocked clean out of her. When she opened her eyes she saw Del peering down at her.

"Are you all right?" Del asked.

"No, I was on the verge of coming, now get down here," Mallory said, pulling Del on top of her.

She could feel both of them getting closer and Mallory held out until she was almost positive Del was right there and then together they collapsed with a mutual "Oh . . ."

Del kissed her softly. "I love you," she said, seriousness and the flush of desire still on her face.

"If you love me, you will get me off this floor and take me someplace soft, preferably the bedroom," Mallory said.

"By all means," Del said, helping her up and then carrying her into the bedroom where the soft and sensuous part of making love would take place.

Alex put out Gigi's birthday card and a single red rose on the coffee table. She pulled the afghan up around Gigi's shoulders. She knew Gigi probably wouldn't wake until almost noon but she didn't want her to feel neglected on her birthday. She felt bad for Gigi about the whole debacle with her family but as she told Taylor what did Gigi really expect? You can only push people so far and then they walk out of your life. Sometimes Alex wondered when Gigi would do that to her. It seemed only a matter of time before Gigi turned. She eventually turned on everyone she was ever involved with, everyone except Mallory, but then Mallory was the one person in the entire universe that Gigi loved with every ounce of her being. So Alex waited and tried to keep herself from falling in love with Taylor, whom she was going to have breakfast with, and then she'd go shopping at Price Club to get the party goods. Alex could not persuade Taylor to come to the party but did get her to at least play golf together before the party.

She felt a slight pang of guilt as she wrote Gigi a brief note as to her morning errands and then dashed out the door to spend time with Taylor. There was a chemistry between her and Taylor that had nothing to do with lust but rather with that wonderful sense of companionship that few people ever really achieve. Those who do find it end up staying together forever. She knew it was only a matter of time before they would become lovers but until they worked out the logistics they seemed to bask in the moment and the promise of an unspoken future.

As Alex drove across town to the Good Egg on Central her mind played over last night when she had come over to Taylor's for dinner. It all started harmlessly enough. Taylor had convinced Alex that having a workout in the middle of the day was not only beneficial but staved off the middle-aged middle-of-the-waistline bulge. They didn't get lunch until they worked out. This was the end of Alex's second week and she was sore.

She told Taylor she was going to have a long, hot bath because for once Gigi didn't have them booked for a gala night of party central; instead she was pulling a shift for one of the other girls at the shop. Gigi was actually excited. Friday was a hopping night for freak watching. Alex was looking forward to a reprieve from Gigi's crowded life. But Taylor had other ideas.

"Well, if she's working late why don't you come and sit in the hot tub and I'll grill you a steak. You need a lot of protein when you're building muscles. We'll watch a flick and just chill. It'll be fun," Taylor said, barely containing her excitement. Any snatch of time she could get Alex was practically a holiday in her book.

"It's sounds inviting . . ." Alex replied.

"Please come," Taylor said, trying to keep pleading out of her voice but her eyes gave her away.

"I can go shopping for dinner right after work while you go home and get your bathing suit and some comfy clothes and then we'll meet at my house."

"How can I refuse?" Alex teased.

"You can't. You're coming."

"All right," Alex said.

Taylor went dancing across the office. Her father noticed and came in to check on his daughter. She was so happy lately and he attributed it to her spending time with Alex, who was also looking a lot happier. He used to worry about Alex because she always seemed like she was just going through the motions of life without really enjoying any of it. He thought this was sad for someone so young and so capable of vitality.

"You're looking rather perky for a Friday."

"Dad, are you alluding to my usual black moods on the weekends because I don't get to see my friend for two whole days?"

"Well, seeing as you mentioned it."

"Alex is free tonight so we're doing a hot tub, steaks and a movie."

"That explains everything."

"Yes, it does."

"You're in love aren't you?"

"Madly," Taylor said, without exhibiting any restraint.

"What about the girlfriend?"

"I'm waiting," Taylor replied.

"Is that going to work?"

"You said love always prevails."

"It does, I assure you. Have a good weekend and be honest."

"Because it's the best policy?"

"Precisely."

Alex showed up with two bottles of Merlot and a bouquet of flowers.

"It's a hostess gift," Alex said, blushing.

"They're beautiful," Taylor replied, sticking her face into the flowers.

"I hoped you'd like them," Alex said, thinking what a pleasant luxury it was to buy flowers for someone who didn't think such an action was an affront, that it was a mimicking of heterosexual values, which was exactly what Gigi would think. Alex had never dared purchase flowers. Tonight she felt so relaxed in doing this small action that gave her such pleasure, knowing for certain that Taylor would enjoy them.

"Let me stick these in water. Why don't you get changed and we'll soak before dinner. Everything is ready so we have some chill time."

"Okay," Alex said, as Taylor led her down the hall to the guest room.

When she came out Taylor put a soft white terry cloth robe around Alex's shoulders.

"It gets chilly until you get in the hot tub and especially afterwards. You want some music, something mellow?" Taylor asked.

"That sounds wonderful."

Taylor put music on and then waited for Alex to disrobe and slip into the hot tub. They stood looking at each other. Taylor spoke first.

"I had no idea," Taylor said.

"No idea what?" Alex said, getting into the hot tub, hoping the steam would cover her blush.

"How lovely you are," Taylor replied.

"You're not so bad yourself," Alex replied, taking what she knew to be a very errant hand and running it down Taylor's flat firm stomach.

Taylor turned beet red and immediately plopped into the hot tub. Alex laughed.

"What?"

"You're shy," Alex teased.

"I can't help it."

"Why?"

The moment of truth had come and Taylor tried not to freak.

"I can't say it."

"Why not?" Alex asked.

"Because you're with someone," Taylor said, immediately hating herself for being a coward.

184

"Say it anyway," Alex replied, feeling her heartbeat rapidly increase.

"I'm in love with you. I know I'm not supposed to be but I can't help it. I hope this doesn't wreck our friendship . . . I mean I can pretend it's not there, I can take it back, I can wait forever . . ."

Her diatribe was interrupted. Alex moved dangerously close and kissed her softly on the lips. It was the first illicit kiss she'd ever given anyone but Alex told herself it was for love, big love that she had committed this indiscretion and she knew after Gigi's birthday she would tell her how she felt about Taylor and leave.

Taylor kissed her back but then stopped.

"I don't want to be your mistress."

"You won't be," Alex said, pulling her close.

And they were good. They talked but they didn't make love. Not that it couldn't have happened, not that the whole night wasn't infused with desire, not like they didn't hold each other as they sat by the fire and talked about how they wanted to live their lives and not like they didn't kiss each other ardently goodbye but they waited, waited for Alex to be free, waited so as not to ruin a birthday and hurt a person who was already hurting.

"It will be all right," Alex said.

"I know," Taylor said.

Breakfast with Taylor was lovely and now as Alex loaded groceries in the house with assistance from Mallory and Del she tried hard not to look like a woman in love with someone else.

Gigi tried not to look like a woman on the verge of a nervous breakdown. Having Fran and Lil come to her party helped. At least, part of her family would be there. Gigi didn't expect her parents to acknowledge anything but there was a part of her that wished for forgiveness, that wished for a moment of respite, one she knew wasn't coming.

As her friends started to fill the house and the keg got tapped and air mattresses littered the pool, Gigi started to relax. After all she did have a family, if not blood at least by choice, and for that she felt a small glowing ember of glee and humility enter her black world. She almost felt happy. Even if Alex wasn't fawning she was at least present and cordial but Gigi knew something was amiss, something she hoped she could fix.

Maybe it was the way Alex kissed her or the way her eyes seemed less than loving, less than full of desire, like she was preoccupied. Gigi crossed it off to hostess stress and began to ease into the party mode, allowing for some fun, if only for the afternoon. There would be time to talk later. She felt now that maybe she could learn to love Alex properly, bringing her back, promising her fidelity and the chance to start their life together the right way.

Gigi sat in a lawn chair by the pool and watched Mallory and Del in the pool wrapped around each other and kissing. They looked madly in love and very sexual.

"For shit sake why don't you two get a room if you're going to behave like that," Gigi said.

"We would if we didn't have to attend a very special person's birthday fete," Mallory said, gently inserting her tongue in Del's ear.

"I don't think Gigi is doing well when it comes to Mallory and Del's love affair," Alex told Kim, who was doing a poor job of not drooling over Angel in a bathing suit. She knew hers were among many admiring eyes at the party. She did redirect them long enough to reply to Alex's observation.

"Gigi had her chance, no offense."

"None taken. I've always known that Gigi was in love with Mallory among others," Alex said.

"Are you all right?" Kim said, picking up a strange vibe from Alex.

"I'm fine, just thinking back on things. You haven't seen Ollie in a while have you?"

"No, thank goodness," Kim said, suddenly wondering if Alex knew about Ollie and Gigi's liaison. She had often wondered if she should have told Alex what she knew about that night in the van when they were fucking each other. She talked to Angel about it and they both decided it was best to let it alone. Time had a way of revealing all that needed to be told. Maybe Alex already knew.

"Pity she isn't here to see the lovely accoutrements of your new girlfriend," Alex said, as they both watched Angel take a perfect dive off the board.

"Yes, that would truly be a precious moment," Kim said.

"One I'd like to see," Alex said.

"So I hear tell you have taken up golf again with a certain partner, a very attractive partner."

"Who told you that?" Alex said, feeling her face flush remembering last night.

"Pink Mafia tells all. Grapevine gets around and we know someone who works at the pro shop at the Country Club," Kim teased. "Good for you."

"You know Shelley?" Alex asked.

"Her girlfriend works at the hospital. She says Taylor is absolutely in love with you."

"How does she know that?"

"The look, I guess," Kim said.

"It's a small world," Alex said, quietly.

"What the hell happened to your back?" Gigi said, as Mallory got out of the pool.

"Del pushed me off the couch," Mallory said, winking at Del, who was instantly mortified.

"It was an accident," Del said.

"Accident my ass, more like a pelvic thrust," Mallory said, doing her best to look lascivious.

Both Del and Gigi stood amazed.

"What can I say—I am now a sexual being. Is there a problem with that?" Mallory replied.

Alex and Kim both started to giggle. Gigi scowled.

"What?" Alex said. "It's cute. Obviously, they were making love and Mallory fell."

"You're talking about my best friend here," Gigi replied.

"So? She has every right to be in love," Alex said.

"Yeah, well does she have to flaunt it?" Gigi grumbled.

"Why? Because you don't like how it feels? Be happy for her," Alex said.

"Yes, be really happy for me," Mallory said, pulling Del close.

"It has been a long time coming," Kim said, thinking back to Mallory's pajama-wearing celibacy days. This was definitely an improvement. Mallory had blossomed into a charming, witty, and outgoing young woman with a few eccentricities. But even those were more an illustration of her individuality rather than any crippling behavior left behind by emotional upheaval. Kim was amazed at the incredible power of love to make or break people.

Whatever Mallory's ex-girlfriend had done to Mallory had now been repaired by Del and it was a beautiful sight. She was beginning to see signs of that same repair in herself because of Angel, who came over to sit next to Kim and see what all the commotion was.

Kim winked at her and whispered, "They finally made love," cocking her head toward the two lovebirds.

"What a delicious thought," Angel said, kissing Kim's ear and moving her hand up Kim's stomach and dangerously close to her scantily clad breast. Kim blushed. She thanked the powers that be for putting love in the universe and for removing Ollie from her sight, she hoped for all time.

Gigi went off to check on Lil and Fran, who seemed to be doing quite well with the younger crowd as she discovered. They were telling tall tales to a rapt audience of Gigi's bar fly, pool shooting, women cruising, buddies. Gigi sat and listened for a while and then went on to explore the rest of her party. Everything seemed to be in order so she slipped off for a quick nap. This not getting any sleep at night was really starting to wear on her but suddenly being surrounded by the safety of her friends in loud noisy numbers she felt comforted and sleepy. She knew the party would rage for hours to come.

When Alex went to look for her later she found Gigi fast asleep with a face like an angel. She kissed her forehead softly so as not to wake her and let her be. Moments of peace to a tormented soul were not to be snatched away lightly. Alex sat on the corner of the bed and remembered how she had first come to know this tattered little soul that lay before her. Gigi hadn't been so raggedy then, rather she seemed like a welcome breath of pure oxygen, volatile, electric, and prone to getting one high by her mere presence.

Alex had not been an easy catch. She was still scarred and very leery of women after coming off a long stint with a woman who came home one day after work and told her she was in love with someone else. Alex did all the usual things, cried, screamed, had insomnia, promised to wait, and then finally moved out. She had tried going out on a few dates but found she wasn't the kind of woman who dated. She couldn't stand the countless awkward moments one had to endure before companionship finally arrived.

One day she went to a party and met Gigi—or rather Gigi introduced herself and then spent the rest of the evening making Alex laugh. But when Gigi asked for Alex's phone number she declined, telling Gigi she was done with dating and perhaps they would run into each other again. From that moment forward Gigi managed to show up at every social event Alex attended. Alex accused her of stalking and Gigi replied that she knew every lesbian in town and always asked if a certain attractive, witty, blond accountant would be attending the event.

Actually, when push came to shove Gigi knew a friend of a friend of Alex's. Gigi professed an incredible infatuation that she pleaded Alex make go away by spending some time with her. Alex finally relented, telling Gigi that she wasn't looking for lifelong love but a fling might do. Gigi said she'd take what she could get. They fell comfortably into mutual acquaintance and it worked until Gigi's grandmother died and left her money. She took Alex on her house-hunting journeys, telling her she would blow the money if she didn't buy something big.

Gigi kept asking if Alex liked each house. Alex kept asking why it mattered if she liked the house, it was Gigi's house. "Because I want you to live with me," Gigi told her. At first she refused until Gigi talked her into it, using the ardent factor. Alex eventually agreed and that was how they came to be lovers and roommates. And now it seemed they were a couple, a couple in love. For a while this worked until Gigi grew complacent and then started the casual cruising that slowly killed what could have been a good love affair.

Now looking at her sleeping, Alex felt the weight of their choices. Choices made of noncommittal behaviors. Choices that said you can walk whenever you want. And now Alex knew she was going to take that walk. It wasn't like Gigi had pushed her away but she had always left that open door, the door that allowed Taylor in. It made her sad looking at her lover sleeping and Alex realized this was going to be harder than she had anticipated.

Gigi woke up and smiled, thinking it lovely that Alex was there and gazing down on her.

"What are you doing?" Gigi asked, pulling Alex toward her.

"Watching you sleeping and wondering what you might be dreaming," Alex said, quickly, trying to hide the sudden vulnerability she was feeling.

"I was dreaming of you," Gigi said, pushing Alex on her back and neatly inserting her thigh between Alex's legs.

"Gigi," Alex said, protesting, only to find herself quickly wrapped up in one of those ardent embraces that she had just been remembering.

"We have guests," Alex said.

"And they would more than understand," Gigi said, kissing her way down Alex's stomach.

Alex's last protest got lost as Gigi's tongue licked the inside of her thigh.

Aunt Lil winked at Gigi as they came out of the birthday party.

"Getting a little cheer are we?" Fran said.

Alex smiled. "You know how she is."

"I do," Lil said, giving Gigi a quick cuff.

"The old ladies are going to bail. We've got a drive ahead of us. Happy birthday Gigi, take care," Fran said, giving Gigi a hug.

Aunt Lil gave Gigi a hug and whispered, "Don't worry kid, the folks will come around."

"I doubt that," Gigi said.

"She has hated me for years but I still get a Christmas card," Lil said.

"Oh, something to look forward to," Gigi replied.

"Something is always better than nothing," Fran said.

Alex found Mallory at the buffet table.

"Where's Del?"

"She got paged. One last weekend at the hospital on call as a favor, set a bone and she'll be back. It's a broken ankle."

"What—the inseparables are separated?" Gigi teased, coming up to join them.

"Del had to go fix someone's ankle. She'll be back shortly," Alex said, picking up a plate and looking ravenously at the buffet table. Making love always made her hungry. Gigi winked at her lasciviously while she shoved a carrot in her mouth.

The party was still going strong when two new arrivals slipped in the front door. At first no one noticed as people had been coming and going all evening. Mallory was standing by the buffet table. Gigi and Alex were across the table. They both saw Mallory turn pale and let the plate she was holding slip to the floor. Puzzled, Gigi turned around, not having a clue, until she saw Ollie and another woman. Gigi felt her stomach tighten as she recognized Caroline. She knew they weren't here to wish her happy birthday. Her intuition told her that doomsday was about to become the grand finale of her birthday party.

"Gigi, what's wrong?" Alex said. She'd never met Caroline but the look on both Mallory's and Gigi's faces told of something terrible.

"Oh, shit," Gigi said, moving to try and intercept them, but Ollie guided them through the crowd like a tribunal set on capturing the victim and beginning the torture.

Mallory stood completely still.

"We thought we would come see you on this glorious day of your birth," Ollie said.

"Caroline?" Mallory said, feeling like she should rub her eyes and try looking again.

"Hi, Mallory. How have you been?" Caroline said, gently. She had anticipated this as being a shock for Mallory but maybe more than she bargained for.

"I thought you moved to back to Brazil," Mallory said.

"Actually, Caroline has a little story to tell you," Ollie said.

"I do?" Caroline said, thinking this wasn't part of the plan. Ollie had told her that going to the party would guarantee them entrance. She hadn't mentioned a word about confessing the real reason she had left Mallory.

"Well, let me get it started," Ollie said.

"Let's go talk," Gigi said, grabbing Ollie's arm.

"Yes, let's talk. Let's tell Mallory why Caroline really left her. It didn't have so much to do with you, Mallory, as it had more to do with Gigi."

"Ollie?" Kim said, coming to join the tribunal with Angel right behind her.

"What are you doing here?" Kim said.

"I'm tying up some loose ends," Ollie replied.

"Ollie why don't you just go away. No one is interested in your stories," Kim said. "This is not the time or the place."

"I disagree. This is perfect," Ollie said.

"Ollie, come on, please," Gigi said, trying to pull her away from the table.

Caroline tried to get closer to Mallory, who was backing away in total fright.

"I'm not leaving until everyone knows the truth," Ollie said.

"It's all in the past. Let it be," Kim said.

Alex felt her stomach flip as she waited for the other shoe to drop.

"The reason Caroline left you was because she and Gigi were having an affair. Gigi wouldn't come clean because of you so Caroline left nursing her broken heart. It wasn't you, Mallory, it was her," Ollie said, pointing an accusatory finger at Gigi.

"You and Caroline?" Mallory said, trying to let this new point of view sink in.

"Mallory, let me explain," Gigi pleaded.

"We didn't mean for it to happen," Caroline said.

Mallory looked from one to the other.

"Why didn't you tell me?"

"I didn't want to hurt you," Gigi said.

"Maybe you shouldn't have slept with her then," Ollie offered.

"We've had just about enough of your shit," Kim said, grabbing Ollie's wrist and then doing a karate move that landed Ollie flat on her back.

"You know karate?" Angel asked.

"My father is a black belt," Kim replied.

"I'm not done. And not only did Gigi cheat on Mallory, she also cheated on you, Alex," Ollie said, just before Kim put her foot on Ollie's chest to keep her flat on her back. Kim glared at her.

"But I'm sure Kim already told you about that night in the van when she found us fucking," Ollie said.

Kim moved in to do something hideous but Angel grabbed her around the waist and raised her aloft.

"Put me down. I'm going to kill her," Kim said, struggling to get free.

"I am not going to have a prison romance," Angel said, dragging her from the room.

"Where are you taking me?" Kim said.

"Home, where you won't get charged with assault."

"But she deserves it," Kim screeched.

"I know she does, but I love you too much to spend all my time writing letters to my incarcerated girlfriend."

"Alex, I'm sorry—I should have told you," Kim said as they made their way to the door.

"It's not your fault. Gigi should have come clean about everything," Alex said, trying to get closer to Mallory, who looked like she was starting to hyperventilate.

"Mallory, are you okay?" Alex asked softly.

"I think I need some air," Mallory replied, making a quick move to the arcadia door.

Caroline came toward her. Mallory freaked and before anyone could do anything she had walked right into the glass door and shattered it. Mallory tripped and fell into the pile of glass, cutting her right forearm nearly clean through. For a moment everyone stood still. Mallory sat up and looked at her arm. Alex was the first to think of first aid measures.

"Oh, my god," Gigi said, starting to panic.

"Gigi, you need to help me," Alex said, firmly. "Get a belt and a towel. Right now."

Caroline moved to help.

"*You* need to leave and take your friend with you," Alex said.

Caroline backed away. Between them Gigi and Alex got a tourniquet on Mallory's arm and helped her into the car.

"Mallory?" Gigi started to say something.

Mallory smiled at her sadly. "I don't think there is anything you could say that would even touch this, Gigi."

Gigi nodded. For once in her life she didn't have a single word to cover this. She doubted even Robert's Rules had a funny quip for this. You deceived your best friend for years because you stole the love of her life and then trashed it because you were a coward. She had loved Caroline, more than she had ever thought herself capable of, more than anyone since, including Alex, but she couldn't make herself tell Mallory the truth, so she had told Caroline goodbye. Caroline in desperation had vacated all three of their lives. It had always amazed Gigi how one act of cowardice could have had such huge consequences.

Alex started the car and then realized the congestion problem. Mallory noted it as well.

"I'll get them to move," Gigi said, going inside.

"That won't be necessary," Alex replied, as she whipped the car across the desert rock landscaping, ripping a jojoba bush up with her front grill.

Gigi stood mouth gaping while Alex and Mallory laughed.

"Never liked that bush anyway," Alex said.

"Me either," Mallory said.

"Next stop Desert Samaritan Hospital," Alex said. "You should really put your seatbelt on," reaching over to help Mallory.

"Oh, no not Desert. Del will be there. I don't want to see her like this."

"Mallory, it's the closest hospital," Alex tried to reason.

"I don't care. Drive fast and we can make it to Saint Joseph's."

"Mallory, in case you haven't noticed you're losing blood at an astonishing rate. You've cut one of your major arteries."

"We can make it."

Alex drove like a maniac until they got pulled over. As Alex slowed the car down with the police lights and sirens kicking up a storm behind them, she said, "You're going to bleed to death."

"I am not. When he comes to the window just point at my arm," Mallory advised. It did look ghastly.

Alex did as she was told. The police officer's eyes got huge.

"I'll give you an escort," he said, running for his car.

"See how easy that was. All fixed," Mallory said, leaning back in the seat. She didn't feel so good.

Alex sat in the emergency room making an attempt at filling in the blanks on the admittance paperwork. Mallory had thrown her her wallet just before they carted her off on a gurney. Finally completed, Alex handed the clipboard back to the nurse and went to get a cup of coffee. She was trying to stave off processing what had just happened, how all her worst fears had been brought to light. Part of her knew Gigi played around, but having someone actually say the words made it real, made it something she could no longer bury. Her partner was a cheat. A cheat with a long history of cheating. There was no going around that and as she sat in the ER waiting for the other casualty of Gigi's history of cheating, Alex knew there was no going back, no overlooking, no pretending it wasn't happening.

She stood in front of the coffee machine waiting for the small paper cup to fill. Mallory came around the corner.

"Hi, we can go now," Mallory informed her, looking around furtively.

"Shouldn't we check out?"

"That won't be necessary," Mallory said, leading Alex by the arm, minus her coffee to the stair exit.

"Mallory, why do I get the idea we're sneaking out of the hospital?" Alex asked as they scurried down the stairs.

"Because we are," Mallory said.

"Why?"

"They want to keep me overnight. I'm not staying."

"Do you have a hospital phobia?" Alex asked.

"You could say that. I'm fine. My arm feels great," Mallory said, as they slunk through the cars in the parking lot.

"You don't look great," Alex said, when Mallory winced as she tried to shut the car door.

"Well, I did almost slice my arm off. I think that is to be expected."

"Are you all right . . . you know, about the other stuff?" Alex asked.

"Oh, that little thing about Gigi?" Mallory replied.

"Yes."

"Not really. I'd like to kill her. As it stands now I don't think I'll ever speak to her again," Mallory said stoically. "How about you?"

"I'm going to kill her," Alex replied, pulling out of the hospital parking lot.

Mallory's eyes got big.

"Not really. I haven't given it a lot of thought yet. But I'm sure there will be some heavy thinking going on before I see her again."

"Would you like to borrow some clothes?" Mallory said, diplomatically.

"No, I'll be fine," Alex replied, taking Mallory's outstretched good hand.

"Where will you go? Want to stay at my place?"

"No, you and Del are just starting out. You don't need a third wheel. Besides I've got somewhere to go."

"And someone to see?"

"Yes."

Taylor clicked off the movie when she heard the doorbell. She thought she saw lights pulling up in the drive. Puzzled, she went to the door.

"Hi," Alex said. "I was wondering if I might stay at your place tonight."

Taylor stood staring. Alex was wearing a white T-shirt that was covered in blood.

"You didn't kill her, did you?" Taylor said, envisioning some grisly scene involving a large kitchen instrument.

Alex burst out laughing, kind of laughing and then she started to cry. Suddenly all the stress and emotion of the last few hours came crashing through. Somehow she muttered the whole story to Taylor, who watched sympathetically as Alex spilled her guts. Then she ran her a bath, got her a brandy and a clean outfit. She put her to bed and stayed until she fell asleep.

Taylor got up to leave and Alex woke up.

"Please stay with me," Alex said.

Taylor crawled in next to her and held her until morning, knowing that despite tragedy they would begin their new lives together in the morning.

When Del pulled up in the drive she immediately sensed something was wrong. Perhaps it was the bush torn out of the front yard, or the trail of blood leading up to the front door. She noticed Alex's car was missing but Mallory's truck was still there. She tried to breathe a sigh of relief. The living room floor didn't look much better and the gaping hole in the glass arcadia door seemed to sum up the situation.

Del looked around for Mallory, Kim or Angel but couldn't find anyone she knew. A group of party animals sat around the couch and were laying out shots of Apple Pucker. A pretty young woman was making an attempt at cleaning up the glass out on the patio. She obviously hadn't made it into the house yet. No one else seemed to care. Gigi was nowhere to be found.

"Have you seen Mallory?" Del asked.

"You must be Del," Caroline said, thinking she fit the description Ollie had given her about Mallory's new girlfriend. Caroline had been rather relieved to discover that Mallory was no longer pining after her. It assuaged some of her guilt.

"Who are you?" Del asked, studying the huge hole in the door and the sticky puddle of blood full of glass. Whoever went through the door had been bleeding badly.

"I'm Caroline," the young woman replied.

It took Del a minute to make the connection. "Caroline, the woman Mallory was in love with, that Caroline?"

"Yes, as a matter of fact."

"This mess, you, it was Mallory," Del said, pointing frantically at the door.

"She didn't take it well."

"Seeing you?"

"It's a little more complicated than that."

"What do you mean?"

"Ollie told her about the affair Gigi and I were having while I was with Mallory. And then she told Alex about the affair she and Gigi had been having. It wasn't pretty."

"Where is she? Tell me she didn't bleed to death."

"She'll be fine. Alex made her a tourniquet and took her to the hospital," Caroline said.

Del flew to the door and turned around.

"Stay away from her," Del warned.

"Don't worry, she won't let me near her. I really am sorry."

Her apology fell on deaf ears as Del screeched out of the driveway.

Much to Del's consternation Mallory had not been admitted at Desert Samaritan, which made no sense, considering it was the closest hospital. The admitting clerk called around and found her at Saint Joseph's. Del flew across town, still trying to figure out why Alex had taken her there. The nurse took her to Mallory's room. It was there they discovered the empty hospital bed and a pool of liquid from where the IV was dripping.

"Where is she?" Del asked the nurse.

The nurse checked her chart.

"She's supposed to be right here," the nurse replied.

"Do you normally let your patients walk around after they've ripped their IV's out?" Del asked.

"No, Doctor, we do not. Let me call the main desk and see if she checked herself out. We certainly didn't let her go. She'd lost a lot of blood."

"I know. I saw the site of the accident," Del said, following her back to the nurse's station.

The nurse called downstairs.

"She didn't check herself out. It seems she must have escaped."

"Perfect," Del said, hoping that when she went to Mallory's house she would find her there.

The living room light was on when Del pulled up in the driveway. Del felt her racing heartbeat begin to slow as she now, at least, knew Mallory was safe at home. Perhaps Mallory had left the hospital because she didn't like it rather than the nagging thought Del kept having about Mallory going straight off the deep end. After all, she had come home and not disappeared off the face of the earth.

Del knocked. No one answered. She rang the bell. Still there was no answer. She tried the knob. The door was locked. She heard someone move inside.

"Mallory, it's me. Open the door," Del called out.

She heard footsteps to the door and then a slumping noise as Mallory slid down the door. At this moment, Del knew all her fears had instantly materialized. Mallory had gone over the edge and if she didn't get her back quick she'd be gone forever.

"Mallory, talk to me."

"Del, you need to go away," Mallory said.

"I can't go away. I love you," Del said, feeling an intense pain in her chest like she couldn't breathe. If she weren't a doctor she would have sworn she was having a heart attack, but as an emotional scientist she knew it was her heart breaking at the thought of never seeing Mallory again.

"Love isn't good for people. It makes them do bad things."

"Not our love, Mallory. I would never do anything to hurt you," Del pleaded.

"That's what everyone says and then your best friend sleeps with your lover and everyone hides it. I can't go there, Del. I thought I was strong enough but I'm not. Now go away."

"I'm not leaving. I'm staying here until I convince you that love isn't bad," Del said.

"Suit yourself. But I hear the temperature is supposed to drop rapidly," Mallory replied.

"I don't care. I'm not leaving," Del said firmly. She was trying to keep a grip on the creeping terror that was threatening to engulf her. There was silence.

"Mallory?"

No answer. *Give her time*, Del's inner voice told her.

Mallory was visiting the almost forgotten Republic. It contained the same vistas she had first seen when Caroline left and her world was suddenly turned upside down. It frightened her how desperate and frightened she had been and the apparitions of inadequacy that had tormented her. She wasn't meant for love and she needed to somehow make Del understand that she would never be free of these apparitions, that she couldn't love because she was afraid of losing. So afraid it wasn't worth trying. She started to cry.

Del heard her sobbing on the other side of the door.

"Mallory, let me in. Please."

"Go away."

"I'm calling Dr. Kohlrabi," Del said, digging in her wallet for the card, remembering that the doctor had warned her that there might be a time like this, a time when all the tumultuous emotion of falling in love would prove too much.

She called the emergency number and woke up a sleepy therapist who made her slow down and tell her exactly what had happened.

"This is not good," Dr. Kohlrabi replied, thinking this was bigger and worse than anything she had ever imagined.

"I know. Please save her. I can't bear to live without her."

"Let me talk to her," Dr. Kohlrabi said.

"Mallory, Dr. Kohlrabi wants to talk to you," Del said, hoping this would mean that Mallory would open the door and let her in.

Instead, the door opened a crack with the chain still on it and a hand snatched the phone. Del never saw Mallory.

"Fuck!" Del said, slumping down on the porch to wait.

What ensued was a screaming match between patient and therapist. Then quiet, intense conversation, then tears.

"I'm crazy!"

"You're not crazy. The world is," Dr. Kohlrabi said.

"I can't love Del. She'll hurt me like Gigi and Caroline," Mallory said.

"No, she won't."

"Can you guarantee that?"

"Yes, no one could ever be as duplicitous, selfish, and polysexual as those two."

"How can you know that?"

"Because the universe only has a finite number of evil lesbians in it. You've already experienced your fair share."

"You're not talking sense. You're supposed to be a therapist," Mallory said.

"I am also a woman who would like to be as revered, adored,

chased and loved as you are. You'll be a fool to let her go. Do you hear me?"

"Yes, ma'am."

"Now open the door and let her in before you break her heart," Dr. Kohlrabi instructed, wondering if her direct order would be obeyed.

"I'm taking you to court and suing you for undue mental stress if this doesn't work," Mallory said.

"And if it does?"

"I'll buy you a new car," Mallory replied, remembering the hunk-of-shit old car the doctor drove.

Mallory opened the door. The look of fear and despair on Del's face pierced straight through Mallory. She was certain it was the same look she had on her face when Caroline had left. Mallory took Del up in her arms and they both started to cry.

"I love you. I'm so sorry," Mallory said.

Alex left Taylor a note. She knew it was a horrible thing to do but she wanted to get clothes and tell Gigi to go fuck herself. They would meet for golf and talk on the golf course like they'd done a thousand times before. She crept from the house and made her way across town. It was still early and the city was unbearably quiet. For once Alex missed the noise of early morning traffic. She needed a distraction and there wasn't one to be found.

As she pulled up in the drive of the house she no longer lived in she saw a few straggler cars. The diehards had spent the night, like they'd done at many a party before and Alex thought she wasn't going to miss getting up in the morning to find uninvited guests passed out in her house surrounded by the party mess of liquor bottles and pizza cartons. She tip-toed over a woman in a leather jacket passed out on the living room rug and made her way to the bedroom. Gigi was nowhere to be found. Someone was in the kitchen making coffee.

Caroline smiled at her.

"I thought I told you to leave last night," Alex said briskly.

202

"I didn't have to, seeing as you did. Want some coffee?"

"No, thank you. Where is she?"

"Out on the couch by the canal . . . drunk."

"Oh, good. Well, tell her to fuck off for me. You can be my emissary," Alex said, making her way to the bedroom.

Caroline followed. "You're leaving her?"

"Shouldn't I? I can't think of a reason to stay, considering our entire relationship was one huge lie," Alex said, barely controlling the urge to slap this impertinent woman sitting on her bed in her house playing twenty questions as she packed.

"It's not as bad as it looks," Caroline tried to explain.

"Spare me. Now if you don't mind I'd like some time alone," Alex said, shoving clothes into a duffel bag.

When she was finished packing she took a last look around and left, half angry, half sad and drove to Mallory's.

Del answered the door. She looked tired and strung out.

"You look like shit," Alex said.

Del ran her hands through her tangled curly hair.

"I didn't get a lot of sleep last night."

"But you did get in the door," Alex said.

"Did she talk to you?" Del asked, getting them both some coffee.

"Not really, but I had a feeling that she would freak," Alex said, taking the coffee and sitting on the couch. She didn't feel so great herself.

"Well, Dr. K persuaded her to at least see me and then we patched things up from there. So far so good but I'm worried," Del said, rubbing her temples. She had a monster stress headache and if she didn't eat something soon she was going to puke up all the coffee she was drinking.

"Caroline is still at Gigi's," Alex said flatly.

They looked at each other trying to figure out what that meant.

"Are you okay?" Del asked.

"No, I'm angry. I don't get all this. Right now I hate them all, Gigi for lying, Ollie for telling everyone and Caroline for showing up."

"I am in total agreement. I was so close to convincing Mallory that this love affair would work and now I'm not so sure that she will ever trust anyone again," Del said.

"Where is she?"

"Sleeping."

"Is she okay?" Alex asked.

"Yeah, I couldn't get her to go back to the hospital so I brought the hospital here. I have her on a drip. She lost a lot of blood and experienced some shock," Del said, remembering rubbing Mallory's back as she puked and pleading with her to go back to the hospital.

"I tried to get her to go to Good Sam's but she wouldn't let me."

"I know. You probably saved her life."

"It was the least I could do seeing as it was my conniving, evil girlfriend who created all this mess."

"What are you going to do?" Del asked gently.

"I got my stuff, thank God I'm not a pack rat, and I need to find a place to live. Taylor wants me to live with her but I can't do that, not yet. I need some time."

"Are you two involved?"

"Not yet. In love yes, having sex no."

"Why don't you take Del's place?" Mallory said, standing in the doorway holding her IV. She looked like the walking wounded.

"And where would Del live?" Alex asked, knowing the answer.

"With me, silly, if it's all right with Del. We should probably do that anyway. I think we've had enough courtship. It's time for the other things," Mallory said, dragging herself over to the arm of the couch and stroking Del's head.

"Really?" Del said, feeling her heartbeat quicken.

"It's time. I don't want to spend another night without you," Mallory said. "Besides you'd be helping Alex out. However, Alex, I must warn you Del's apartment adheres strictly to the idea of minimalism."

"Like I'm any different," Alex said, thinking she had packed her stuff in a matter of a half an hour.

"What is it with you two?" Mallory teased.

"We're just waiting for that right woman to come along and decorate our lives," Alex said.

"Come on, I'll get you set up, and then I'll be back to cook you breakfast," Del said, hopping up.

"Are you in a hurry?" Mallory teased.

"I don't want you to change your mind," Del said.

"I heard what you said. That you're worried I won't trust you. But I do trust you. Actually, there are a lot of people I can trust. I just can't trust Gigi. I love you and I want to be your partner. Simple. So you need to stop worrying," Mallory said, pointing her finger at Del, who sucked on it slowly.

"I know what you two will be doing this afternoon."

"Yes, now get going. I need a bath. What do I do with this thing?" Mallory said, holding up her bandaged arm.

"Stick it in a trash bag and keep it out of the water," Del advised.

As Del and Alex left the house, Mallory started her bath and then got on the Internet. She ordered Dr. Kolhrabi a two-door Saturn Coupe in bright red to be delivered by the end of the week. She smiled. Alex may have saved her life but Dr. K had saved her heart.

Ten

Taylor sat at the Country Club waiting for Alex to arrive. She was puzzled by Alex's sudden departure and wondering what the future would hold for them. She felt less than certain. She hoped Gigi hadn't talked Alex into returning, because Taylor was no longer in control of her emotions and being so close to Alex and yet not able to touch her was definitely starting to mess up her brain. It reminded her of other times when she thought love was perfect only to have it fail. She did not want another failure.

"Hi," Alex said, coming to sit next to Taylor on the hood of her car. They watched the golfers on the driving range.

"Good morning," Taylor said, looking at Alex, trying to find something in her face to give her a clue.

"Sorry about bailing and leaving the note. I just had some things to take care of," Alex said.

"Are they taken care of?" Taylor said, trying to keep any emotion out of her voice.

"Yes, they are. I got my stuff. I found a place to live and it's over."

"You can live with me."

"I know. It's not that I don't want to. I just think it would be better if I didn't . . . not yet at least."

"I love you."

"I know you do. I need you to be patient," Alex said.

"I'll try."

"That's all I ask. Don't give up on me," Alex said, taking her hand.

"I won't. Let's go shoot a few holes," Taylor said.

Taylor smiled, but Alex read disappointment in her face.

"I won't let you down."

"I know," Taylor said.

Angel woke up to Kim holding a cup of tea and a plate of oranges. Her mind briefly recalled the night before.

"You're not mad at me are you?" Angel said, sitting up in bed.

"Because you saved me from a prison sentence," Kim teased.

"Well, yes."

"Actually, now that I am of sound mind and judgment, no."

"It would have been a horrible waste and I'm not a very good letter writer," Angel said, taking a sip of tea.

"Neither am I so it's probably for the best," Kim said, sticking an orange slice in her mouth and then moving toward Angel.

Angel took the other half out of her mouth and felt their lips touch.

Kim took the cup of tea and set it on the nightstand. She pushed Angel back on the bed, lowering her body down on her.

"I was dreaming about you," Kim said, lifting Angel's T-shirt and caressing her breasts.

Angel let out a soft moan. "Was it good?" she asked, pulling Kim's shirt off.

"Very good."

Kim kissed her stomach and then moved lower. taking Angel in her mouth, lifting Angel's legs on her shoulders, her tongue gliding softly between the folds, watching her lover's face. Angel put her hand behind Kim's head and pulled her in tighter.

"I love you," Angel said, feeling the shower of love wash her body clean of the past, her mind ready for the future, aching for the moment of release as Kim entered her.

As they lay quiet together, Angel said, "You know, I was proud of you last night."

"Why?" Kim asked, running her finger around Angel's soft brown nipple.

"Because you stood up for yourself. Ollie didn't intimidate you anymore."

"I think what really happened was that I was so damn mad at her I forgot to be scared. Suddenly, she didn't have that same hold on me. I finally saw her for what she is—a pathetic woman who only knows how to hurt people. It's sad that someone can be that damaging to everyone around her," Kim replied.

"This much is true," Angel said, running her hand up Kim's thigh.

Caroline finally succeeded in ousting the last of the party guests and had sufficiently rendered order to the house. She knew she was staving off the inevitable. Gigi was still on the couch out back by the canal. Caroline knew she had to talk to her, that's why she had remained, but she dreaded it because Gigi was going to be full of nothing but animosity. She knew how difficult it would be to make Gigi understand that what she had done wasn't what she had intended, that was Ollie's doing and she should have had enough foresight to see it coming. Caroline had been desperate to repair a past that was haunting any chance of having a future. She poured two cups of coffee and went out back.

Gigi sat with a bottle of Jack Daniel's between her legs, fishing with a children's plastic play reel.

"Mallory and I used to do this all the time. I guess you put an end to that."

"I didn't mean for that to happen," Caroline said, offering the cup of coffee. Gigi waved it away.

"For Mallory to lacerate herself, for Alex to pack up and move away, for me to lose my best friend and my lover in one evening. What did you intend to do? Bring a *'welcome to the neighborhood basket, I'm back now, doesn't everyone still love me'* card attached to your lapel. What the fuck," Gigi said, standing up and whipping the fishing pole into the canal.

"Gigi . . ."

"Go way. What are you still doing here anyway?"

"Waiting for you," Caroline said.

"We're over. We were over before we even got started. We should have never started," Gigi said, climbing down the bank of the canal.

"Where are you going?" Caroline asked.

"Away from you, as far away from you as water, mud and garbage will take me," Gigi said, starting to wade upstream.

The police officer led Gigi from her cell into the custody of Aunt Lil.

"Couldn't you have cleaned her up a bit?" Lil asked the police officer, as she held a tissue to her nose.

"She wouldn't let us. She's lucky we didn't throw her in detox except that she kept pleading for us to do so. The ones that beg aren't good candidates. Besides she never got the DT's so we figured she wasn't in need."

"No, she's not. What's she in for?"

"Trespassing and disorderly conduct. Pay the fine and she's free to go," the officer said.

Lil paid the fine.

"I'm taking it out of your allowance," Aunt Lil said.

"You stink," Fran said.

"I'm having a nervous breakdown. Do you think you could cut me some slack," Gigi said.

"What happened?" Aunt Lil asked.

"Take me to breakfast and I'll tell you," Gigi said.

"Do you have a trash bag we could have?" Fran asked.

"Sure," the officer said.

"I'm not letting you ruin the upholstery in the car," Fran said.

"We have rules," Aunt Lil teased.

"Yeah, yeah, thanks for coming to get me," Gigi mumbled.

They rolled the windows down and got Gigi some breakfast.

When they dropped Gigi off, Aunt Lil asked, "Do you have a better grip on things or do you want us to stay?"

"I'm fine."

"Are you sure?" Fran asked.

"Yes. I just had to get it out of my system. Now I don't give a fuck," Gigi said, getting out of the car.

"Call me if you feel like you're going to have a relapse, understood?" Lil said.

"Yes, ma'am," Gigi said.

Gigi went in the house and stripped off all her clothes, leaving them in a pile by the front door. She sat on the couch, sipped her coffee and munched on her breakfast burrito.

Caroline came in. "You're naked."

"Have you smelled my apparel lately?" Gigi said, pointing to the pile of discarded filthy clothes.

"Obviously not," Caroline said.

"What are you still doing here?" Gigi said, spreading ketchup on her hash browns.

"I was waiting for you," Caroline said, sitting down in the easy chair.

"Why?"

"I want to talk."

"I don't see any purpose in that. You accomplished what you set out to do."

"Which is?"

"Punishing me and everyone I loved for my one act of cowardice.

Now go. I don't want to see you anymore. I never wanted to see you."

"That wasn't what I set out to do," Caroline replied.

"Sure," Gigi said, finishing her breakfast.

"I came to tell you I love you," Caroline said, looking at Gigi's naked body and remembering happier times.

"Gee, that's a handy thing. Perhaps you should have thought of that before you ran off, devastated Mallory and made it virtually impossible for me to find you. You're a little late to be saying that you love me. In fact, you're fucking pathetic. Now if you don't mind I'm going to take a shower and then nap, seeing as I just spent the night in jail," Gigi said, getting up.

Caroline sat and listened to the shower running. She got up and collected Gigi's clothes and threw them in the trash. She wasn't going anywhere until she talked to Gigi and told her the story of the last few years—how she had roamed the earth, tried to find love only to disappoint herself and several innocent women. She had come to realize that until she reconciled the past she could not know a future. She would wait.

Taylor sat across the dining room table from her father, looking glum. She played with her pearl onions and peas and hadn't touched her stuffed pork chop.

"What's wrong?"

"What makes you think anything is wrong?" Taylor said, avoiding his gaze, knowing he was practically reading her mind.

"Because you seem preoccupied and you haven't talked about Alex in several days, which makes me think that something extremely important is happening and as your dear old dad that makes me nervous."

"Well, since there appears no way to avoid your studious psychological intuitions I suppose I will have to tell you," Taylor replied.

"Only if you want to."

"You are a smooth one," Taylor teased.

"So tell and I won't have to stay up nights worrying about you."

"Alex broke up with Gigi after a horrendous night in which various episodes of infidelities were revealed and she moved out."

That's good. Isn't it?"

"The problem is I wanted her to move in with me and instead she moved into a friend's place."

"Taylor, I don't think that is necessarily a bad thing. In fact, it is probably for the best. Alex shouldn't be expected to jump into another relationship having just left one."

"Somehow, I knew you would say that. I love her and I think she loves me so why can't we start. I've been waiting patiently," Taylor replied.

"From the sounds of it you're going to have to continue to be patient if you want this to work. Anything worthwhile is worth waiting for," her father said, looking sagely over the top of his spectacles.

Taylor sighed heavily, "I know."

"Now eat your dinner. We've got to keep your stamina up."

"For what?"

"The love thing."

"Oh, that," Taylor said, smiling.

Del rolled over in bed and stroked the side of Mallory's cheek. Mallory nestled in closer, placing her head on Del's chest and listening to her heartbeat, thinking how exquisitely wonderful life can be. In the early morning their bodies glowed with sweat and were flushed with lovemaking.

"Are you happy?" Mallory asked.

"Right this minute or overall?" Del said.

Mallory slowly moved her hand down Del's leg and pinched her inner thigh.

"Ouch!"

"I suggest you answer the question properly," Mallory advised.

"Your behavior is truly indicative of a Catholic school upbringing," Del teased, remembering their late night talk about childhood and how it had made her feel even closer to Mallory knowing that these secrets were not freely shared with many others.

"Blame it on the nuns," Mallory replied.

Del took Mallory's face in her hands and looked deep in her eyes, seeing her own reflection within them.

"I am happy. You make me happy and there is no other place on the planet I'd rather be."

"What a charming woman you are," Mallory said.

"Let me show you how charming I can be," Del said, rolling Mallory on her back.

Mallory smiled and looked at the clock.

"All right but I've got to meet Dr. Kohlrabi in an hour," Mallory said.

Mallory left Del in the shower still panting from her efforts and raced across town to barely make her therapy appointment. The receptionist didn't stop typing when she came in. She nodded her head toward the door of Dr. Kohlrabi's office indicating that Mallory could go in. Mallory followed her cue and entered the office.

"You look a little rushed this morning," Dr. Kohlrabi said, looking up from her notes.

"I got up late," Mallory said, averting her eyes and wondering if she looked like she had been making love twenty minutes earlier.

"How is Del?"

"She's fine, lovely in fact."

"And the two of you are living together? How is that working out?" Dr. Kohlrabi inquired.

"Better than I ever imagined."

"And that is why I have a brand-new car in the parking garage?"

"Yes, it is. I always keep my promises."

"Mallory, you can't give me a car," Dr. Kohlrabi said.

"Sure I can. Today is my last day of therapy and because you have so diligently stuck by me and essentially brought myself to me, you will have saved me thousands of dollars in additional therapy; thus I consider this an investment in my future," Mallory said.

"Mallory . . ."

"Besides, I can't take it back and I already have a car," Mallory said, taking a hard look around the office, thinking that she had spent a lot of time here.

"You're sure about this?" Dr. Kohlrabi said.

"Yes, I want to be on my own. I don't want to always be analyzing and fretting about my life. I'd like to just live it now. I can't do that and therapy. It has to be one or the other."

"I don't want you to consider it a failure if you want to return, and you are welcome to return . . . without charge," Dr. Kohlrabi said, her eyes getting moist.

"I do have a favor to ask," Mallory said, getting up.

"Yes," Dr. Kolrabi replied.

"I'd like to refer a friend," Mallory said.

"All right," Dr. Kohlrabi said, digging out a business card and handing it to Mallory. "Who is it?"

"You'll find out soon enough."

Dr. Kohlrabi laughed. "You always were such an enigma."

"Now if it will not violate your professional protocol I would like a hug," Mallory said.

"Of course," Dr. Kohlrabi said, getting up from behind her desk.

"You're short," Mallory said, taking a good look at the doctor.

"Yes, five foot one to be precise. You've never noticed," Dr. Kohlrabi said, giving Mallory a hug.

"No, your psychological demeanor belies your stature."

"I will miss your stunning vocabulary. Now you better go before I get mushy and you discover that not only am I short but also embarrassingly emotional."

"Thank you . . . for everything," Mallory said.

Dr. Kohlrabi nodded and pushed her red spectacles back up her nose.

When Mallory got to the car she pulled an envelope out of the glove box and scribbled the address. She drove directly to the post office and placed it in the blue collection box, knowing that if she didn't do it now she would lose her nerve.

Kim was reading the latest cartoon script while Angel showered. At first it was odd seeing a rendition of yourself in the weekly paper, but Angel was always adamant about having her check the script first to see if it met her approval. Kim thought this was cute and considerate. It seemed foreign to her to have a lover who was kind and loving, yet sexual and passionate. She knew it was a sick and twisted statement about her life albeit true. Being with Angel was the first correct step in what she discerned as the beginning of her life as it should be, not as it had been. Life now had the possibility of being a beautiful experience. She sat glowing with this knowledge, feeling it grow inside her filling up all those empty spaces until she was suddenly full, like the cartoon characters Angel sketched and then inked in to give them complete dimension.

Then she saw the brochures for houses sitting on the desk. She picked up a brochure and looked at the houses circled for perusal. Kim thumbed through the pages trying to figure out exactly what was going on and whether it was Angel that was thinking about moving or one of her many friends.

Angel walked into the room with a towel wrapped around her waist. She peered over Kim's shoulder.

"What are you looking at?" Angel asked.

"Right now, I'm looking at you," Kim said, tracing a line down Angel's flat stomach with her fingertip, which made both of them quiver.

"Do you like what you see?" Angel teased.

"Would it offend you completely if I told you I am in a state of total lust when it comes to your body?" Kim said.

"Well, it is sort of non politically correct, but I think I can get past it."

"Are you serious?"

"Not really. It is what it is and I'm glad you like it. Now pick a house and move in with me," Angel said, before she could stop herself. She didn't want to stop herself but fear and decorum ruled her inner hemisphere with only an occasional foreign body getting through. Moving in with Kim was one such body.

"What?" Kim asked.

"I want to get married and move to suburbia."

"You don't really mean that," Kim asked, getting alarmed. This was more than she had planned on for this evening. They were supposed to be going out to dinner and then to see a movie. Kim wasn't prepared to decide the fate of their future.

"I've been thinking about it for a while now. I know you already have a house but . . . I want to start fresh, to slough off our old selves."

"Do you have your period?" Kim asked.

"No. Why?"

"Because your behavior is erratic, which could definitely be hormonal."

"Meaning?"

"You're not usually this spontaneous. Normally you plan, ponder, discuss and then decide. It's very methodical."

"That sounds boring," Angel said, moving closer to Kim, who sat perched on the stool. She'd show her spontaneous, Angel thought as she took Kim's leg and wrapped it and then the other around her waist.

Kim raised an eyebrow. "It's not boring. In fact, it's a very admirable trait," she said, as she put her arms around Angel's neck and softly kissed her. The fluttering butterfly wings of desire that lived in her lower abdomen and upper thighs began to quiver and take flight.

"I want to live together, in our own house," Angel said, lifting Kim from the stool and carrying her to the bed. Her towel dropped from her waist of its own accord as if agreeing with her decision.

Angel laid her on the bed and inserted herself between her

thighs, lowering herself down onto Kim, their two bodies coming together like missing puzzle pieces. As Kim felt Angel taking her she recognized the difference. Before when they made love Kim had always initiated it. Not that it was a bad thing. Angel was a kind and generous lover, but now as she watched Angel's body rise and fall against her own like waves rolling up onto the shore, their journey brought to fruition only to begin again, Kim knew their separateness had disappeared. Angel exhaled and her body shuddered. Kim ran her fingertip along the vein on Angel's forehead that only showed itself in times of intensity, passion, anger, and physical exhilaration.

"I would love to live with you," Kim said.

"You mean it?" Angel said, hoping this was not the postcoital voice of utter submission.

"Yes, but I have one request."

"Anything."

"I want you to teach me to play soccer."

"Really?" Angel said, bewildered that anyone else other than she and her soccer buddies ever thought of the game.

"I know it's difficult but I'd still like to learn," Kim said.

"You got it. Now can we look at house brochures?" Angel said, leaping off the bed and making for her stack of real estate advertisements.

"Sure, and then can we get something to eat?"

"You'll make a fine soccer player, a good appetite is a prerequisite," Angel said, lying on her stomach, her new life spread before her on the glossy pages of a real estate monthly.

Caroline waited outside Mallory's house until she saw Del get in her car and pull out of the drive. She felt like a police officer on a stakeout. Right now her whole life felt like a mystery chase involving her younger self and tracking her earlier indiscretions. She had failed to bring Gigi around but she wasn't giving up.

Someday she would make Gigi understand that she was the love of her life and they should be together. Caroline knew how psychotic this sounded but she had traveled halfway around the world only to discover that the woman she left behind was the only one she needed to fill the seeping void of loneliness that kept spreading across the landscape of her soul creating a dangerous bog that allowed no foot travel. She did not want her emotions to become preserved yet buried in those marshy waters.

She needed to repair the damage of five years ago, and most of it had to do with Mallory. If she could make amends for that, her chances of getting Gigi back were increased tenfold. She took a deep breath and prepared to go into the confessional booth.

Mallory opened the door and Caroline saw the look of complete terror on her face.

"What are you doing here?" Mallory asked.

"I want to explain."

"I see no reason for that. Now you need to leave."

"Maybe not for you, but for me it is one of the primary reasons for coming home," Caroline said, wondering if she would ever get past the threshold.

"I thought Brazil was home," Mallory said, savagely.

"You know what I mean."

"I don't know anything about you, obviously, or I never would have trusted you with something as delicate and vulnerable as my heart."

"Mallory, we can talk or I am going to camp on your doorstep until you let me in. It's your choice," Caroline said, firmly.

"You have exactly five minutes," Mallory said, thinking she did not want Caroline on the doorstep when Del returned.

"Thank you. How's your arm?" Caroline asked, noticing her gauze-wrapped forearm.

"Healing nicely. It'll be one hell of a scar," Mallory replied, thinking it was the battle wound she'd never had when Caroline left. Now she had it forever marked on her body, a testimony to the morning she woke up to find Caroline packed and leaving.

218

"You could have died," Caroline said, her eyelid quivering.

Mallory remembered that quiver. It occurred whenever she felt strongly about something. Mallory had once thought it an endearing personal mannerism. Now it brought back only a rush of painful memories.

"It wouldn't have been the first time," Mallory said.

"That's what I want to talk to you about."

"And what will you say that would make it better, that would make it go away, that would heal the jagged, gaping hole in my heart. What could that possibly be?"

"I'm sorry."

"Somehow that seems like you're offering me a quarter when you owe me ten grand. That doesn't cut it. I want you to tell me how, why, when and where. You tell me every torrid detail and I'll consider letting you walk out of here alive," Mallory said.

"To what purpose?" Caroline asked.

"So that I can stop imagining what happened and start knowing. You may want closure but I need closure."

"All right. I will tell you everything," Caroline said, thinking this must be the final ring of purgatory. If she could confess then maybe she could free herself as well as Mallory.

"Completely uncensored," Mallory said.

"As uncensored as memory allows," Caroline said.

"I'll make tea."

"Please," Caroline said, glad for the distraction. It was hard looking at Mallory, remembering the woman she had fallen in love with and then left so abruptly.

Caroline waited for tea and then took a perfunctory sip before she began.

Del saw the car in the drive. It wasn't one she recognized. She tried not to panic. Anything new or different in their lives was still cause for panic. She tried to take three deep breaths as Mallory in her Buddhist-gone-therapy mode always advised. Mallory hadn't mentioned anyone coming over and she didn't usually have anyone over. Home was a sacred place. She walked past the large picture window and something caught her eye. She looked in to see Mallory and Caroline wrapped in an embrace. She stopped. Caroline wiped the tears on Mallory's face and then kissed her forehead. She said something and Mallory nodded. It took everything Del had not to burst in the house and demand an explanation.

Caroline came out as Del walked in. Del stared at her.

"Hi," Caroline said. "I was just leaving."

"You better be," Del snarled.

"Are you all right?" Del asked, feeling panic take complete hold.

"I'm fine," Mallory said, trying to get control.

Del held her.

"You're trembling," Del said. "I'm going to kill her."

"Del, wait. Don't please. I need you right now," Mallory said, pulling her tighter.

Del kissed her. "I love you and I can't bear to let anyone hurt you."

"She only hurt me by telling me the truth I needed to hear," Mallory said.

Mallory kissed her softly. Del kissed her back harder. Before Caroline was down the street they were both on the floor making ardent love as if making love would make them both clean again.

"Wow," Mallory said, as Del lay on her stomach. "Maybe we should invite Caroline over more often."

"You're mine," Del said with the frightening look of intense love, of love that if it went wrong would totally undo her.

Mallory knew that look. She had had it once herself.

"I am yours utterly and completely," Mallory murmured, wondering if Caroline had seen that look and if it had scared her.

Mallory knew there had been things about her that frightened Caroline. Caroline had told her so, saying that when they first met she had been extremely intimidated by Mallory and had grown more so as time went on. Mallory never thought of herself as intimidating but Caroline had said that she was an overachiever, finishing college in three years, starting her own business, always so certain of her place in life, never questioning her direction. It was funny. Mallory never thought of herself that way. Sometimes she wondered how two people could hope to communicate when impressions and illusions covered their relationship like a stack of overlays that changed the image over and over again until its original form was no longer visible.

She pulled Del closer and prayed for some kind of miracle that would keep them from the tactics of delusion that love created. Perhaps love needed a patron like Saint Christopher to keep it safe from the harms of shadows and dreams.

"What are you thinking?" Del asked, suddenly fearful of the silence.

"That I want us always to be as fresh and truthful as we are this very moment, that time won't distort our vision or stain our love, taking what is clear and making it cloudy."

"Tall order," Del said, stroking Mallory's cheek and gazing into her eyes.

"Can we try?" Mallory said.

"Of course," Del said, with her usual commonsense confidence.

"I'm going to hold you to that," Mallory said.

"Think of who you're talking to, I'm just a simple Midwestern girl without a duplicitous bone in her body. I'm not even certain I know how to lie," Del said.

"Del . . ."

"All right, I might understand the basics of deceit but I do not practice any of them."

"It's a strange thing but I believe you. In a basically evil world, I think of you as one of the good entities."

"I won't let you down."

Chapter Eleven

Dr. Kohlrabi waited for her next patient. When her secretary had told her who it was she had had instant reservations. She could have backed out and referred her to someone else but she knew this particular client would not seek help from another therapist. She was coming to see her because Mallory had told her to do so. Dr. Kohlrabi felt like Mallory was passing on her legacy of insanity by having Gigi come here today.

A small woman entered her office. Dr. Kohlrabi was surprised, not that she expected Gigi to be a giant but definitely more formidable. She had a large bruise on the side of her face.

"What happened to your face?" Dr. Kohlrabi asked.

"Someone threw a shoe at me," Gigi replied.

"Someone?"

"Shall I tell you the story?" Gigi asked.

"If you like."

"Isn't that what therapy is about, telling stories?" Gigi said.

"True stories," Dr. Kohlrabi amended.

"May I?" Gigi asked, pointing to the couch.

"Certainly."

Gigi flounced down on the couch, closed her eyes, and said, "Would you mind if I pretended you were Freud?"

"Why?"

"Because he would have had a heyday with my mother."

"I don't think fantasies are a good idea at this point," Dr. Kohlrabi warned.

"This isn't going to be fun."

"I'm afraid not. Tell me more about what happened to your face."

"Oh, all right. I was standing on the canal late one night listening to the part of a song that I had taped on my headphones. The refrain of the song is 'I don't know the answer.' I thought I should try scream therapy, so I screamed 'I don't know the answer' about a hundred times until someone threw the shoe."

"Why did you choose that part of the song?"

"Because that's how I feel. I don't know the answer to anything."

"I see."

"Do you?" Gigi said, sitting up.

"Well, I don't think it was very nice to throw the shoe at you," Dr. Kohlrabi said, lifting Gigi's cheek toward the light.

Gigi flinched involuntarily and pulled away.

Her response gave Dr. Kohlrabi her first clue. Gigi's mother was not a physically affectionate parent. Smart alecks like Gigi were usually the result. They grew up tough in order to survive the abuse of being treated in a less than ideal manner.

"Tell me what else is going on," Dr. Kohlrabi said, taking a seat in the wingback chair. She'd decided to change her locale ever since Mallory had been surprised by her height, having never seen her without the protective front of her large cherrywood desk. At first it seemed odd but she was getting used to it, practicing her new location with her new or relatively new clients. She didn't want to upset her long-term patients with a change in routine, nor did she want to explain her reason for changing.

"Caroline, who I'm sure you've heard about, is living or rather squatting at my place. She won't go away."

"Have you considered calling the police?" Dr. Kohlrabi suggested.

"Yes. However, as an anarchist it would be totally against my political and philosophical ideals and secondly, I did ruin her life."

"She hasn't exactly done wonders for yours."

"No, but I deserved it."

"Because?" Dr. Kohlrabi prompted.

"I am a coward."

"You also appear to be a masochist."

"With sadistic undertones. Maybe I'm bipolar," Gigi said, momentarily weighing the possibilities.

"I think we'll need a few more sessions before we draw any such conclusions."

"If you say so," Gigi said, admiring the ethnic artifacts that covered the walls in the office.

"What is it with you shrinks and your interest in the primitive? Dr. Freud had all this same kind of shit in his office."

"Perhaps we are fascinated with the primitive because it is basic and we must always start at the beginning and work from there. Now why don't you tell me about falling in love with Caroline?" Dr. Kohlrabi said, redirecting her client.

"Shouldn't we start with my mother and move through my fucked-up childhood?" Gigi suggested.

"We will get to your mother. Trust me."

"All right. Falling in love with Caroline was the most frightening, intense, passionate, surreal, painful experience of my entire life. At one point I thought I could only live and die in her presence. And then I came to my senses and realized that she was Mallory's girl-friend and it needed to stop."

"Was this before or after you slept with her?"

"You know a lot already."

"It is one of the pitfalls of having a mutual therapist."

"Mallory won't speak to me."

"When did you try to talk to her?"

"I haven't," Gigi replied.

"Then how do you know she won't talk to you?" Dr. Kohlrabi inquired.

"Would you talk to me after what I've done? I'm probably fortunate that Mallory is a pacifist or I would really be watching my back."

"I don't think you can decide that Mallory won't talk to you because you decided you wouldn't talk to you. Did it ever occur to you that how you felt about Caroline might have been heightened in some way because you knew it was taboo, or perhaps by sleeping with Caroline you were really acting out your true desires for Mallory?"

"I think you're way off base there, like you slipped into Freud hyper-drive," Gigi replied.

"I don't think so."

"Look, I slept with Caroline because she seduced me and she's really hot and quite talented in bed. End of story."

"Is the same true of Ollie?"

"You know about that too?"

"Consider it therapeutic shorthand."

"Well, sure. It was pretty much the same with Ollie."

"Why do you do that?" Dr. Kohlrabi asked.

"Because I'm horny."

Dr. Kohlrabi raised an eyebrow.

"I do it because I suffer from low self-esteem and having someone desire me, even if it's illicit, or maybe because it is so, I succumb to the moment," Gigi replied.

"That was very good."

"So this is therapy?"

"Yes."

"You saved Mallory. Can you save me?"

"Mallory saved herself."

"Surely one or two of your suggestions helped. You get paid for doing something."

"I guide."

"Guide me then."

"As you wish."

Taylor was sitting on the edge of her desk going over the final details on an account. It was almost six and her neck and shoulders felt the torment of being tied to a desk for nine hours. She could hear Alex in the next office over clicking away at her computer and she wondered at her fortitude. Fortitude was a desirable quality in a partner, Taylor told herself. They still weren't lovers, although Alex had tried to seduce her on more than one occasion. Taylor was holding out. In this Alex was amazed by her fortitude. They had sessions of teenage heavy petting, foreplay with no resolution.

The clicking on the computer stopped and Alex came into the office. She sat on the edge of the desk next to Taylor.

"Almost done?" Alex asked, taking a loose tendril of Taylor's hair and tucking it behind her ear.

Taylor smiled at the gesture of sweetness. Alex was full of them. Small acts of kindness that spoke of intense love.

"I love when you do that," Taylor said, kissing Alex softly.

The phone rang. Alex got up to answer it.

"Don't go," Taylor said. "Work is done for today." She pulled Alex in between her thighs and held her.

"I guess you're right. I don't think your father is going to be as happy with my performance now that I hang around with you. I get less work done," Alex said.

"You've worked too hard and too long already. I think a little slacking is in order," Taylor counseled.

"If you say so," Alex said, nestling her face in Taylor's neck.

"I am the boss's daughter," Taylor replied.

"The boss's very attractive daughter," Alex said, kissing her ardently and then wrapping Taylor's legs around her waist.

"Where are you taking me?" Taylor asked.

"Just over here," Alex said, kicking the office door shut on their way to the couch.

"To do what?" Taylor asked.

"Do you remember that thing we did the other night?"

"What thing?" Taylor teased.

"In the kitchen, the thing your first girlfriend taught you to do."

"Oh, that," Taylor said, remembering kissing Alex in the kitchen and then proposing something more.

Alex had teased her about how wet Taylor made her and trying once again to end the moratorium on not making love until Alex moved in. Taylor said she wanted proof. Alex put her hand in her shorts and came up with the goods. She stuck her finger in Taylor's mouth. Taylor sighed heavily as she sucked on Alex's finger. Then she suggested an old trick. She took Alex's hand and put it back between her legs, her hand on top of Alex's guiding it inside Alex, then she pressed herself on top of both their hands, gently pushing against Alex with her hips. They kissed with open eyes, watching the other's face, feeling each other, and ultimately making them both come. Alex closed her eyes, and pulled Taylor close.

"Did you?" Alex asked.

"Uh huh," Taylor said, still shaking.

"I think that constitutes making love," Alex said.

"No it doesn't. We still have our clothes on so technically it's more like dry humping."

"I like it anyway."

"That was just a teaser."

"When do I get more?" Alex said.

"You know when."

Alex eased her back on the couch and inserted herself between her thighs.

"I think I need more teasing, in fact I've been thinking about you all day," Alex said.

"You have," Taylor said, pulling her closer and kissing her.

"What do you say?"

"I say you should just move in with me so we can end all this torment," Taylor replied, as Alex took her hand and placed it between her legs.

"Persuade me," Alex said.

The office door opened and Taylor's father walked in to find his daughter and his head accountant tangled in a compromising position.

"What do we have here?" he said, his eyes twinkling.

"Dad, what are you doing here?" Taylor said, trying to straighten herself up.

Alex sat up and blushed profusely, muttering "It's not what it looks like."

"I'd say it looks pretty nice," Dad replied.

"I feel like a teenager," Taylor said.

"You are certainly behaving like one. I tried to call your house to see if you wanted to go to dinner and then I came by the office," Dad explained.

"We were just leaving when all this started," Taylor explained.

"I can leave and you can resume," Dad offered, "if I haven't ruined the moment."

"Why don't we all go to dinner," Taylor said, looking at Alex.

"Sure, if that's all right," Alex replied.

"I'd like that," Dad said.

"What did you have in mind?" Taylor asked.

"I was thinking Durant's," Dad replied.

Taylor went to Alex's office to see if she was finished. Her office was empty. She went out to the receptionist's desk.

"Sally, has Alex left for the day?" Taylor asked, puzzled. They had a golf date for after work.

"Yes, she has. She wants you to call her when you're finished."

"Okay, thanks," Taylor said, going back to her office.

"Hello," Alex said.

"I thought we were going golfing. What's going on? Is everything all right?" Taylor asked, trying not to sound panicky.

"Nothing's wrong. Something came up," Alex said, shoving clothes in her suitcase.

"What are you doing?"

"I'm packing," Alex replied.

"Where are you going?" Taylor asked, her voice cracking, her mind instantly conjuring up images of Alex walking out of her life forever.

"To your house," Alex said, trying to sound nonchalant but knowing the weight of her words was immense.

There was silence on the line.

"Taylor?"

"What did you say?"

"I'm packing. I want to live with you and I'd like to be making mad, passionate love within the hour," Alex replied.

"You mean it?" Taylor said.

"No, I'm just fucking with you."

"Alex!"

"I'm teasing."

"Are you sure you want to do this? I don't want to pressure you into doing something you're not ready for. I can wait. I can wait forever."

"Taylor, will you relax? I don't want to wait. I have sufficiently processed my failed love affair and I want to be with you. We are well adjusted, grown women and we're both great with details. We'll work everything out. Don't worry. Go home and take your clothes off."

"Really?" Taylor said, feeling instantly like a teenage boy whose girlfriend had finally agreed to have sex with him.

"Really. I'll be there in a half an hour," Alex said.

Taylor nearly floored her father as she flew out of the office.

"Taylor, what's wrong?"

"Nothing. I have to get home fast."

"Why?" Dad asked.

"Alex is moving in."

"How nice. Does she need some help?"

"No."

"Are you sure?"

"She's already packed and on her way."

"I can come help unload stuff."

"Thanks Dad, but I think we can handle it."

"Okay, well don't hesitate to call," Dad said.

"Have a nice weekend," Taylor said to Sally and her father.

"She's in an awfully big hurry," Dad said to Sally.

"Wouldn't you be if moving in meant you got to finally make love to the woman of your dreams?" Sally replied.

"Oh, I had forgotten about the chastity issue."

"Nothing is a secret here. I do have to say that having all this sexual tension in the office has been exciting," Sally said, fanning herself with a portfolio.

Alex rang the doorbell and Taylor answered the door stark naked.

They both blushed.

"You look absolutely beautiful," Alex said, taking Taylor in her arms. She kissed her ardently.

"I didn't want to let you down for your first request," Taylor said as Alex kneeled in front of her and took her in her mouth. Whatever else Taylor had meant to say got lost in the soft groans as Alex gently brought her to climax. Taylor ran her fingers through Alex's still damp hair, pulling her head in close.

"I don't think I can stand anymore," Taylor said.

"Then don't," Alex said, pulling Taylor to the floor.

Together they removed Alex's clothing, kissing and murmuring words of love.

Halfway through seducing Alex, Taylor stopped. Alex looked up alarmed.

"What's wrong?"

"I never saw any bags," Taylor said, eyeing her suspiciously.

"Taylor, please don't stop. They are in the trunk. I swear," Alex said, pulling her back down.

"For sure?" Taylor asked.

"Yes," Alex said, putting Taylor's hand between her legs and giving her some gentle guidance.

Taylor could feel Alex tighten around her and she smiled at her.

"I love you. But do you think we could go somewhere softer?" Taylor inquired.

"Are you implying that making love in the front hall is not appropriate?" Alex teased.

"With you I'd make love anywhere, but right now I think I have rug burn."

"Maybe somewhere softer is a good idea. How about the bedroom?" Alex said.

"Sounds wonderful."

Later as Taylor lay on her stomach with Alex still on her back with her fingers inside her, she started to cry.

Alex rolled off.

"Are you okay? Did I hurt you?" Alex said, alarmed that in the throes of passion she had gotten carried away.

"No, I'm just happy," Taylor said, trying not to be embarrassed at this sign of intense emotion.

"They're good tears?" Alex inquired, wiping one from Taylor's face and putting it in her mouth. She wanted to taste all of Taylor.

"My mother used to collect my tears when I was little and then freeze them," Taylor said.

"That's beautiful."

"Until my overly helpful aunt defrosted the fridge and then threw them out. My mother was furious," Taylor said.

Alex stroked her face, suddenly wanting to be all those people Taylor had lost in her life. With Taylor she felt she could totally commit, save jars of tears, and never intentionally throw one moment of happiness away. She jumped up.

"Where are you going?" Taylor asked.

"To get my bags. I don't want you to change your mind," Alex said.

"Like I would," Taylor said, getting up to help her.

Mallory got the mail and began sifting through what was important and what could immediately go into the recycle bin. She had a soft spot for letter carriers now that she knew what Angel went through to deliver the mail she was stuffing into the trash. Angel on their long walks together during Mallory's recuperation from her broken foot had explained the various methods of the postal service to her. Now she understood why they all received so much bulk (or as she referred to it as junk) mail. Still, it was hard to grasp how one person had to go to all the trouble to put this stuff in her mailbox only to have another throw it away. But today's mail contained something different.

She tore open an invitation to a housewarming party. It seemed Angel and Kim had finally found the house they had been looking for, bought it and now were inviting their nearest and dearest friends. Mallory wondered who would be coming. She knew who wasn't and that caused her a twinge of regret. Not that she would miss some of the usual party crowd. Mallory tried hard to put out of her mind those people who had caused havoc in everyone's life but one of them was Gigi and try as might she still missed her long-lost best friend.

Dr. Kohlrabi had telephoned her to ask how she felt about her treating Gigi. Mallory had no problem with it. At least Gigi was getting some help and that was an important step forward. Mallory had no idea how they could ever get back to the place they had been before. It seemed there could be no going back. Even though

Mallory missed Gigi she doubted they would ever patch this one up. This wasn't like any of their other disagreements. It was a broken trust, and they had always been able to trust one another.

She had relived that moment a zillion times, dreamt about it, talked to Dr. Kohlrabi about it but the idea, the thought, the vision of Gigi cheating on her with the woman, the one and only woman Mallory had loved still seemed like some nightmare lesbian drama that wasn't supposed to exist except in film and Naiad romance novels. It wasn't supposed to happen in real life. In real life people were supposed to be better, supposed to have a conscience, supposed to restrain themselves from moments of unbridled lust.

But Del said otherwise. People do things like that. They shouldn't but they do. Together they got through that tumultuous time and now as Mallory walked in the house to find Del perched over a mountain of books, writing an article for a medical journal, she knew it was worth all the turmoil to have this incredible woman sharing her life.

"What are you doing Saturday night?" Mallory said, nibbling at Del's ear.

"Whatever you're doing," Del said, looking up, her blue eyes catching the light and sparkling.

"Kim and Angel are having a housewarming party."

"Really? Good for them."

"What are we going to get them for a present?" Mallory asked, suddenly panicked with the idea.

"How about a vending machine?" Del teased.

"That's a great idea. I have one of the old Coke machines at the warehouse. It's vintage. Now that would be an outstanding present," Mallory said.

Del nodded, thinking that Mallory having been the most difficult woman to date was an incredibly easy person to live with. She had yet to experience one of her emotionally claustrophobic moments that usually accompanied moving in with someone. They worked everything out in a matter of days, cooking, cleaning, grocery shopping, social times and work times. In fact, Del kept peeking around corners looking for something to be wrong only to find a peaceful existence full of early relationship passion. Kim had told her that she shouldn't be so leery of Cupid's gift. Del told her that Cupid had not always been kind to either one of them. He's a capricious little monster boy. A boy in charge of love is not good. Male images of love are comprised of conquer, copulate and cuckold, Del told her. Kim laughed and told her she didn't think any one of their relationships were going in that direction.

"Did you want a new house?" Mallory asked, still sitting on the corner of Del's desk contemplating how to wrap the housewarming present.

"Excuse me?" Del asked, closing her book and hearing her stomach rumble. She'd never gotten around to having lunch.

"Well, I was thinking about Angel and Kim starting over someplace fresh. Should we do that?"

"Why? I didn't think Caroline ever lived here."

"She didn't."

"That answers your question. I love this house. It is in the perfect location and it so reminds me of you that when you're not here I don't feel lonely. I feel surrounded by you. I'm never leaving."

"I guess there's no need to move."

"No, now how about some egg rolls on a bed of cabbage with a hot and sour soup."

"Starving?"

"Famished."

"You really like it here?" Mallory asked, staring intently at Del as if she had x-ray vision.

"I love it here. Now are you ready to experience another one of my cooking delights?" Del inquired. She had been taking a cooking course via the Internet and had only managed to blow up the kitchen once.

"I'll get the takeout menus ready just in case," Mallory teased.

"This one might work," Del said, picking up her directions and heading to the market.

"There's a good Chinese takeout just down the street," Mallory offered.

"No, it's not the same. I'm a doctor and that was no easy task, certainly I can learn to cook you a decent meal," Del said, putting her jacket on with that slightly lost look she got whenever she was required to do something practical.

"All right. I'll call Angel and tell her we are definitely coming to the party."

"I won't be long and don't snack. I can just feel that this time everything will work out," Del said.

Mallory rolled her eyes. She went and made a peanut butter and jelly sandwich, knowing it would be hours before Del gave up and they ordered takeout. It was sweet of her to try being domestic but it never worked out. They had pink laundry, had to disembowel the vacuum cleaner after Del got the Persian rug stuck in it, and the kitchen disasters were beyond measure. And still Del tried. Mallory just laughed and told Angel the stories. They had it planned to put Del's Household Adventures in the comic strip.

"So you're coming?" Angel asked.

"Of course," Mallory said.

"You don't want me to invite you-know-who," Angel said.

"No, we're still not speaking. Doubt we ever will."

"It is probably for the best. Want to hear something even stranger than that oddity?"

"Sure."

"Guess who Jennifer is dating?"

"Who?"

"Ollie."

"That is so positively lesbian," Mallory said, making no attempt to hide her disgust.

"Isn't that the truth? They can't have the ones they want so they sleep with their lover's ex-lovers. We are an incestuous bunch,"

Angel said, peeking around the corner to see what Kim was up to. Angel hadn't told Kim the news about Ollie and was thinking better of not telling. It didn't really concern them but at the same time the thought of the two of them together didn't sit well with Angel. Together they knew too much about Kim and herself and that gave Angel instant trepidation. They seemed like an odd match; their only similarities were for degrees of manipulation they routinely inflicted on their partners.

"Maybe they will find incredible happiness in each other's arms," Mallory said, snidely.

"You never know."

"But we both doubt it," Mallory said.

"I wouldn't put money down on it. So what's the newly crowned Queen of Domesticity doing?"

"She's going to try and blow up the kitchen again. We're having egg rolls. In fact, I better let you go. I need to make a quick trip to the hardware store."

"What for?"

"Another fire extinguisher."

Angel laughed. "See you at the party. I'll watch the news tonight but hopefully they won't be showing your house going up in flames."

"Maybe I'll get two extinguishers and a couple more smoke detectors."

"Good idea."

The new house was coming into its own, Kim thought as she put the last touches on the buffet table for the housewarming party. Angel was in the backyard finishing up the decorations. She had strung Chinese lanterns and hanging candles all over the yard. The veranda was filled with large pots of flowers and an odd collection of old furniture that Angel and Kim had refinished. The backyard of the fifty-year-old ranch house had a matured landscape with large shade trees, hedges and flower gardens as well as a small pond. On the whole it looked more like an overgrown English garden than it did anything native to Arizona. "Our oasis in the desert," Angel had told Kim. They had decided to stay with that theme and improve upon it. Now as Angel sat in the backyard surveying her handiwork she liked what she saw.

"You know for an apartment dweller you sure make a motivated house restorer," Kim said, wrapping her arms around Angel's waist and kissing her forehead.

"It was all those years of pent-up feelings toward remodeling that just gushed forward when I first saw this house. In fact, I might just give up the post office and take to restoration," Angel said.

"You're joking," Kim asked, concerned.

"No, I'm totally serious," Angel said, smirking.

Kim pinched her.

The doorbell rang and Kim went to answer it.

It was Del and Mallory.

"What happened to your hand?" Kim asked, looking down at Del's bandaged right hand.

"She doesn't like to talk about it," Mallory said.

"It is kind of hard not to notice it," Kim said diplomatically.

"She was going to wear this absurd oven mitten, but I absolutely refused to be seen in public with her," Mallory said.

Angel came around the corner into the foyer.

"The egg rolls?" Angel said, her eyes getting big.

Mallory nodded.

"Did you have to use the fire extinguisher?" Angel asked.

"No, but we did have to go to the emergency room for a spell," Mallory replied.

"It's not as bad as it looks," Del said.

"What constitutes not bad?" Angel asked.

"Well, suffice to say Del can become a career criminal now as her right hand will most likely not have fingerprints anymore," Mallory replied.

"That's the up side?" Kim inquired.

"No, the up side is something much better," replied Mallory, looking pointedly at Del.

"I've given up cooking. We've both decided it's much too dangerous," Del said.

Everyone laughed.

"I don't think the culinary world will be any poorer for that," Angel teased.

"Speaking of food," Mallory said, eyeing the buffet table. "It looks outstanding."

"Can we have a tour?" Del asked.

"Come this way," Angel said.

Later after the guests had eaten and everyone was sitting around outside Angel asked Mallory if she minded that Gigi wasn't around.

"It does seem odd that she isn't here with all the others. I don't think about it much until I see the rest of the group together and then I feel her lack of presence but then if she were here, Alex wouldn't be with Taylor. Gigi would be off cruising someone and Alex and I would be pretending not to notice. I would feel bad because she's my best friend and I can't stop her from doing it. Alex would feel bad because she must not be the lover she's supposed to be or Gigi wouldn't be interested in other women, so I think it's best this way. Does that make sense?" Mallory asked, suffering her first crisis in confidence in weeks.

It seemed not being around Gigi made Mallory feel more adequate in dealing with her life. Maybe Dr. Kohlrabi was right. Gigi had been her crutch all these years. She had always been there to remind Mallory how socially inept she was, especially when Gigi wasn't there to fend for her. With her gone, Mallory was discovering new parts of herself and she found she liked most of them. It was a pity that to find herself she had to lose Gigi. The universe was truly a capricious place. It only gave you what you wanted when you'd forgotten you needed it.

"Of course, it makes sense. Gigi will grow up one day and she might even become a decent person. She has it in her. Perhaps she just needs to find the right person to bring it out," Angel said.

"I think she lost the right person already," Mallory said.

"You mean Alex?" Angel said, looking at Taylor and Alex cuddled up together in the hammock.

"No, Caroline. If only she'd done what she was supposed to have done, everything would be so different right now," Mallory said, rather glumly.

"I'm not so sure that's a good thing. I'm kind of liking it right now."

"Well, yeah, I guess things didn't turn out so badly after all," Mallory said, looking over at Kim and Del.

"Except for Gigi," Angel said.

"For now. She could be doing penance."

"Being the good Catholic girl she is," Angel said brightly.

"Only time and the Astral Goddess will tell," Mallory said.

Publications from
BELLA BOOKS, INC.
The best in contemporary lesbian fiction

P.O. Box 10543, Tallahassee, FL 32302
Phone: 800-729-4992
www.bellabooks.com

BLOOD LINK by Claire McNab. 159 pp. 15th Detective Inspector Carol Ashton Mystery. Is Carol unwittingly playing into a deadly plan?   ISBN 1-931513-27-9 $12.95

TALK OF THE TOWN by Saxon Bennett. 239 pp. With enough beer, barbecue and B.S., anything is possible!   ISBN 1-931513-18-X $12.95

MAYBE NEXT TIME by Karin Kallmaker. 256 pp. Sabrina Starling always believed in maybe next time . . . until now.   ISBN 1-931513-26-0 $12.95

WHEN GOOD GIRLS GO BAD: A Motor City Thriller by Therese Szymanski. 230 pp. Brett, Randi, and Allie join forces to stop a serial killer.   ISBN 1-931513-11-2   12.95

A DAY TOO LONG: A Helen Black Mystery by Pat Welch. 328 pp. This time Helen's fate is in her own hands.   ISBN 1-931513-22-8 $12.95

THE RED LINE OF YARMALD by Diana Rivers. 256 pp. The Hadra's only hope lies in a magical red line . . . Climactic sequel to *Clouds of War*.   ISBN 1-931513-23-6 $12.95

OUTSIDE THE FLOCK by Jackie Calhoun. 224 pp. Jo embraces her new love and life.   ISBN 1-931513-13-9 $12.95

LEGACY OF LOVE by Marianne K. Martin. 224 pp. Read the whole Sage Bristo story.   ISBN 1-931513-15-5 $12.95

STREET RULES: A Detective Franco Mystery by Baxter Clare. 304 pp. Gritty, fast-paced mystery with compelling Detective L.A. Franco   ISBN 1-931513-14-7 $12.95

RECOGNITION FACTOR: 4th Denise Cleever Thriller by Claire McNab. 176 pp. Denise Cleever tracks a notorious terrorist to America.   ISBN 1-931513-24-4 $12.95

NORA AND LIZ by Nancy Garden. 296 pp. Lesbian romance by the author of *Annie on My Mind*.   ISBN 1931513-20-1 $12.95

MIDAS TOUCH by Frankie J. Jones. 208 pp. Sandra had everything but love.   ISBN 1-931513-21-X $12.95

BEYOND ALL REASON by Peggy J. Herring. 240 pp. A romance hotter than Texas.   ISBN 1-9513-25-2 $12.95

ACCIDENTAL MURDER: 14th Detective Inspector Carol Ashton Mystery by Claire McNab. 208 pp.Carol Ashton tracks an elusive killer.   ISBN 1-931513-16-3 $12.95

SEEDS OF FIRE:Tunnel of Light Trilogy, Book 2 by Karin Kallmaker writing as Laura Adams. 274 pp. Intriguing sequel to *Sleight of Hand*.   ISBN 1-931513-19-8 $12.95

DRIFTING AT THE BOTTOM OF THE WORLD by Auden Bailey. 288 pp. Beautifully written first novel set in Antarctica.   ISBN 1-931513-17-1 $12.95

CLOUDS OF WAR by Diana Rivers. 288 pp. Women unite to defend Zelindar!   ISBN 1-931513-12-0 $12.95

DEATHS OF JOCASTA: 2nd Micky Knight Mystery by J.M. Redmann. 408 pp. Sexy and intriguing Lambda Literary Award-nominated mystery.   ISBN 1-931513-10-4 $12.95

LOVE IN THE BALANCE by Marianne K. Martin. 256 pp. The classic lesbian love story, back in print! ISBN 1-931513-08-2 $12.95

THE COMFORT OF STRANGERS by Peggy J. Herring. 272 pp. Lela's work was her passion . . . until now. ISBN 1-931513-09-0 $12.95

CHICKEN by Paula Martinac. 208 pp. Lynn finds that the only thing harder than being in a lesbian relationship is ending one.   ISBN 1-931513-07-4 $11.95

TAMARACK CREEK by Jackie Calhoun. 208 pp. An intriguing story of love and danger.   ISBN 1-931513-06-6 $11.95

DEATH BY THE RIVERSIDE: 1st Micky Knight Mystery by J.M. Redmann. 320 pp. Finally back in print, the book that launched the Lambda Literary Award-winning Micky Knight mystery series.   ISBN 1-931513-05-8 $11.95

EIGHTH DAY: A Cassidy James Mystery by Kate Calloway. 272 pp. In the eighth installment of the Cassidy James mystery series, Cassidy goes undercover at a camp for troubled teens.   ISBN 1-931513-04-X $11.95

MIRRORS by Marianne K. Martin. 208 pp. Jean Carson and Shayna Bradley fight for a future together.   ISBN 1-931513-02-3 $11.95

MIRRORS by Marianne K. Martin. 208 pp. Jean Carson and Shayna Bradley fight for a future together.   ISBN 1-931513-02-3 $11.95

THE ULTIMATE EXIT STRATEGY: A Virginia Kelly Mystery by Nikki Baker. 240 pp. The long-awaited return of the wickedly observant Virginia Kelly.   ISBN 1-931513-03-1 $11.95

FOREVER AND THE NIGHT by Laura DeHart Young. 224 pp. Desire and passion ignite the frozen Arctic in this exciting sequel to the classic romantic adventure *Love on the Line*.
ISBN 0-931513-00-7 $11.95

WINGED ISIS by Jean Stewart. 240 pp. The long-awaited sequel to *Warriors of Isis* and the fourth in the exciting Isis series.   ISBN 1-931513-01-5 $11.95

ROOM FOR LOVE by Frankie J. Jones. 192 pp. Jo and Beth must overcome the past in order to have a future together.
ISBN 0-9677753-9-6 $11.95

THE QUESTION OF SABOTAGE by Bonnie J. Morris. 144 pp. A charming, sexy tale of romance, intrigue, and coming of age.   ISBN 0-9677753-8-8 $11.95

SLEIGHT OF HAND by Karin Kallmaker writing as Laura Adams. 256 pp. A journey of passion, heartbreak and triumph that reunites two women for a final chance at their destiny.   ISBN 0-9677753-7-X $11.95

MOVING TARGETS: A Helen Black Mystery by Pat Welch. 240 pp. Helen must decide if getting to the bottom of a mystery is worth hitting bottom.   ISBN 0-9677753-6-1 $11.95

CALM BEFORE THE STORM by Peggy J. Herring. 208 pp. Colonel Robicheaux retires from the military and comes out of the closet.   ISBN 0-9677753-1-0 $12.95

OFF SEASON by Jackie Calhoun. 208 pp. Pam threatens Jenny and Rita's fledgling relationship.   ISBN 0-9677753-0-2 $11.95

WHEN EVIL CHANGES FACE: A Motor City Thriller by Therese Szymanski. 240 pp. Brett Higgins is back in another heart-pounding thriller.   ISBN 0-9677753-3-7 $11.95

BOLD COAST LOVE by Diana Tremain Braund. 208 pp. Jackie Claymont fights for her reputation and the right to love the woman she chooses.   ISBN 0-9677753-2-9 $11.95